Gwyneth Becoming

Also by Reg Quist

The Church at Third and Main
Hamilton Robb
Noah Gates
Terry of the Double C

Danny Series
Just John Series
Mac's Way Series
Reluctant Redemption Series
The Settlers Series

Gwyneth Becoming

FRONTIER DREAMING
BOOK ONE

REG QUIST

Gwyneth Becoming
Paperback Edition
Copyright © 2025 Reg Quist

CKN Christian Publishing
An Imprint of Wolfpack Publishing
1707 E. Diana Street
Tampa, FL 33610

cknchristianpublishing.com

Paperback ISBN 979-8-89567-863-3
eBook ISBN 979-8-89567-862-6

Dedicated to all those hardy souls, women especially, who conquered the trials and difficulties of doctoring on the frontier. Often with little training they faced the near impossible.

The three Gwyneth books follow the career of a teenage girl who volunteered in the medical tents of the Civil War, moved on to nursing on the Kansas prairie, fell in love with a cowboy, married, built a ranch in the wilderness and ended up going to medical school, graduating with a medical degree. With grit and determination, she built the life she had dreamed of. It was neither quick nor easy but, in the end, -- well, you're just going to have to read the books.

Special thanks to my friend Bill, MD (retired), who wishes for no credit, but who put in hours walking me through Gwyneth's many medical and surgical adventures.

Author's Note

A WORD ABOUT FRONTIER MEDICAL
PRACTICES

Until early in the twentieth century, the practice of medicine had changed little for hundreds of years. It is true that in many places in the world, individual men—and a few women—were diligently studying aspects of the medical arts. This was essentially the beginning of a new, more scientific and tested era in medicine, but the new discoveries were often slow to be put into practice, only becoming more acceptable after the end of the US Civil War.

But even as some of the new discoveries were being eased into the world of medicine, at the same time, practices such as Bloodletting, meant to restore fluid balance in the body, Mercury Treatments, with its devastating results, used to treat venereal disease and other infections, Arsenic and Lead Medications, both deadly, used to treat infection, Trepanation, where doctors drilled holes into patients' skulls to relieve headaches, Tobacco Smoke enemas to cure intestinal issues, Heroin and Opium, used for coughs and pain, Cocaine used for toothaches and fatigue, and many other long forgotten practices, persisted.

To render the patient unconscious during surgery, both Chloroform and Ether were put into practice before the Civil War. However, there were serious side effects to both, including post-surgery vomiting and nausea, the dangerous flammability of ether, the occasional sudden death from the overuse of chloroform, among other problems.

The unavailability of anesthetic in any form on the frontier or remote locations forced doctors to sometimes do surgery with the patient awake and suffering.

Doctors with no significant formal training at all were common until the turn of the century. Few medical schools offered more than a two-year course of study, and often that study was classroom only, with no lab or actual patient experience. It was common for a young man to hang up his shingle as a doctor after simply working alongside an older doctor, entering into an apprenticeship of sorts, as a carpenter or blacksmith might.

The doors of medical schools only gradually opened to women in the years before 1900. The schools themselves were virtually unregulated, with no authority governing what was taught or judging whether or not a student was adequately trained to hang out his shingle.

As the frontiers of America opened for rapid settlement, there were never enough men with even a rudimentary knowledge of medicine to fill the needs in the hundreds of new towns. Many towns had little more than a midwife to assist with birthing, and someone who may have an idea of how to set a broken bone. Early or untimely deaths were common. The experience of childbirth was filled with hazards. Many babies and their young mothers died on lonely ranches or farms with no one to help.

It is into this medical world that Gwyneth entered, offering her skills and experience wherever it was needed.

Gwyneth Becoming

Chapter One

TRENT WYCOME WAS A CAREFUL MAN, THE OPPOSITE of his happy and loving parents, who appeared to thrive in the midst of chaos. The young man was wearied by the never-ending mistakes, changes, and corrections that seemed to rule his father's life, and the many times the family started over, while living on the sharp edge of fiscal disaster. That they somehow seemed to arrive on the other side of the changes smiling, and with more wealth than they started with, did little to balance Trent's longing for stability. He was determined to live differently.

Under his father's easy-going nature, barely hidden, but seen from time to time by the family, there was an explosion, set and primed, waiting for someone or something to light the fuse. The source of this scourge was a mystery to Trent, as was the willpower that held it in check. Trent had found nothing similar in his own makeup.

Easing into adulthood, Trent had become a man whose driving habit was to study things out. That didn't mean he was the least bit timid or afraid of life. In fact, if anything, he was, at times too bold—in his work, in his daily activities, and, as would be seen in the future, in his courting. He was simply a man who attempted to live life without surprises. His goal, always making allowance for the will of the Creator, whom he had acknowledged in worship since his youth, was to be forward-looking, to attempt to see where the likely events of his life's decisions were leading him. And to make no more restarts than the situations demanded.

Trent Wycome liked to plan. Later, looking back in time, he had to grin as he acknowledged that the working out of one of his earlier impulsive and less thought-through actions had set his life on a different, and long-term path. At least it was different from the constant milking of his father's small dairy herd and the hoeing of weeds in the market garden that brought the family mere pennies for all the work involved.

As he was preparing to escape both his youth and his family home, he made the impulsive decision to tag onto a herd being driven to the Kansas market. It was a new temptation springing to life unbidden. But when the drovers of a herd that had come north from down near the Nueces country pulled into a shallow, well-watered, and grassed valley for the night, a short five miles from the Wycome family holdings in central Texas, he waited until his evening chores were done and then rode over to take a gander. He eased himself, sitting the saddle slightly askew, as his riding animal rested hipshot on the fringe of the camp.

Fascinated by the orderliness of the gathering, with everyone seeming to go about their jobs, from the cook to the riders, with little shouting or talk, if you'll overlook the frustrated horse wrangler who was attempting to rope out night horses that didn't want to be roped, he studied the actions, attempting to figure out how a cow camp worked.

A tall, well-built man, one of the few he had seen with a clean-shaven face, loped in from the herd. Seeing a rider who was not part of the crew, the man turned a bit to the side and slowed to a restless stop beside Trent.

"Someth'n fer ya, kid?"

Startled, and just slightly frightened by the rumbling voice and the evident authority of the man, Trent fumbled his first few words, but finally managed to say, "No. No, just look'n. Never seen a trail herd this close up before. Try'n to figure it out is all."

"Ya live around here, kid?"

"Folks got a truck garden and a few milk cows just outside that town you must have seen as you passed by this afternoon. Over east just a bit. Few miles to the south. Milkn's done for the day, so I'm free till just before first light in the morning. Thought I'd take me a ride around. Saw your camp smoke and then heard the cattle. Rode over to take me a look-see, is all. Curious. Aint mean'n no harm."

"No harm done, kid. You et yet?"

"Time I ride home it'll be on the table."

"Come join us. Cook always has a-plenty. Two things—tie yer animal well away from the chuck wagon and wash yer hands. Cook's awful fussy that way."

The invite was still kind of settling between Trent's ears as the foreman spurred his horse toward the wrangler. With no words or instructions, the foreman stepped to the grass, tossed the reins to a rider no older than Trent himself, and stepped toward the dinner fire. Trent noticed that he went first to the wash basin resting on a hinged, fold-down shelf attached to the side of a heavily loaded wagon.

The men sat in every relaxed posture possible as they took on their evening meal. There was little talk. Eating was purposeful, filling a need that would have to last until morning's first light and the holler from the cook to "come and get it." The typical joshing and ribald humor among the saddle-weary men wouldn't begin until the dinner plates were dropped into the crash bucket and the heavy porcelain mugs were filled with coffee. But Trent knew nothing of that long practice. On special evenings, there would be baked pie or some other such sweet treat. This wasn't one of those times.

The foreman, who had taken a seat across the lightly treed

natural clearing from Trent, picked up his coffee and strolled toward where Trent had chosen to sit for the meal, cradling the metal plate on his folded legs.

"Name's Shade, kid. Foreman on this drive. Triple C Ranch. From down south. We could use another rider or two. You want'n to see the world from the saddle and make a few dollars along the way?"

A rider sitting close by laughed and said, "Don't let him fool ya, kid. Mostly what you'll see is the south end of north-bound longhorns. And one 'a 'em looks pretty much like the other. From that vantage point is what I mean to say. Anything further away you can't see fer the dust anyhow. Of course, you'll maybe see an Indian or two along the way. Was I you, I'd ride for home and be thankful fer the cot you roll into come the night."

"That's enough, Taylor. You've got a good home too. And a good woman waiting. You could ride for home this very minute if you wanted to."

Taylor grinned at Trent and said no more.

Trent turned his eyes from Taylor back to Foreman Shade. He had made the most rushed decision he had ever made, but he held that fact to himself while he said, "Got no riding animal of my own. You got one to spare?"

"Got horses enough and all types, from gentled till they're near useless, to some that'll stretch your bones, and your horse sense, come a cold morning."

"That offer still be good in the morning?"

"It'll stand till you make yer decision. Or till we've moved on. One or the other."

Trent stood and said, "Thanks for the dinner and the offer. I'll think on it."

～

TRENT SLOWLY RODE HOME, knowing his decision was already made, feeling excited at the possibilities but also feeling foolish that he hadn't asked about the pay. The conversation with his parents was short. He was the youngest of four offspring in the family and the last to live at home. Now it was his turn to venture forth and see what the world would lay before him, problems or opportunities, and probably enough of each.

"We'll miss you, Trent. Your ma and me will. But we'll pray for you too. Pray that the Lord will show you the way. His way. His way for you. But we surely will miss you here on the farm. Can't keep up with the garden and the milking, just the two of us. But it weren't more than a week ago, when I hauled that last load of garden truck in, that Filbert, he who owns the grocery store and trading post down to town, suggested he might be willing to sell out if the right buyer came along with a comforting amount of jingle in his pocket. And Pinky, strange name for a man I always thought, he's often said that our two places, being side by side, could be joined together and both be the better for it. You do what you're of a mind to do, son. I can do the milking for a few days until I get the chance to talk with Pinky, and your ma and I have looked at possibilities. Go if your hearts leading you that way. Stay if you're working your way through serious doubts."

Chapter Two

The Wycome family couldn't spare a horse, so a five-mile walk faced Trent the next morning if he was to join the trail crew before they left the campgrounds. Misjudging the walking speed of a trail herd, he was afraid that if they ever pulled away from the campgrounds, he might never catch up to them. He shoved his few belongings into the bottom of two Civil War haversacks his father had dragged home after that conflict ground to an uneasy stop. The canvas sacks had seen much use in the family's several moves.

Trent tied the two carrying straps together, making a single sling that would drape over his shoulder, leaving his hands free. In one of those hands, he carried a well-used 44-40 caliber Henry rifle. Around his waist was strapped a scratched and sweat-stained leather belt with a single holster on his right hip, carrying his Smith and Wesson 32 caliber Army six-shooter. Like the haversacks, the two weapons had found their way into the senior Wycome's possession on the long walk home in '65. It was laughingly rumored by his older siblings that his father had arrived home from the conflict thoroughly loaded down with weapons salvaged and canvas bags hung from his shoulders, weighted with useful items. All that his father did in battle was never talked about. His mother had mentioned one time that her husband was a changed man, not at all the man who went to war.

On top of the other possibles Trent had in the haversacks were a sewing kit put together by his mother and a bundle of clean rags, torn into strips and rolled, in case he needed a bandage or anything of the sort. On the very top, completing the bundle of clean clothing, and easy to reach, was a lunch and a canvas-covered metal canteen he had filled with fresh well-water. He wouldn't be leaving home totally unprepared.

Starting out before first light, he naively convinced himself that he might be the first to stand in line at the camp kitchen when the breakfast call went out. It turned out to be a bitter lesson on the short nights the riders lived through as normal. In the cowboy's life, the days ended late, and the mornings started early. The truth was that the driving of cattle was governed by the weather and the disposition of the animals. And little enough the men could do about either.

He had walked perhaps three miles on the familiar trail before he heard any sound except for the normal night sounds of birds awakening to the needs and possibilities of the new day, and the scurrying of small grassland critters drawing their nightly hunt for food to an end. He knew he was still too far from the drover's camp to hear cattle or men rising to greet the morning, so when the sound of quickly moving hooves and the clacking of a few horns—such as would be made by cattle being pushed through the darkness—caught his ears, he stopped to listen. He knew enough about cattle to recognize that the animals were heading his way, south, away from the big herd. And that they were being driven at a faster-than-normal pace. That alone set Trent to wondering. Other than the neighbor's milk cows and a yard animal or two, there was only the Triple C herd anywhere close by, as far as Trent was aware.

When the first of morning's light gave him a glimpse of a rider lashing a small bunch, perhaps fifty in all, with the double of his catch rope, warning signals took over Trent's thoughts. He was sure he had seen no other herds in the area the evening before, and there were no neighbors that close who would be driving animals in the dark of night. They had to be Triple C cattle cut out of the northbound herd. Not only were the animals trotting, just short of a full-out run, but they were being driven dangerously close to where he was walking.

The first indication that the rider saw the walking man brought about three quick actions, one following closely on the heels of the other. The first was the riders startled, pulling back on the reins. The second was the quick coiling of the rope that the man had been lashing the cattle with. The third was the lifting of a saddle gun from its scabbard. All of that was only a prelude to the whining of a ricochet dangerously close to Trent's feet. A split second elapsed before the crack of exploding powder awakened what was left of the silence of the night.

Trent hollered out and dove to the ground. In quick succession, two more shots were directed his way. None struck anywhere near so far as he could tell. The roar of an angry voice split the morning's peace.

"What's going on? Who you shooting at over there? You've got the whole country awake by now, you fool."

"They're already after us. First one's right here. But I think I got him."

"Never mind him. Get those animals to moving."

"Gotta make sure he's dead or he'll be coming along again."

Trent could see the rider break away from the herd, heading toward him. He had scrambled thirty or forty feet away from where he had fallen, hoping the early morning mist and a hedge of low-growing shrubbery would hide him a bit longer. The hope was in vain. The rider spotted him and pointed his rifle, carefully this time, taking the time for a steady shot.

The first shots had come from a moving horse, a fact that most likely explained why Trent was still among the living. As his strong desire was to continue in that condition, he rolled three times to his left, ending up in a half-sitting position, lifted the Henry only to waist height, resting the barrel on his one raised knee. Fearing his attacker's next shot, and with a fierce desire to continue living, for the first time in his life, he squeezed the trigger against a living human man.

The shot went true. As the rider clutched his chest and was slowly slipping from the saddle, the second man rode into view, riding fast. Trent saw the pistol in the man's hand and understood immediately what the situation was. He had only to turn the Henry a few degrees to the left, accomplishing this by sloping his knee in that direction, and again squeezing the trigger. In spite of his own fear and nervousness, the lead smacked against flesh, producing a sickening sound. The rider screamed, dropped his pistol, and gripped his thigh.

Trent shot again, holding high this time. The buzz of the lead mere inches from his head was enough for the man to lose his balance and drop to the grass. Trent had shot without lifting the weapon to aim, something he recognized only later as he relived the event for the hundredth time. The cattle, startled by the shots, had set out on a short track back to the Nueces at a hard run.

Slowly, carefully, looking for a third rider but seeing none, Trent rose unsteadily to his feet. He had no desire to check on the condition of either man. Whether dead or wounded, neither was paying him any more attention. The rising rim of brightness on the eastern horizon showed that the running and fatigued cattle were, one by one, either standing, with their heads dropped to the grass, or they were looking for distance. Some were confused by a couple of confining fences, the resistance and screeching of barbed wire causing them to back off and drop to a slow walk. Some had stopped, about one-quarter mile south, looking around in confusion. A few determined animals were splitting off in other directions and would soon be out of sight in the brush.

Trent had no trouble catching up to one of the loose horses. He swung aboard and moved toward the cattle. At the sound of hooves, a few animals again moved into a trot. It became quickly obvious that the horse knew more about rounding up cattle than he did, so Trent did little more than point the horse at the escaping bunch and ride along as the gelding turned the cattle back into a weary mill. With just a bit of trouble, Trent got the herd bunched and turned back to the north. The few stragglers who had charged into the brush would have to be dealt with later. When he got back to where the shooting had taken place, several Triple C riders came boiling around some brush and into the clearing.

The rider in the lead, a man Trent had not seen at the dinner hour the evening before, held up his arm and swung it from side to side to indicate the men behind him should slow down and spread out.

"Hold it right there, fella. Hold and raise your hands or be shot from the saddle."

Trent, befuddled with all that had been going on, hesitated, looked around him, and started to say, "I'm coming to join—"

He was shouted into silence with another warning, "Raise them."

A voice from the rear hollered, "I'll get a rope, fellas. One of you scout a suitable tree over in that bush." The voice was one he had heard guffawing at another rider the evening before.

The man who had hollered for Trent to raise his hands said, "There'll be no lynching on this drive. Settle down, all of you."

Trent, without lowering his hands, managed with the dexterous use of arm and shoulder to push his much-damaged hat out of his eyes and over his brow to rest once again where hats are meant to rest. His face was now fully exposed.

"Why, he's just a kid."

"Ya, kid he may be, Cob, but he sat at our dinner fire last evening. Studying up on the operation appears to me. Guilty as sin. Was casing the joint for a gang, sure as shoot'n."

"So, tell me, where's the gang. I don't see but just the one rider and him a kid. He didn't run this bunch of longhorns off by himself. Look around. Might find a trail to where the others have run off to. If there are any others. And someone get the kid's guns and get him off that horse."

With some relief, Trent saw Shade riding in. Boldly, he spoke up, "Shade. I was coming to join you, walking I was, on account of the family has but the one riding animal, as I told you last night, and he can't be spared. I ain't no thief. Fact is, I shot a couple of riders. Brought the thing to a stop. I gathered this bunch and brought them back to here."

"All right," said Shade. "Where are the two you say you shot?"

"Over there to the north by maybe a quarter mile. Closer on to the brush. My kit is lying on the grass over there too."

Shade turned and led a couple of the other riders to where Trent was pointing. Three or four others turned their attention to the cattle. Trent's kit lay not more than a couple hundred yards to the west of where the two bodies lay. One rider stepped down and picked up the haversacks, looping the handles over his saddle horn. Shade had stopped beside one fallen man and stepped down himself. As he turned the body over, he heard a gasp of pain.

"You're still with us, are you? Where are you hurt?"

"Leg. Dang kid shot me in the leg. Bleeding. Hurts like all perdition. Get me to a doctor."

"No doctor out here that I know of. You should have thought of that before you set out stealing other folks' beef animals."

"Rich rancher won't miss that little bunch. More than likely branded them wild himself anyway. Belonged to no one before that. He's got no special right to wild cattle."

"Well, you lie here and think what you want. Keep telling yourself that if it pleases you. We get ready to ride back, we'll drag you along on the end of a rope unless you can sit a horse. Cook's helper knows some about wounds and such."

A new voice broke in on the conversation. "There's another one over here, Shade. No rush. He's as dead as he's ever going to be. Shot clean in the heart."

Shade turned back to the wounded man, saying, "Just the two of you?"

"Just Poke and me."

"And the kid?"

"Ain't ever seen him before. Wish'd I'd never seen him now. Nor heard of him, neither one."

Shade and Cob walked together to where Trent was now sitting on the ground. "What about it, kid?"

"I was walking. Coming to join up with you. Was carrying my kit over my shoulder and the Henry in my hand. Heard the cattle. They was driving the animals just short of a full-out run. That one fella saw me. Thought I was one of y'all. Commenced to shooting. Dang near got me too. I dove to the ground and crawled off while those two were arguing, shouting over the backs of the cattle. But that one, he looked back and spotted me and was about to commence shooting again. I rolled away some, hoping to put his aim off. Set off just the one shot myself."

Trent hesitated, gulped down some mixed saliva and guilt, and said, "He dead? I didn't go to kill anyone or even to shoot. Just didn't want to get killed myself, is all."

"Stand up, son. Get back on that horse. No, leave your guns where they are. Cob, take those guns and hold them safe. You two ride on ahead, back to camp. If they aren't moving the herd yet, Cob, get them up and going. Hold Jan and his wagon back in case this fella should live till we get him to where he can be helped. Tell Jan to heat up some water."

Shade then turned to the two riders standing beside the wounded man. "Get him up on that other animal and throw the dead man on behind. Get them to camp. Best get to digging a hole to put these two in." With that, he rode off following the slowly walking bunch of stolen beef. The two riders who had gone after the runners were left to do their jobs, digging the animals out of the thorny brush.

Chapter Three

BACK AT THE DRIVE CAMP, THE COOK AND HIS HELPER were loading the last of the camp gear. The fire was smoldering, mostly down to ash and small ends of wood. With the chuck wagon ready to roll, the cook climbed to the high seat. With a holler and a slap of the reins on the backs of the team, he would be ready to roll out of camp. He would follow the herd until he had the chance to pass and move on ahead, seeking a location to set up for the evening dinner. The riders had stuffed leftover breakfast makings into their jacket pockets. It would do for them during the day.

As they rode into camp, Cob turned aside for just a moment while Trent rode directly to the second wagon. He saw nothing left of the camp but worn and trampled grass and the second wagon, with the cook's helper picking up the last of the camp gear, stuffing rolled bedding into every corner of his crowded wagon.

The wagoner chose to say nothing, only looking sideways at Trent out of the corner of his eyes. Finally, the men hauling the dead and wounded trotted into camp and rode directly to the shade of a few trees, where the men had slept the night before. Roughly, the wounded man was dragged from the horse and dropped to the ground, a scream of agony rising from his lips. Another rider had gone to the wagon with word for the driver. "Jan, Cob needs you over to the trees." When Jan, as it seemed the wagon driver's name was, neared the gathering of men under the trees, Cob leaned from the saddle and spoke. Trent was too far away to hear what was said. It seemed logical to believe he was laying out orders for the care of the wounded rustler.

He wished he was miles away and had never seen or heard of the Triple C drive. Without guidance, his horse took several steps toward where the other horses were gathered. Trent finally drew him to a stop. He sat his saddle in silence until Cob hollered. "Get yourself back over to the wagon, kid. Shade left word. Said he wasn't quite sure of your story yet. Says you're riding the wagon this one day. I'll be hanging back till the riders find those stolen cattle, but I can't hold off the wagon no more. Turn that horse over to the wrangler and step it up. Soon as Jan's done with that bullet wound, he'll be heading out."

Jan looked up from where he had been attempting to plug the wound and stop the bleeding. He didn't seem too concerned about whether his efforts were paying off or not. He hadn't bothered to heat any water. To no one in particular, he suggested, "We dally much longer, we'll be eating trail dust the whole long day. Cook's already miles away. Me, I'm most usually at the front of the bunch, leading the way. Me and the cook."

In less than five minutes, the wagon driver sat back on his haunches, studying the man on the ground. Reaching to the side a bit, he wiped his bloody hands on the grass before rising to his feet. With no comment about the wounded man, he turned and walked back to the wagon. Still silent, but with a troubled look on his face, he turned the wooden spigot on the water tank and ran a goodly wash over his hands. With the sideboard up and fastened in place, he had trouble fumbling out a bar of lye soap, but he finally found it and rubbed his hands with soap and water for so long that Trent thought he might go right down to bare bones.

Studying on Trent as he scrubbed, with no comment on the wound repair he had attempted, he said, "Never known Shade to be undecided about a man before. He musta seen something in you he liked. Or mayhap it was suspicion. Or mayhap, again, it's something else the rest of us knows noth'n about. Heard some shooting. Was that you?"

Trent ignored the question.

Nothing more was said about the wounded man, but Trent couldn't ignore the fact that Jan, who apparently knew something of wounds, had glanced over to the treed hollow for one more look at the man he had ministered to, and then straightened back up and climbed onto his high driver's seat. With a motion from Jan, Trent joined him on the seat.

As the wagon wheels slowly rolled north, following the chuckwagon tracks, he spoke to Trent, saying, "I don't know the deal yet, but don't you go to thinking Shade's liking of you will earn you any breaks nor no easy time. Shade, he runs a tight camp. If'n he chooses to sign you on, you'll earn your keep, or you'll be walking home. You got a name, kid?"

"I have. And it's not kid. Trent Wycome. And am I to assume you have a name too? More than just Jan is what I mean."

"Jan Renfrew."

"Jan Renfrew. Okay by me, but I never heard no such name before."

"Short for January, which my old man thought was a right good handle to lay on his firstborn. Never did like it my own self. Makes me think of the cold, and I surely don't like being cold."

Trent figured that was all the information he needed to round out his knowledge and opinion of the wagon master. Instead of pursuing the matter, he asked, "What do you call this here wagon all stuffed to the gunnels?"

"Depends on whether it's raining or if the sky's draping the whole land with sunshine, like it's doin' this morning. And how this team of mules decides to pull. I've called it some mean things, and any of them will most often do. Rightly it's not got any particular name. Heard one like it called a hoodlum wagon once last year. Name doesn't seem to have stuck though. Carries bedding and such, and maybe some supplies as what the cook can't carry on the chuckwagon. Just call it a wagon, I suppose. Never thought about no name before."

Cob rode into view saying, "Kid, don't you pay no attention to Jan. He'll run off at the mouth all day less'n you put a stop to it. Ain't no telling what he discusses with them mules as the days go by. Now, Jan, you get a good look at that wounded man?"

"As good as will help any. You find a wanted poster I may recognize a drawing, although most are poor pictures at the best of times."

As Cob turned and rode away, Trent was afraid to ask what that short speech meant. In any case, to ask, he would have had to holler over the instructions being shouted at the mules, the grinding of the iron-rimmed wheels on the gravely soil, and the squeak of one wheel that was crying out for attention. He didn't bother.

With the flatness of the country around, Trent could see a far way, back toward the camp. Two men were digging a hole. He guessed it was a grave. Trent figured he wouldn't know till the end of the day if he had killed one man or two.

AT THE NOON STOP, Shade rode to where Trent was studying on a wool-fuzz-covered biscuit the teamster had dug out of his pocket earlier, offering it for the breakfast Trent had missed. It was his first nourishment of the day, and there would be no more until evening camp. He was sorely tempted to take it in, fuzz and all. He was longing for his haversacks and the lunch his mother had prepared, but he didn't bother asking where Jan had stowed it.

Trent watched the foreman approaching with some concern. To be driven off now would mean a long walk home, and to be accepted onto the crew might mean a visit with a lawman at the next town. Neither possibility did anything to brighten his day.

"Kid, you want to tell me exactly what happened?"

Trent didn't really want to, but with no real choice, he started in. The telling took no longer than the incident itself had taken. As the words of the sad tale were drifting off on the prairie winds, Trent gulped down some fear and guilt. Having looked back at the hole the crew was digging, he thought he knew the answer, but he asked the question anyway. "Did that second man survive?"

Shade didn't really show any emotion when he answered, "No, he'd lost too much blood. Jan did what was to be done. Two men. One hole. Unfortunate, but a man sets his own trail through life. There's work enough available for any able man who can fork a bronc. No excuse for stealing what others have worked for. Don't you get all worked up with guilt. You protected yourself, and that's to be expected in a lawless land."

"Am I going to have to report to some sheriff in the next town?"

"No sheriffs. No talk. What happened is over and done with. Leave it lay."

"Well, I'm happy it's me still breathing, but that won't do much for my guilt."

"I'm saying to forget it. What you do is entirely up to you. I would advise, though, that the less said, the better. Now, are you riding with us, or no? If you sign on, you're on for the whole of it. I'll have no quitters on the crew."

Trent built up his courage and said, "I'm assuming there's pay at the end of the trail? Mind if I ask what that will be?"

With that settled, Shade said, "The booty those two fellas left behind is yours to choose from. Claim a horse and saddle, or both if that's your wish. Rummage through their saddlebags. Might be something of value there."

"I'd as soon turn the horses loose, saddles, bags and all. I want nothing to do with any of it."

"Your choice, but we'll not waste good stock and gear. We'll run the animals into the remuda. But you're going to need a saddle. Best you adjust your thinking on that bit at least."

Chapter Four

From that point in Trent's life, it was cattle drives, long days and short nights, rail towns, and temptations he had never faced before, all the while doing his best to avoid trouble in trail's end towns. He saved his pay, purchasing small herds to include in the drive, saving his cattle sale money at the end of the trail cow towns, adding it to the saved wages, and finally, purchasing one much larger herd to wrap into the last drive. Prices were up, and that bunch paid especially well at the end of the trail, adding nicely to his already considerable savings. It was time to put it all behind him. The trailing days were about over. The rails were creeping through the land, going every which way. Soon they would be making the big, walking herds, and the rough and ready men who drove them, a thing of the past.

Along the way, Trent had made special friends with Cob Fleming, a rider from the south of Texas. Cob was the son of a large Nueces area ranching family. With the other brothers available for the ranch work, he had done as Trent was doing, cutting out fifty or one hundred head from the family's Sombrero Brand herd to carry along to market. And as Trent was doing, he saved his wages and his sales profits. On the last drive, just completed, Trent's bunch had made up nearly one-third of the beef animals. Cob's accounted for about one quarter. They turned a very nice profit.

Thinking it through and laughing about the ups and downs of trailing, Trent and Cob, who had become great friends, figured they had raised enough blisters and calluses in unmentionable places. Trent had plans that included a move into the western lands, and Cob, who was free to return to the family's South Texas spread anytime he wished, decided to tag along with his friend to see how this tough, hardened range man, whom he remembered as a green farm lad, faced up to the new challenges a move west would bring.

OVER THEIR SEVERAL trips from Texas to Kansas and back again, Cob and Trent had faced dust storms, a couple of hard runs by the cattle, two attempts from rustlers, and one small group of intruding Indians. It was the Indian matter that had set Trent apart among the crew. The first warning had come from a terrified point rider, a kid who was probably too young for the job.

"Indians. They're armed and waiting. Shade, Shade, what we gonna do?"

But Shade was away off on the other side of the herd and didn't hear the distressed shouting. Trent looked all around him and didn't see anyone carrying authority. And if it was left to the frantic point rider, who was in the process of unlimbering his saddle gun, there would be one dead or, at least, shot Indian and probably more dead or shot herders than anyone wanted to consider, or explain. Someone had to do something. It was Trent's horse that made the decision. Tossing his head, putting pressure on the reins Trent carried loosely in his left hand, he stepped forward. The action seemed strange. Trent wondered if he was riding an Indian raised animal, but there was little time to consider. The Indians were only a couple of hundred yards away, approaching slowly, but definitely approaching.

Trent waved the point rider to silence and covered the distance to the Indians in less time than it took to think about it. In his total ignorance of Indians, he could have made a costly mistake, but when he rode close, he said, "Howdy. Anyone of you speak English?" just as if he was walking into the general store back home. He then relaxed, slumped back into his saddle, and grinned at the lead rider. He hadn't planned the words he had spoken and didn't know what to do next, so he sat silently and waited. He had seen no sign of aggressiveness from the Indians.

"I speak."

The words came from a striking-looking man who wore white man's pants draping down over his moccasins, with a worn and faded blue rebel shirt under a beaded, tanned leather jacket. The rest of the riders wore a catch-can of miscellaneous clothing, none so grand as what the speaker wore.

As the herd trundled slowly past, Trent held his eyes on the speaker while he somehow found the courage to say, "My name is Trent. We want no trouble here. We're not staying on the land. Just riding over. We'll be gone in a day or two."

"I am called Daniel. We want no trouble either. But we are hungry. The women and children in the village are hungry."

"Where is your village?"

Daniel pointed to the northwest. "Maybe ten of your miles."

"Do you not have cattle? There's grass and water enough."

"I have told the chiefs. They are still waiting for the buffalo to return."

"I'm thinking they're in for a long wait. For my part, I've never seen a buffalo. Never expect to."

The two men studied each other, neither speaking. Finally, Trent made a decision he had no authority to make.

"We will be stopping for the night right soon. I will ride

ahead and speak with the cook. We killed a fat steer just yester-day. I'll try to get Smokey to cut off some steaks for your evening dinner. And I'll give you one animal from my share. You ride off a mile or two and stay away until the herd stops. Then you come closer, but not right into camp. I will come out to you. Will you do that? And will your men keep their guns silent?"

"We will be back. No guns. No trouble."

With that, Daniel wheeled his horse around and rode over a small hill. The thirteen men riding with him followed. A few yips and a couple of meaningless shouts rent the air.

Again, pushing on authority he didn't have, Trent rode past the drive and within a few miles found the night camp set up and the fire going.

"Got good news for you, Smokey. I heard you grumbling last evening about never seeing any but the same ugly faces day after day. So, I went out and found you some company. Good-looking fellas, some of them, at least. Don't talk much. I invited them for dinner. Fourteen in all by my quick count. I'm thinking they'll be happy with just a steak speared on a stick. I didn't see much sign of what you might call sophistication in the bunch. Just hungry faces. You want me to hack off fourteen steaks or can you get 'er done?"

"What'cha prattl'n on about, kid? Fourteen men? Where did you find fourteen men out here?"

"Seems as if they live here. Always been here. Or somewhere around at least. Seemed only right to invite them for dinner. I gave them one steer too. To take home with them. Kind of as a thank you for letting us ride across their land."

As if a light had suddenly shone from the clouds, Smokey turned his eyes up to Trent. "Indians? You invited Indians to camp? Shade will have a fit. Fourteen Indians could eat a whole steer and come looking for more. You're crazy, kid."

"Well, I'll admit it was a decision that was kind of pushed on me. Seemed better than shooting each other though. I'd appreciate if you got to cutting out those steaks. I'd not like to appear as a liar to those boys. I didn't see any real sense of humor anywhere in the bunch."

A couple of hours later, as Shade stood watching the Indians ride away, driving two reluctant steers ahead of them, Trent's, and one from the larger herd, he spoke to Trent without turning his head toward him. "Young man, you lucked out this time. I'll admit you made a good choice, but it doesn't always work out that way. I've seen...well, never mind that. I'd say we were lucky the whole thing only cost us some beef and a couple of live steers."

"One steer was mine, Shade. I offered it and that's done."

Shade challenged that statement with, "No. That's generous of you, but we'll take them both from the overall count and not talk any more about it. But I'm going to ask you to call me the next time."

"I'm hoping there won't be a next time."

There was only the single day's ride north to the rails following the meeting with Daniel and his bunch. Trent had decided he'd seen enough of longhorn hind ends, dust storms, and hard sleeping grounds. And he had enough in the bank to give him at least a modest start somewhere to the west, although he hadn't decided exactly where. Just one more drive with a herd made up largely of his own animals, and he should have enough capital to gain a good start on his new life.

WITH THE HERD sold and the riders paid out, they rode back south to gather one final herd. The ride back north, with several new riders, moved along more slowly than before. With so many cattle pointed toward Kansas, the grass had suffered heavy use. But finally, Trent knew they were closing in on their rail town destination. He couldn't see the town yet, but he recognized the signs. The strongest sign was the severely chewed-off range and the clear indication of four trails converging into just the single path ahead. He was contemplating this and looking for some wisdom to define his next move, and trying to outguess the drive foreman, when the shout arose.

"Smoke rising, off to the northwest. Range is on fire. Either that or Gladys is burning the dinner steaks again over at the hotel."

Smiley, the speaker, sure he was the accepted one-man humorous entertainer on the crew, burst out laughing as if his observation was the one thing that would lighten up this last day on the drive.

"Swing 'em," shouted Gates Sampson, the foreman who had replaced Shade for this last drive, pointing at the smoke. He was just a touch late in giving the order. The point riders had seen the smoke before Smiley had made his out-of-time observation and taken it as their marker buoy. No one bothered correcting Smiley or the foreman. The men were too tired, too rump-sore, too much in need of rest, a bath, and several decent meals, to care. In any case, their dust-punished throats were already set more for whispering than shouting.

There were perhaps eight miles left to the closest bedgrounds. There was scant grass anywhere. There had been a steady run of herds arriving for several months. The cattle, acting as if they were in a trance for the past half week, would have walked the rest of the way without guidance if they were turned loose. The men, almost as a unit, slumped in their saddles, expelled satisfied breaths, tipped their hats back, and looked forward to a final ride, leading to that woman-cooked meal and perhaps a drink. Or two. By evening, another long trail would be behind them, and they would either be soaking their outsides with hot water and soap, or their insides with cut-rate whiskey or warm beer. And waiting to collect their pay when the sale was wrapped up the following day.

The pleasant thoughts were interrupted by the sharp crack of one Colt .45 revolver shot, followed by a long series of similar sounds. Over those sounds was the deeper thunder of what sounded to Trent like a Henry 44-40, like his own, fired quickly and freely.

With the first shot, every man sat back firmly into his saddle. Some were reaching for their own carbines or Colts, some were busy bringing frightened horses back under control, and a few were lost in the dust and turmoil of a suddenly turning, milling, charging herd of startled longhorns.

No shots seemed to be directed at the riders. But if the intent was to scramble the herd, making it possible for a small number of riders to cut out a bunch they could pick off under the cover of dust and running cattle, holding them away from the rest, and eventually driving them for sale at some other rail town, the attack was a success. The attack was eerily like the one Trent was involved in the first morning away from the farm. He wondered if this was the new way of rustling—just take a few, making a long chase more trouble for the drovers than it was worth.

Leaving the bulk of riders to gather up the main herd, Trent, again making his own decision, rode at a full run around the stolen herd and gave chase. The rustlers had probably three hundred head, but at the rate the beasts were dropping out and scattering, they would be lucky to hold fifty under control.

As yet, Trent had no idea how many thieves were involved or how many of the animals wore his road brand, but he knew it was his job to give chase. He glanced back when he heard hooves pounding over the turf, and then a shout. Fearing he was being overtaken by one of the rustlers, he lifted his Henry and took a second glance back. He was relieved to see Cob and Gates Samson, the new, tough, drive foreman brought on after Shade decided he'd swallowed enough Indian Country dust. Three men. It wasn't many and didn't represent much firepower, but the main herd had to be the priority for the crew. Three only. He hoped it was enough.

No matter how the rustlers whipped their doubled ropes

over the backs of the cattle, they couldn't hope to outrun the horses the trail crew were riding. Of course, the thieves knew that, so they must have had some other plan in mind. Perhaps the desperate rustlers were hoping it would take the entire drive crew to save the bulk of the herd. All these thoughts were working their way in a jumble through Trent's mind when he thought of the river. The river his own bunch had crossed just a few miles south the day before.

Trent's best guess was that the rustlers were hoping to have the cattle driven across, and running on the south side, while other riders dropped off to hold the chasers at bay on the north side. It was a desperate move. The chances of success were medium at best. There were always a few renegades, Indian and white, who would work hard stealing a few head. Work harder than they would at a legitimate riding job. Still, the rewards for such a small steal hardly seemed worth the risk. But Trent had never understood the criminal mindset, so he shoved all the thoughts away and bore down, hoping to reach the river before the gang could cross.

The land to the south would one day be productive farms, but right at the time, it was barren, with some small hills, thick brush, and rough hiding places here and there.

Trent had swung to the right while Cob and Gates had maintained their course, crashing into the brush before Trent again reined his mount to the south. The noise the other two were making would gather all the attention of the rustlers' rear guard. Trent slowed to a fast walk, riding through and under the covering brush as silently as circumstances allowed. Suddenly, gunfire blocked out any sound Trent might be making. He stepped to the ground and, with his Henry in one hand and the reins in the other, he moved forward, hoping to see before being seen. He tied off his mount in the last fringe of bush before the river shore and dropped into a crouch, easing toward the sound of firing. Before him rose a small hillock of river sand. The dulled shooting was coming from somewhere beyond that barrier.

Cradling his Henry across the crooks of his elbows, he wormed his way up the sandhill. He took his hat off just before he cleared the ridge. Peeking over the top of the sandhill, he found himself less than fifty yards behind the two rustlers who had done the shooting. He couldn't see his partners, but the powder smoke rising through the tree limbs gave a pretty good indication of where they had gone to ground.

Hoping to stop the shooting while everyone was still alive, he rose to his knees, lifted the Henry over the peak of the sand, and shouted, "It ain't worth it, boys. Lay 'em down and raise your hands."

As fast as Trent had ever seen anyone move, the two rolled onto their sides and half turned around, stopping with their rifles pointed toward him, with both flaring flame and smoke. The unexpected move startled him into immobility for a precious second. He had suspected nothing of the sort to happen. Sand flew, altogether too close for his comfort. He could have ducked back down, but that would again leave his friends exposed to the shooting, and it wouldn't stop anything. And he wanted it to stop. The sooner, the better.

He was still thinking these thoughts while his finger tightened on the trigger. With an ugly scream, one man literally threw his rifle into the air with an involuntary reaction and then fell backward onto the sand. His hands grasped the front of his shirt. With wild eyes, he turned to look at the man beside him. Blood was frothing on his lips. The second man threw another shot toward Trent before attempting to roll under some thorny brush and toward the river. Perhaps he hoped to follow the river, swimming all the way to Arkansas. Trent would never know. And he couldn't ask because a shot from Cob, who had run up close while the other shooting was going on, downed the man. From the way he fell into an unmoving, crumpled heap, it was obvious that he, too, had ridden his last raid.

Trent rose to his feet, sick at heart and wondering what would drive a man to such hopeless lows. Coming to believe there had only been the two of them, but unwilling to bet his life on it, he held the Henry ready, with thirteen shots still available.

Cob and Gates met Trent at the foot of the sand hill and stood in silence as they surveyed the wreckage of a theft gone wrong and two lives wasted. A long, slow thirty seconds dragged past before Gates said, "Let's get back to the herd. We'll send a few of the boys out to gather up this bunch."

"We'll go get them now," Trent replied, before coming to realize he had just contradicted the foreman, his boss on the drive.

He pushed his mount into the river, ignoring his verbal misstep, again taking up the lead on the matter.

They found the cattle grazing lazily on the river's edge a short distance from where they had been abandoned by the thieves. There was no sign of any more rustlers. Nor did any of the three have any desire to chase them, if in fact there were any. It was possible that the two they had shot were alone, hoping to hold them off and gather up the cattle later.

Driving the animals back to the herd, Trent asked, "What do you figure that was all about, Cob?"

"Can't be sure, but if I was to take a guess, I'd say those two either had a bunch of renegade Indians that wanted beef and found a couple of white men to help them with the rustling, or there's somewhere close by that could be used as shelter before driving the herd off to another buying point. But them is just guesses, you know."

Gates completed the conversation with, "We'll report it in town and to the Army if there's any around. Then we're done with it. If we lost any at all, it isn't more than a half dozen, and we're not spending any time, nor are we risking our lives looking for a bunch that small."

Chapter Five

THE RUSTLING ATTEMPT PUT A HALT TO THE DRIVE, forcing the drovers into one last camp. It also meant that the cattle, although weary from their short, frightened run, were restless and difficult to hold. The grass had all been eaten off by previous herds, leaving little forage for the Triple C bunch. But they made it through the night, and before first light, they had the animals up and moving. Most were already awake and alert, some never having settled down. They were a day late, but the buyers would still be there, and the saloons would still be open. Considering the time and overall trouble a drive from South Texas could take, the extra day was not even to be considered.

But everything changed for Trent at the end of that last day when he, on foot and ready to close the big gate on the railway corral when the last animal was driven in, was hooked under the belt by a big, red-eyed, wide-horned steer, half mad with thirst. The horn didn't break skin, but Trent was tossed over the animal's head and under the feet of the following animal. The result was a crushed and ruined hat and a badly broken arm. After the railway crew pulled him to his feet and to the side, out of the way, he stepped back quickly to rescue the hat. He brushed the damaged headgear against his shirt tail, which was already hanging out, and carefully looked it over. He decided he would make do with the hat, pushing it back into shape enough to serve. The alternative was to dig into his savings. And the fact was that good hats didn't come cheap. He could avoid unnecessary expenditures, but he couldn't avoid the broken arm. He would need help with that.

With his good hand gripping the saddle horn and the fingers of the damaged arm gripping his shirt front awkwardly, he gritted his teeth, did his best to ignore the pain, and climbed onto the gelding he had tied on the outside of the corral. Ten minutes, at a slow walk, with one hand holding the broken arm, and following pointed-out directions from townsfolk, put him outside the doctor's small house. Before the doc would even look at the arm, he insisted his nurse help him out of the remains of the torn shirt. With a firm grip on a pair of scissors, she cut Trent out of the filthy and badly torn garment. Watching with a disinterested look, the doctor simply said, "Take that vermin-infested excuse for a shirt out to the burning barrel. Then show this man where the wash rack is."

Minutes later, while the doctor was tugging the arm into position and then wrapping it with a plaster cast, Trent was reveling in the light touch of the nurse's slender fingers, a touch he concentrated on as a way of dampening the pain of the doctor's somewhat flippant treatment. He couldn't keep his eyes off the young woman. Never having had any close experience with the opposite gender, he wasn't sure how to begin a conversation, especially with the doctor there, close by and curious. But by the end of the repair job, once he managed to lessen the pressure on teeth he had held gritted to their near breaking point during the worst of the pain, in his innocent and stumbling way, he had found out that the nurse's name was Gwyneth and that she had aspirations of someday becoming a doctor.

Although the townfolk, the young ladies especially, were justifiably cautious of trail drovers, Trent, having managed to retain some of his inherited mannerisms, somehow talked the pretty nurse into having dinner with him that evening. There were two provisions for the dinner date. One was that they would meet in public, at the hotel dining room, and the consumption of alcoholic beverages would not be included as part of the evening. The other was that Trent would have a bath, always taking care to keep his arm dry, and purchase clothes that would replace the near rags that were showing the thousand miles of travel on them. She didn't mention a shave, but Trent added that into the deal of his own free will.

Trent, mulling over his overall planning and knowing he had completed his last trail drive, was ready to move on. Move on to a more stable and, hopefully, permanent new life.

Even knowing nothing at all about women, or girls for that matter, he sensed that having Gwyneth share that new life with him was a comforting thought, even if he didn't dare speak of it so soon after they had first met. She was pretty beyond the ordinary, clearly self-assured and competent, which she demonstrated during the doctor's rough handling, and was mature several steps beyond that of most girls her age. The dinner date resonated with possibilities.

WHETHER IT WAS HIS SMILE, enhanced by the application of the toothbrush he had purchased at the small apothecary shop tucked into the corner of the general store, the first he had ever seen, or used, he would never know. It may have been the bath and the new clothing, or the shave and haircut. It might have been his explanation of the planning that had put him in the cattle town with wages to collect and a fine payment on the several hundred head that were his on the most recent drive. Or it was possible that Gwyneth was bored enough with her low-paying job and was ready for an adventurous change. Whatever had touched off her interest, she clearly indicated that she might like to get to know the young cowboy better and hear more of his story.

One long, adventurous month later, with Trent doing everything possible to protect the healing arm with a mind to getting back to full usefulness as quickly as possible, the two would-be trailblazers were studying rail line routes and their schedules.

The young couple had spent many happy hours riding the Kansas hills. There had been even happier hours spent planning the ideal ranch of the future. All of this bode well for Trent, for he truly loved to plan. And he finally admitted, to himself at least, that he loved Gwyneth May Scanlon, perhaps even more than he loved the idea of a fine ranch.

Trent had taken a good part of the day building up his courage. His intent was to ask the pretty nurse to marry him. To travel west with him into an unknown land and venture into something neither of them had been born to. The small farming ventures Trent's father had led the family into could hardly be considered as ranching, and certainly not wild, hill country ranching.

When Trent recovered his senses enough following Gwyneth's positive response to his proposal, he said, "It will be different for you. For me too as far as that goes. I'm still virtually a stranger to you and I'm asking for your life to be woven into my life and for us to use what little money I've saved, along with our collective wits and strengths, to travel to a new land, new to us, is what I mean to say, and to make a life. It's a bold thing I'm asking you to take on. You've never told me much about your family or upbringing, but I can scarcely believe a lady such as yourself comes from the kind of situation our first years are likely to entail."

Gwyneth thought for a few seconds before finally replying.

"See here, Mr. Wycome, I'm no shrinking violet. And as to my raising, I did indeed have good parents. We had a good and loving, and well-provided-for home. During the early years, anyway. But I must stretch my memory to bring back those early times. They all happened before Father took ill. We lived in a small town in rural Illinois. We had a couple of acres of land, a milk cow, and chickens. I remember that much, although I was young. Father was a printer. He ran the small weekly paper, which was really not much more than a rag that carried the advertisements of local retailers, along with a bit of news here and there, whatever father was able to dig up.

"When he took ill, he was incapable of doing much more than getting up in the morning and sleeping through most of the day. Mother was unable to find a buyer for the paper, so she sold off the press and whatever else they had that could be hauled away. We lived on the sale proceeds until that small horde ran out. Mother found a few hours of work in the store and took in laundry. But with four children to feed and care for and so little income, the ending was easily foreseeable. By the time I was ten years old, Father was gone, and Mother's health, too, was breaking. Breaking from overwork and bitterness. I hold it out as possible that the experience is a driving factor in my wanting to be involved in medicine.

"It seems strange now, looking back, that there were so many widows and young, single women in the east, after the war, and so many single men in the west seeking wives. There were advertisements in the larger papers. Lonely men hoping to gain a wife and move her west. Mother even answered a couple of the ads, but no one wanted to take on a ready-made family. Not a family as large as ours, in any case. Then, to add mystery to mystery, a man a few years younger than Mother, a man she had known all her life, came calling. Rupert was his name.

"After she got over her shock of finding him outside her door, Mother invited him to the table, where he shared a skimpy lunch with the whole family. I remember as if it was yesterday. He ate his soup delicately, almost hesitatingly, his hand shaking a bit with whatever ailment his war service had left him with, more like an elderly woman might do. He then laid his spoon down and said, 'Mrs. Scanlon, I would speak with you, were you to give me permission. I have family matters in mind. The children may stay and hear my thoughts, if you would approve.'

"Mother laid her own spoon down, leaned back in her chair as best she could, her weary body rebelling at the slight forced discipline of the move. I remember her saying, 'Since this is obviously not a social call, Rupert, and since you and I have known each other most of our lives and yet have had no social interaction, I had already assumed that you had a matter in mind that you wished to discuss. I keep no secrets from the children. Speak. We will all listen.'

"'Well, it's like this. Most of the town knows that I came near to meeting my maker during the war. I recovered as best as the medical people could hope for. That does not mean I am either healthy or strong. But it does mean that I am likely to live for a while yet. I own a nice house that I inherited, a house much larger than one man needs, and I have no debts. I make a few dollars here and there writing articles and stories of the nature around us. I seem to have an innate ability to see, and at least partially understand, the birds and the animals that are so familiar to all of us. But beneath all of that, among the grass, the mosses, and the undergrowth, there lies a world of insects and bugs. I study these and write about them.

"'From that and from my periodic labors about town, enough coin flows into my small bank account to keep body and soul together, and just a little bit more. Enough more to provide care for you and the children. What I'm trying to say, Mrs. Scanlon, is that I would treasure the opportunity to take you as wife and provide for you. Of benefit to me would be your company and meals placed on the table that would exceed my own attempts at cooking. I eat poorly, and the evening hours are immeasurably long. I am some years younger than you, Mrs. Scanlon, but if you can overlook that small issue, perhaps you could see the merits of my proposal.'"

Trent had been listening with rapt attention. He had a question on his tongue, but before he could ask it, Gwyneth said, "And that, Mr. Wycome, is a near letter-perfect rendition of the conversation across that lunch table. I have it indelibly imprinted on my mind. That practice and ability must be a gift from my printer father."

Trent chuckled in wonder and amusement. He gestured with a palm-up open hand and said, "It's a wonderful story, but you mustn't stop there."

"I have no intention of stopping there. The ending is very short. There was a marriage. A happy one from a child's point of view. Our small home was sold. The cow and chickens were moved across town, and with a borrowed team and wagon, all our earthly possessions were transferred to our new home. The change in Mother was almost immediate. I even heard her humming from time to time as she stirred something in the cookpot. Cooking and cleaning were within her diminished ability, and true to his word, Rupert's small income did provide for us. But it wasn't long before my older two brothers ventured off on their own. My younger sister and I were left. We were both putting on a bit of weight with our maturing. We had been scarecrow thin after the years of struggle. We have all spread our wings now, while Rupert and Mother live a quiet life, often going afield together, crawling among the grasses, studying the life habits of the creations that live there."

Trent was still grinning a bit. Perhaps inappropriately, he said, "I can't picture you being scarecrow thin, but I must say you have overcome that situation in a most delightful fashion."

A few seconds eased past before he said, "And they all lived happily ever after."

"Ever after," Gwyneth repeated quietly.

Chapter Six

TRENT AND GWYNETH WERE TAKING THEIR EASE ON the bench outside the hotel, sheltered from the westerly setting sun by the boardwalk overhang. There had been little talking after the shared evening meal. They both appeared to be quite content with that situation. But after a few minutes, Gwyneth said, "You haven't told me how it is that your parents followed along on your last drive up from Texas. They've been very quiet since they got here, staying in the background. How does their presence fit into our plans?"

Trent chuckled a bit, almost to himself. Then, with no further preamble, he said, "You've met them and spent enough time with them to see that they are a happy and agreeable couple. Perhaps happy-go-lucky is a more apt description. I couldn't even begin to tell you all the things they've done, and all the changes made over the years. Changes that often didn't make a whit of sense to anyone but themselves. Whimsical. That word almost describes Father to perfection. Don't take that as a careless or weak whimsy. There is nothing weak about Father. Or Mother either, when it comes to that. They will be front and center, taking a stand and showing their determination when trouble arises. And trouble always arises. If the trouble boils down to them having to make a change or two after the issue is settled, they will merely shrug and move on, almost as if making the change was in their minds the whole time.

"When I pulled away from home, I had to walk. We only had one riding animal, and I was never quite sure where that one came from. It just seemed to show up one day, and Father offered no explanation. The gelding wasn't stolen, I could rest in that truth. Although Father dragged armfuls of booty home from the war, none of it was stolen. Plunder in exchange for pay never received is how Father explained it. Anyway, I left the one horse and headed out, walking. When we had last talked, the evening before I left, Father was considering selling out and purchasing the store in town. He had never once mentioned doing anything like that, but my leaving had pushed him into a corner. So, he adjusted, as seamlessly and painlessly as he had adjusted to all the other changes. He knew absolutely nothing about storekeeping, but little things like that never bothered him.

"Readying myself for this last drive, I left the herd with Cob and rode the two days to see my folks. They were still running the store and were happy as clams. But when I mentioned my new venture, they looked at each other and grinned. The next thing I knew, the very next morning, they had sold the business, bought a wagon, one of the largest wagons I've ever seen, plus a staunch team of Clyde's, and were all set to load up half the stock from the store and set out. Mother was insistent that she would help the cook and drive the wagon. Father purchased a saddle horse and was all set to become a cowboy. He did all right too. Put as many hours in as any of us, sitting the saddle until he couldn't sit another minute. I often saw him standing in the stirrups to give his backside a rest. They've spent most of their time since the drive resting in the shade and asking me when we're going to be ready to go."

"They sound like a fun, easy-going couple."

"Oh, they're that all right. What they aren't is settled. But perhaps age will take care of that."

"Or perhaps we'll find just the right place and build up a ranch that will hold their interest until the end of their days."

"Perhaps."

Chapter Seven

During the month-long interval between his marriage proposal and the planned time of departure for the west, Trent sought advice and information about several locations on the frontier. He bought and shared several gallons of beer, one small stein at a time, and an equal quantity of coffee. The men he shared with fell into two categories, both of which Trent was soon to recognize and respond appropriately to. There were any number of traveling men—cowboys, railroad workers, and hangers-on—willing to tell a story, true or false, in exchange for a drop of liquid refreshment. These he soon learned to identify and to hold to a single stein or cup. But there were others, fewer in number and more cautious with their words, who had actually been to the places they talked about, or nearby at least, and had some knowledge of situations, settlements, grass, weather, and the local Indians.

At the end of all that, with a few repeat visits being taken in Gwyneth's company, the decision was made. They would trail the herd of breeding heifers they had cut out of the larger herd and follow the wagon across the western part of Kansas and into Colorado. The cattle were longhorn crosses, with most of the horns bred out of them. They were, overall, a heavier breed of animal, leaning toward the reddish color of some of the eastern breeds while retaining much of the multi-coloring of the longhorn.

Large work gangs of broad-shouldered, hard-muscled men from many lands had sweated the westward rails into place. The company leaders had taken their massive payouts, while the laborers moved on to their next back-breaking task, perhaps another rail line or swinging a double jack in some hard rock mine. So, the continent-crossing rails were completed, and steam transport became available. But the cost of moving their entire outfit by rail overwhelmed Trent's budget.

After thinking it all over and jotting down some simple numbers for Gwyneth to confirm his thinking, Trent said, "I've come to believe God gave these animals four legs to make their walking easier. I'd not want to be found thwarting the Creator's good intentions."

Gwyneth smiled a somewhat hesitant smile before saying, "So we're driving them? Cattle, horses, and a wagon? With just three men and two women to do all the riding? All the work?"

"You forgot to mention this dog, who seems to have adopted us."

"All right, all that and a dog. But since I'm one of the women involved, perhaps you can outline my duties. We're not married yet. I still have options."

A slow, careful look didn't find a grin or a smile on his beloved's face, so he chose his next words carefully.

"Mother would be insulted if she wasn't allowed to cook. And you're a good rider, plus you tell me you know how to drive a wagon. That big wagon team of fathers are like friendly giants. I dare say they'd follow along with no hand on the reins. And that breed of animal doesn't have much run in them. They behaved every mile of the way, coming up from Texas. I'm thinking you and Mother could share the wagon duties, allowing you lots of time to enjoy the scenery along the way while planning our future home."

"Have you looked at the scenery around here? How long do you think it will take to absorb most of it?"

"It's not the treed green meadows of the east you've talked about; I'll have to give in on that point, but I like it- endless grass, a few small trees here and there, rolling hills. Wonderful cattle country."

That ended the conversation, leaving Trent just a bit uneasy. But from that point onward, he figured the less said, the better, until they both promised *I do*. Those two words, falling from Gwyneth's smiling lips, would be answer enough.

THEIR GOAL WAS SOMEWHERE in the eastern lee of the northern portion of the Sangre de Cristo mountains, in central, western Colorado. Or at least that's what it was, by Trent's rudimentary understanding of the geography of the country. The main portion of the mountain range veered off to the west at that point. But he didn't figure they'd be going that far. They would take a good study of the possibilities before they got into the actual mountains. So far, all they had to guide them was the word of previous travelers and a couple of roughly drawn maps. They would keep their eyes open for a better rendition of the lands before them.

The plan, when they got further west, was to follow the Arkansas River wherever they could sort out a wagon trail. The word they had was that, after leaving the river and working their way through some rough and challenging country, there were valleys and unclaimed grasslands as they closed in on the nearly impassable hills to the west. The man who seemed to know that country best, a retired military man, had told them the land was filling up, to the north, at least, driven largely by the discovery of gold some years earlier. But gold miners don't need grass. They need beef. There was likely a goodly number of options for the cattleman who was prepared to live off the main trails.

They were warned that Colorado was not yet altogether a settled or well-governed land, especially in the frontier areas. The larger centers and their surroundings were reasonably civilized, but at times, away from the big city, circumstances could become a bit unpredictable. The news was that the gunmen and other lawbreakers were pretty well focusing their efforts on the gold country, having little interest in grass or beef animals that would, if stolen, have to be driven many miles to a market to secure a profit. There were easier ways to get eating money and a stake toward a life of leisure than rustling cattle.

Overall, if a cattleman could hold his animals on his own claim, not bothering his neighbors, and somehow steer clear of, or try to make friends with the local Indians, the future of ranching sounded promising. In the closed-in mountain valleys that had been described to Trent, the land tended to be dry, the sloping plains showing a good growth of golden yellow grass, although where rainfall was more abundant, or the small creeks fanned out over the land, the grasses greened up, at least in the spring and early summer. The high, western mountain valleys were said to be a far cry from the arid, open ranges of Texas, Wyoming, and much of Montana.

With the forests thriving on and among the folded hills, separating the blocks of land, there need be little mingling of nearby ranchers' herds. Roundups would be simple affairs, not requiring the great sweep of land and the hard-riding cowboys, so familiar in other parts of the west. Trent wouldn't be satisfied with this information until he saw the land for himself. His planning left room for some doubts as to the actual facts.

The Federal Homestead Act of 1862 applied, so each of them could claim a quarter section of water for a minimal fee. The mountainous portion they were aiming for wasn't as water-starved as other parts of the west. It was a good bet that there was still land that would make a fine ranch, having dependable water of its own. Claiming large acreage around a stream or river was a long held western tradition and the basis for most ranches. Trent would have to size up that situation when they arrived in the area.

There was much talk and planning, but it had to take second place to branding of the separate herds. Trent tracked down a local smithy and together they designed and built a branding iron. Trent had chosen the double *W*, one mark facing the other, with the top one upside down. He called it the Mirrored W. Cob copied his family's hat brand but built the iron smaller to differentiate the two ranches and then added a dash and a numeral two. At the finish, he had the *HAT–2*.

THERE WAS no shortage of paid-off riders whose services were no longer needed, hanging around town. It was also common for portions of any trail crew to choose not to return to Texas with the remainder of the riders. Trent strode into a saloon and glanced around to see if there were any sober riders who might want a few days' work. He considered his choices, and finally, shouting over the din of the drinking men, he said, "Got a bit of branding to do if any of you men are wanting a few days' work and if you're sober enough to know which end of the cow to lay the iron on."

He spoke and waited. A hush took over the room until one jokester hollered out, "You got the jingle to cover the wages, or are you another of those fly-by-night'rs hoping to take advantage of us poor-home and heartsick fellas?"

The talker followed that outburst with an uproarious laugh as if he had just spoken the funniest words ever used. No one joined him in laughter, and Trent struck the questioner off his mental list of possibles. A fella standing at the bar set his mug down on the hardwood, half turned to cast his eyes over Trent, and finally said, "I've about et up my wages. I'm near enough to my last dollar, so's the offer sounds good. Where and when?"

Addressing the speaker, Trent replied, "I could use three

good men, and yes, you will receive the pay earned. How about you pick two good men to join you on the job? And since you're all on vacation, resting up, sort of, how about you lie lazy in the sack in the morning. We won't start until seven. Flats out past the depot. Bring your own riding animal and rope. We'll have the rest of what's needed."

~

WITHIN LESS THAN A WEEK, the work was done, the men paid off, and the wagon loaded to capacity with the necessaries of life, plus a good load that Trent's father hoped to stock his new store with.

On their last day in the Kansas trail town, Trent and Cob were walking the single street when a disreputable-looking Indian, dressed in near rags, his big-brimmed hat angling down over his face, who had been leaning against the wall of the saloon, pushed himself away from the sun-warmed siding and thumbed his hat back. Looking directly at Trent, he said, "You. I know you."

The two men stopped, startled by the claim and by the looks of the raggedly dressed man in front of them. Into the momentary silence that followed the statement flew the critical question: friend or foe. Is this leading up to a fight or to a plea for money? Then, as if recalling a faint voice from the past, Trent's memory came to his rescue with a single name. He spoke it aloud. "Daniel?"

"Ah, you do remember. You remember that time on the prairie when you gave the men the steaks and the two beefs to carry home to the people. It was not much. It never was much, or enough, the drovers offered, but if we could get a couple of animals from each herd that passed, there would be meat in the pot. At least enough to stay alive."

"Well, Daniel, you're speaking better English than you let

on that day, but you must have your own good reasons. What
are you doing here?"

"The winter winds were cold these past months, with the
snow piled up around the shelters, and there was no more meat
to put in the pot. Some ate their horses. Some dogs, too, went
into other pots. Some of the old grandfathers died. Died waiting
for the buffalo to return. I did not want to live like that through
another winter. I came to town. Maybe find work."

Cob entered the conversation. "What kind of work are you
figuring on doing, Daniel?"

"Riding. See to the cattle."

"Are you a cowboy, Daniel? Can you ride and care for the
herd?"

"I ride."

Trent entered back in. "You did a good job fooling me with
your speaking back then. Where did you learn the English?"

"I am half white. I lived in town when I was young. Not
this town. Another. In Texas. But my mother died, and my
father's new white wife wanted nothing to do with a half breed
kid. Our happy home became an unhappy cabin. I went to the
barn one morning to do the milking. Only, instead of milking, I
threw a saddle on my horse and rode out the back door. I was
maybe twelve or thirteen then. I was never sure about that.
Ain't never seen them, nor them, me since that day. After
wandering over half the country for near enough to a year,
being chased from here to yonder by half-breed hating folks, I
joined up with a welcoming Choctaw Band and spent the next
few years learning Indian ways. I came into my manhood with
the band. Couple of weeks ago, I rode off again."

Trent studied the man as he spoke, wondering at the story,
although situations like that were common enough. The rugged
west, desperately short of women, fostered many make-do
marriages, or so-called country marriages, and distrust of
Indians of any sort was common and expected. Trying to see
through the rags, the obvious hunger, and Daniel's disreputable

appearance, Trent looked into his black eyes, wishing to see the man, the inward man. Deep down, where the soul resides. Finally, he shrugged at the incomplete picture and said, "Well, Daniel, we were just thinking of taking on some lunch. Come with us. We have no work we can offer you, but at least we can have a meal and a visit."

THERE WERE business places on the frontier, in the more settled and established towns, where such as Daniel would not be welcomed. The dust-filled and fly-specked establishment Trent and Cob had chosen was not of that outlook. The owner and cook, a rotund man of indeterminate age, but certainly too old to return to driving a chuckwagon, feeding a pack of hungry and unruly range riders, was in business to make money. That and nothing more. He was not in the least squeamish about whose pocket coughed up the coins he would gather to care for him in his older years.

The special of the day was steak and fried potatoes, the steak having been taken from a tough old longhorn bull, well past its age, that he had dealt a drive foreman out of. The price was right, and both men wound up content with the deal. The hungry cowboys that made up his clientele offered few complaints. The special of the day hadn't changed in the eighteen months the Double Down Café had been opened.

The three men sat down after helping themselves to a mug of self-serve coffee. There was no table waiter. None was needed as there was, among the many other lacks in the eating house, a lack of a second choice on the menu. Williard, the cook, simply counted the heads gathered around the six home-built tables and carved an equal number of steaks from the remains of what had been, a couple of days before, the hindquarter of that muscle-bound range bull. He flopped these down on the big flat iron grill beside the heap of sliced potatoes liberally spread with sliced onions and waited for the fire to do its magic.

Trent continued to stew around a thought while Cob and Daniel talked of cattle drives, Indians, and the weather. Only half listening to his tablemates, Trent burst right into the middle of the conversation, hardly even aware that he had done so. But he was conscious of the well-thought-out question he placed before Daniel.

"Daniel. You moved from a Texas town to a Choctaw Band, which is to say that you left the white world behind and took up with a band you had no blood connection with. Were you welcome? Were they suspicious at first? Did some want to reject you?"

Daniel studied Trent and his questions for a solid half minute before he said, "Why do you ask this?"

"I ask because I'm wondering how you would be accepted and trusted by other bands. Being half white might be a problem with some less trusting folks. The Choctaw are not noted as an especially warlike or troublesome band. Have you had any contact with Apache, Cheyenne, or any other western people? Perhaps the Utes?"

"I have never been more than a few days' ride west of where we are right now."

"You don't seem to be doing much here to bring you either wealth or happiness. Perhaps you would like to come to the west with us. Who knows what might happen in a new land where the Utes have reigned supreme for centuries if the stories are to be believed? We plan to settle among them and establish a ranch. We're hoping to keep the peace, and we'll start by respecting the people and their claimed land. But it might be good if you were to be a part of our ranching venture. Kind of like an emissary of peace. A diplomat of sorts.

"We'll have lots to do. Building a house and bunkhouse, corrals, a barn, well-digging, and everything else a ranch needs. We won't have more cattle right at first. Just the ones you may have noted held out on the grass a bit to the southwest of town. It'll be slow going at first, but I can cover a wage for you if you can do the work. Ranch work when you're there, and peace-pursuing work when you're riding the hills seeking the Ute, who call the place home. You could explain our plans and our desire for peace. When the job of ranching and building starts, there will be no time for us to be burdened down with Indian troubles."

"You say we. Are the two of you partners? Is that what you mean?"

"No. I should have been clearer. *We* is me and Gwyneth, who is to become my wife tomorrow if the earth doesn't open up and swallow me whole before that time. Cob is riding west with us to show me how ranching is done and to push his own herd along with ours. We'll share grass at the beginning until Cob finds a place he likes for himself. His family are longtime ranchers in southern Texas. He has a lifetime of learning behind him. My hope is to absorb much of that learning."

There was more talk, ending with Daniel saying he'd think about the offer. Trent dug into his pocket and dropped a gold coin before Daniel. "Get yourself some new clothing and maybe have a bath. And you'll need a warm coat if you ride with us. Gets cold in the high country, or at least that's what I'm led to believe."

TRENT THEN WALKED over to the doctor's office to tell Gwyneth that he had taken on another man, although that was, yet, no way certain. Daniel had said neither yes nor no to the offer, and Trent had no way of knowing if Daniel would follow the suggestions or walk over to the saloon and get drunk. And Gwyneth was too busy on her last day with the doctor to care much. In Gwyneth's eyes, some days it seemed cowboys were the most careless people in the world, abusing their bodies in shocking ways. It appeared that way in her medical world at least. If it wasn't a broken bone that needed mending, it was a gouge or a puncture caused by the sharp horn of some animal that took exception to his situation.

She still harbored the hope of one day studying medicine to the point where she could hang out a sign advertising Dr. Gwyneth May Scanlon. Or perhaps she would use Dr. Gwyneth May Wycome, which tomorrow would be her brand-new married name. There was a lot of time ahead of her to think that through. In the meanwhile, she was learning all she could, doing the rough healing the doctor practiced on his patients.

She listened to Trent's story for only a few seconds before she elbowed him aside. "You're in the way. Do whatever you want but do it somewhere else."

With her back now turned to her husband while she concentrated on helping the doctor with the cleansing of a nasty wound, she didn't see the look on Trent's face. It may have been just as well she didn't.

Chapter Eight

FINALLY, THE DAY CAME WHEN TRENT AND GWYNETH, freshly excited and starry-eyed at the possibilities that lay before them, stood, declaring their love and pledging their troths, in front of the only church minister in town. Cob Fleming, the logical choice to stand beside the groom, stood nervously, first on one foot and then the other, anxious to get the ceremony concluded. Trent hadn't responded in any intelligible way when Cob had suggested that the growing trend to have another man standing in the marriage group was to keep the groom from slumping to the floor, in the event of a sudden realization of reality should overcome the groom.

Now that Cob had taken a break from Texas trail driving and was determined to move his small herd west, along with Trent's, he was anxious to get started. Nevertheless, he was standing beside the smiling groom, silently wishing it was his arm the bride-to-be was hanging onto. He would die before he said a word about those feelings.

The pastor's wife, only a few months older than Gwyneth, stood beside the bride. And dressed in clothing Trent didn't know they possessed; his parents sat quietly to one side.

There had been no more mention of duties that would be

required during the long drive west, between him and Gwyneth or anyone else. Trent was content to leave well enough alone.

No search for flowers, even scouring the plains hillsides and the river valley as best Trent could, brought success. The few flowering weeds to be found were alive with insects. Passing those by, he mumbled to himself, "It's as if there isn't a flower in all of Kansas." Gwyneth stood empty-handed and didn't seem to mind.

The ceremony itself took hardly any time at all. The tea, fresh-baked buns, and home-churned butter served up by the pastor's wife at the completion of the ceremony took a little longer. But finally, the newly married couple was set free of the well-wishers. Hand in hand, they strolled toward their new, if temporary home, room 201 in the Cattleman's Hotel. Their next home, for the following several weeks at least, would be the small tent purchased and stored in the wagon.

Gwyneth had caught on to Trent's bent for planning. In one of the final conversations before the wedding took place, Trent had pointed to a town on a sketch map of Colorado and explained, "This here is Pueblo. It offers up mostly warm weather, from what I'm told at least. It suffers just a bit of winter, driven down from the mountains to the west, but escapes the dreadful heat of the dry, open grasslands further east. Or so the best information I can find assures us. It feeds into a mountainous territory to the west. Lies along the Arkansas River. Close around the town, most of the land is already taken up, but further west, there's grass enough in the lowlands and through the hills, in some places at least, to establish a solid ranch.

"There's grassed canyons and uphill benches where cattle can be left to themselves for weeks or months. Water almost anywhere you walk or ride. We're not the first. There're others on the land already, but we should be able to find a piece of land to claim. We're not looking for a Texas-sized ranch, just a few hundred acres to raise our breeding beef on. I'm thinking the day of scrub cattle is well over. I'm planning on having the best heifers for sale anywhere around.

"And there might be a ready market for beef in one of the several mines further to the north. If there's steer calves to buy at a reasonable price along the way, perhaps we can take some on, feeding them up and offering them as butcher beef to the miners. We might make a more immediate income from that source.

"I figure to use Pueblo as a jumping off point for our drive west, into the foothills of the Sangre de Cristo. We'll stock up in Pueblo. Shop carefully and prepare for a snowy winter. Father will probably reload his wagon with sale goods, although the wagon is already groaning with stock for his store. I've never known him to plan before, so I'm not about to criticize. Anyway, that's all up to him."

WHEN TRENT and his blushing bride emerged onto the dirt road on the morning of their planned departure, a quick glance showed three men and one woman, plus several saddled horses gathered around the wagon. The team was harnessed and ready. They had been left in the shade of the barn, waiting for the departure time.

Trent pulled to a stop, causing Gwyneth, who had her arm linked through his, to stop also. He was taking in the sight, before him and mumbling under his breath.

Gwyneth chuckled and said, "You might just as well say it loud enough for me to hear. I can't say as that mumbling is a credit to an intelligent man."

"I'm just counting. There's one too many men and one too many wagons. I'm almost afraid to ask."

"Why, didn't you get the news? Daniel signed on a couple of days ago. That's him there now, beside Cob."

"I must have been preoccupied."

"And perhaps you were too preoccupied to hear when your father said he had purchased another wagon. A pup he called it, due to its being smaller than the other."

"What does he want with another wagon. And where is he going to get a team to pull it?"

"My dear, loving husband. You're going to have to pay closer attention if you expect to be our leader on this cross-country expedition. Your father has had that small unit attached to the back of the bigger wagon for a couple of days now. He's been driving that team and wagon over hill and dale outside town to assure himself that it's not overloading the horses. Apparently, it's going to be running empty until Pueblo."

Trent listened and simply nodded as if he had known those details all along. Gwyneth turned her head away so her new husband couldn't see her smile.

"Everyone ready to hit the trail?"

Trent's father answered slowly, "Well, son. Since we've all been here for the most of an hour while you two sat over your morning meal as if we had all the time in the world, I suspect we've pretty much thought of everything except when you'd get yourselves ready. We were about to take up bets around town. We was just sett'n the odds."

"What do you expect to be hauling in that second wagon, Father?"

"Never you mind my wagons. You git yer horses saddled and catch up to us. We're leaving out of here now. We'll push those beeves into a drivable group, and you'll catch up some-where down the trail unless you find that you've forgotten something and have to turn back for it. Speed y'all 'r moving, we might be a good bit ahead."

Cob and Daniel listened to this family, back-and-forthing, but added nothing to the conversation.

The talk was interrupted by the terrified squealing of a horse and the angry, profane shouting of a man. It came from the corral at the rear of the barn. All attention turned in that direction in time to hear another loud curse followed by a whack, as of leather striking flesh. The cursing and threats became a steady stream, interspersed by more whacks and more squealing, this time from two horses.

Abe forgot what he was about to say to Trent and ran toward the trouble. Trent and Cob were close behind. Daniel followed at a slower pace along with the women. A gruesome sight greeted the men as they closed on the corral. A large, rumpled man, filthy and rough-looking in all his ways, was shuffling from one horse to another, swinging his leather strap and trying to dodge the flying hooves of the two frightened animals.

Doing something Trent would never have guessed his father was capable of, without breaking his rapid stride, Abe laid one hand on the unpeeled top corral rail, and as easily as if he was a much younger man, lifted his feet and sailed over the fence, to land on his feet beside the angry brute of a man. In his blinding fit of rage, the fellow with the leather whip was unaware of Abe's presence until Abe grabbed his shoulder and hollered, "Hold up there. No more!"

The brute's response was to half turn toward Abe with his arm outstretched, swinging the leather toward his intruder. It all happened so fast that all Abe could do was hold his empty hand and arm up in self-defense. The inch-wide whip wrapped itself around Abe's wrist, pulling him off balance and toward his adversary. The trailing end of the leather knocked Abe's hat askew and opened a wound down his forehead, splitting his eyebrow before Abe finally shrank back and away. Blood flowed freely into his eyes, but the old man didn't seem to notice. With a turn of his own body and the yank of his arm, he pulled the whip from the other man's hand.

Trent, now nearing the fence, hollered, "Dad!" with considerable alarm. Neither of the quarreling men paid any attention to the shout.

The horses, now forgotten for the moment, were still snorting and prancing. Cob cleared the fence less gracefully than Abe did and went to the animals. The one closest had pulled back on the tied reins that held him to the corral rail. One rein had snapped under the tugging. The horse's continuing tug had pulled the bridle and bit sideways, tearing a nasty wound in the animal's lower lip. There wasn't much blood, but the tear looked painful. With a gentle touch and soothing words, Cob settled him down enough to untie the second rein. When the animal was loose, Cob turned him away from the still-fighting men and slapped him lightly on the rump. Sensing freedom, the horse charged to the far rail and stood down, his lungs and breath heaving.

It took only a moment to free the second animal, who turned and trotted toward his mate. Daniel soon had them both gathered up. Leading them from the corral, he turned to see that the two men were still fighting, now trying to rise to their feet after the antagonist slipped and fell, ducking from his own whip, which was now in Abe's hand. The momentum of the swing had caused Abe to lose his balance and fall. Sensing an advantage, the horse beater jumped to his feet, pulling a wicked-looking camp knife from a sheath at his side.

"Interfere in a man's private business, will ya. Stand up and take it, old man, let's see how you like the cold steel."

Trent was reaching for his Colt in order to protect his father, but Abe surprised them all again, rolling over a few times to gain distance and then rising to his feet, drawing a twelve-inch-long Confederate bayonet from its hide scabbard that hung from his own belt.

"I've seen the steel before, you fool. And yes, I've felt it too. How about you? Are you ready? I'll give you a meal that's hard to digest."

Neither man was wise enough to call a halt. The shouts from Trent and the pleas from the women went unnoticed. The horse beater decided on a charge, with the camp knife leading his way. It took only three long steps to close on Abe. Those steps were taken quickly and with unwarranted, extreme self-confidence. Almost casually, Abe stepped to the side, dropping his own weapon in a downward sweep as the man roared past, cutting a neat rip in the man's jacket, from shoulder to wrist. The bayonet didn't halt its damage at the filthy material of the jacket. It continued on, cutting until it had opened a bloodletting wound almost as long as the tear in the coat, cutting deeply into the bicep and a little less deeply after opening the flesh covering the elbow.

With a scream, Abe's assailant dropped his knife and fell to his knees. The fight forgotten, the fella was trying fruitlessly to use his left hand to staunch the bleeding by wrapping the torn jacket sleeve together. Abe stood over him, the bayonet ready for more action if more was called for. But the fight was gone from the wounded man.

Abe wiped the blood from his bayonet on the wounded man's jacket before sheathing it. He then kicked the man in the ribs with an order, "Stand up. Stand up and get out of here."

Pleading, the man said, "My horses."

Whatever he intended to say next was lost in Abe's angry words. "You got no horses. You're not fit to care for horses, or any animal, far as that goes. I'm buying the animals. Fifty dollars, team and harness. Wagon too if you've got such as that. Now get up and get out of here."

"Fifty dollars? That's theft. That's a good team."

"It's fifty dollars or more of this good southern steel, placed where it'll do the most good."

To bring the matter to a close, Abe turned to his wife. "Helen. Go dig into your reticule and bring this man his fifty dollars."

Glancing at the several townspeople who had gathered outside the corral, he added, "You're all witnesses that I'm paying this man his asking price."

The statement wasn't quite the entire truth, but no one chose to question it.

Gwyneth stepped to the corral gate and swung it open

enough for the wounded man to step out. She then closed it again before saying, "You got a name?"

"Gabe."

"Well, Gabe, get rid of that filthy coat and shirt and have a wash in the trough. When you've cleaned that arm as best you can, come to the wagon. I'll see what I can do to put you back together."

"You'd do that?"

"I'll do it. And do it to the best of my ability. It's no more than I'd do for any man, deserving or not."

DANIEL HAD LED the team through the back door of the barn and tied them together in a double stall after allowing them a quick drink at the trough. The hostler, who had stood back silently while the skirmish wound itself down, greeted him with a shotgun secured in his folded arm. "Y'all beat me to the rescue. Can't abide the abuse of an animal. Have no idea what came over that fella."

Daniel, who had learned patience in his speech during his years with the Indians, made no comment until the horses were tied and secure. A brief nod of his head, along with a stern look at the horse beater, followed by, "Wasn't here yesterday."

"Came in late. Near enough to dark. Interrupted my dinner. Pulled his wagon under the hay shelter, stalled the animals, went back to his wagon, rolled up in his blanket under the wagon, and went to sleep. Said nary a word."

Daniel found nothing to say following that bit of information, holding out that it was Abe's business, and none of his own.

ABE, Trent, Cob, and the hostler all went to work on the horses, washing what blood there was and then currying the tangles out of manes and tails. The hostler arrived with a tin of ointment.

The hostler then checked their feet. "Shoes will last a while as long as you're walking on this soft Kansas grass. You'll want to check them before you head into the mountains, if such is your intent."

The long-suffering animals appeared to thrive under the attention. When the hostler mentioned the wagon again, Abe passed his curry comb to Trent and followed the hostler to the hay yard. Twenty feet away, Abe stopped and studied the rig. After a short few seconds, he said, "Liable to fall apart when it's most needed. More trouble than it's worth." With that, he turned back to the barn, the matter settled in his mind. A glance was all it took to see there was nothing more the team needed. The early morning was easing into noon, a sinful waste of daylight to Abe's thinking.

"You boys gather up that harness. Filthy and hard-used, but we'll need it by and by. Lay it in the pup wagon. Now let's get a move on. Run this pair in with the other loose horses."

As if taking charge of the venture, Abe stormed out of the barn, hollering about wasted time. He didn't see it, but Trent was grinning, walking behind him. He finally said, "Dad, I ain't never seen you in such a rush before."

"My age, a man has to hurry a bit. Ain't all that much time ahead to be lollygagging around come noon and nothing accomplished."

"It's nowhere near noon, Dad. But we'll get underway just as soon as Gwyneth gives the word."

Abe grumbled some more under his breath, but no one paid any attention. Trent approached the wagon tailgate where Gwyneth was carefully sewing up the gash left by Abe's bayonet. Her only response to her new husband's presence was to tell him to move. He was casting a shadow over her work. He shuffled to the other side, studying on the long, still-bleeding gash. To his amateur eyes, the work appeared to be about one half done.

"Don't ask. I'll be finished when I'm finished."

WHEN GWYNETH HAD GIVEN her hands a thorough wash and returned her medical tools to the proper place, she joined Helen. The two women were fussing over a few things in the wagon that they felt the men hadn't placed quite right. But finally, everyone was ready. Helen took the seat on the wagon, lifted the lines, and, with a couple of garbled words that no one could have interpreted, and a slap on the animals' backs from the leathers, the team tightened into the harness and the wagons rolled ahead, leading the group. Both Trent and Gwyneth were soon mounted, ready to take up their part in the long drive ahead of them. Helen held the team to a slow walk along the shallow trail as the four men and Gwyneth trotted their barn-rested animals to the grazing grounds.

Quietly, not wishing to be overheard, Trent leaned toward his bride, saying, "Never seen such as that before. That might have been the only time Dad let his anger loose since the war. He's most always pretty even-tempered. Wouldn't believe he had it in him without I saw it."

Gwyneth's only comment was, "Seeing that, I suspect he could get downright nasty, supposing the situation called for it."

The newlyweds grinned at each other before kicking their mounts into an easy lope to catch up with the others.

IT TOOK a few minutes to convince the cattle to leave the plentiful water of the stream they had been grazing beside, but by the time Trent paid off the two young boys who had been minding the animals, the men had bunched the herd into a manageable drive.

"I almost feel as if I should be waving my hat in the air and pointing the way west, or something of that sort. Theatrical, you know."

"You go ahead and do it, Father. I can't see as how any of the rest of us are honing for the honor."

"Maybe we'll just let er be."

They camped that night fewer than ten miles from their starting point. Abe spent his evening currying and running his gentle hands over the new team.

Chapter Nine

THE FIRST NIGHT ON THE TRAIL WAS A DRY CAMP, BUT they were back on the Arkansas before noon the next day.

Trent shouted to the scattered men, pointing at the river.

"Well, that's proof enough that at least one piece of information is turning out to be true. Cost me a beer, but the fella didn't lie. I think he was kind of doubtful when I asked where the big river was, as if everyone already knew. He said we could shortcut straight west while the river meandered in a big loop to the north. And there it is. We'll let the animals get a good drink and an hour's rest before we push on."

It took six days to reach Dodge, and another two weeks before they spread the animals on the flat ground surrounding the abandoned site of Bent's Old Fort. They were out of words to describe the constant wind by that time. In their search for good grass, they had wandered away from the Santa Fe Trail from time to time but had picked it up again a few days before. They had seen a few scattered cattle along the way and a couple of abandoned shacks, but no established ranches. Trent wondered if the cattle were strays, but he fought off the temptation to drive them into his own bunch. They saw no other travelers, except two riders heading back east. And no Indians.

Everyone was ready for a rest and an opportunity to heat bath water for the ladies, and for the washing of clothing and bedding. The men, one by one, waded into the river with a bar of homemade soap and called it good enough.

"Just get dirty again," commented Daniel.

The third morning at Bent's, they awoke to see a large dust cloud drawing their attention to the eastern horizon.

Cob took a long study before saying, "That can't be anything but another herd. I'd wonder about buffalo, but I do believe the big bunch will be north of here this time of year. Best we move on out. Keep generous space between us. We get tangled with another bunch, we'll be here the summer long sorting them out."

A week of slow plodding put them within sight of Pueblo. The dust cloud had followed them the entire time, pushing them a bit faster than they wished to travel. They drove past the settlement a few miles before calling a halt on ungrazed grass. Trent rode up to the wagon where his parents were setting up camp, and said, "Dad, you'd best ride in first thing in the morning and scout the place. We'll want to know where to buy rations and you'll want to see if you can find whatever salable goods you can find to fill that pup wagon. We'll rest up here. Set up camp and have dinner ready for you when you get back."

Taking turns, leaving the others to mind the herd and their camp, starting the next morning, two by two, they went to town. Daniel and Cob went together. Again, each had a bath and a change of clothing. But this time, they laid out a two-bit piece at the Chinese operated laundry and bathhouse. A stroll around town and a café dinner completed each one's day. In less than one week, the herd was rested, the horses were grain-fed, and their shoes cared for by the blacksmith. Trent's father, now called Abe by everyone but his own son, had cautiously loaded his pup wagon with additional salable ware, storing it at a small expense with the hostler. "May think of some additional things to lay on 'er. Best I leave 'er in town till we're ready to hit the trail."

TRENT AND GWYNETH were the last to go to town. Their first order of business in Pueblo found them standing before the brass-barred teller's cage at the bank. Trent laid down the paper he had received and brought with him from the small trail-town bank and said, "I don't pretend to understand this, but the Kansas bank told me this is as good as cash money if I bring it to another bank. I'll be wanting to open an account and deposit this."

The teller smiled across her desk as if she was about to instruct a schoolboy in the elementary workings of arithmetic, and replied, "This is a bank draft made out to the credit of a Mr. Trent Wycome. Are you that person?"

"Have been all my life. Don't know of any other."

"And do you have any proof of this? Any other document with your name on it, perhaps an addressed letter, or any such?"

"I've stashed a few letters in my kit back out at the camp. I'd hate to have to ride all the way out there and back just to prove that I'm me."

The teller turned her eyes to Gwyneth. "And who might you be?"

Gwyneth fought back the temptation to say she might be almost anyone and simply said, "I am Mrs. Gwyneth Wycome. I married a man named Trent Wycome just a few weeks back. If this isn't him, I'm going to be really annoyed. I have a copy of our marriage papers if that would help you."

"Yes, that would most certainly help."

It took another minute to complete the filling out of the simple documents before the teller passed a little blue book to Trent, saying, "Every time you come into the bank to make either a deposit or a withdrawal, the numbers will be noted in this book. So, bring it with you when you come. If it is all kept accurately, the bottom number will be the amount of money you have on deposit."

Trent took a quick study of the deposit book before tucking it into his shirt pocket. His work-swollen and marred fingers fidgeted with the little button that secured the pocket, but he finally managed to push the bit of mother-of-pearl through the hole and pat the flap down with satisfaction. Gwyneth had glanced at the teller, silently advising the woman to say nothing as Trent struggled. Gwyneth, herself, had to fight the temptation to push the clumsy fingers out of the way and do the job herself, but a single attempt shortly after the marriage was enough to warn her off.

With that bit of awkwardness behind them, the teller explained that the funds were not actually transferred yet, but that they should be in the account within a couple of weeks at the most. Trent nodded in a hazy understanding.

Gwyneth then said, "I, too, would like to open an account."

She dug into her reticule and extracted a small roll of bills and an equally small canvas sack with drawstrings at the top. The clink of coins sounded across the space as she laid the sack on the counter. Saying nothing more, she watched the teller straighten out the bills and count them, noting the total on a slip of paper. Gwyneth already knew the sum, down to the last penny, which she had set aside and held against the temptation to purchase a penny candy or two. The teller then dumped the coins into her own hand. Although her job was to handle money in its several types, she couldn't help taking a long look at the gold, each coin representing a goodly sum. Banks all across the nation, in addition to the government printing presses and mints, were printing paper and stamping coins under their own names. The teller quickly studied each document or coin to see that they had recognizable names that identified the issuer. Without that, their value would be seriously questioned.

"Mrs. Wycome, it is unusual for a married woman to have her own account. Are you sure this is how you wish to proceed?"

"I am very sure."

"And your husband...?"

The words came from Gwyneth's mouth in a pleasant enough form while still letting the teller know there was to be no further inquiry. "My husband, ma'am, is a good man, and he will prove to be a good and faithful husband, I am sure. But this is my money, earned and saved from my nursing work. And some gifted to me by my mother when I left the home-place. Now, we have a busy day ahead of us. I would appreciate it if you could complete the account so we can be on our way."

While Trent had been discussing his account, Gwyneth had taken note of a roughly garbed and lightly bearded man at the counter a few feet away. Without being obvious about her attention, she peered periodically at his reflection in the window. There was something about him that frightened her. The man was not trying to hide his stare. He may have noted Trent as well, but there was no doubt where his attention lay. A few more minutes passed when, his business apparently completed, he left, walking slowly and unnecessarily close to Gwyneth, and turned for one more glance before pushing the door open. Gwyneth shuddered a bit at what she guessed the attention meant.

When their banking was complete, they stepped outside into the late spring sunshine. Trent was studying the town, his roving eyes taking in the various businesses. He couldn't help noting that the supply stores were aimed mostly at the mining industry. He could see only one ranch supply outlet.

A single, well-mounted rider rode past. He was the same one who had ogled Gwyneth in the bank. Back in the bank, Trent had pretended not to notice. He studied the street before lifting his eyes to the surrounding mountains, as if he hadn't noticed the rider, but in truth, he was fully aware of all that was before him.

Trent and Gwyneth had planned a visit to the land office for their next stop. Before they could head off in that direction though, the thud of heavy boots reverberated off the wooden planking of the boardwalk. From behind them came the greeting, "Morn'n, folks." It was a call to get their attention as much as it was a greeting.

The newcomers turned in unison to see a big man wearing western garb, along with a large white, wide-brimmed hat, approaching. The star pinned beside his shirt pocket left no doubt about his position in town. With his eyes focused on the new faces, he was clearly intent on speaking to Trent and Gwyneth.

Unnecessarily saying, "Good morning, folks," again, he completed his introduction with, "Beuford Hamlin here. Sheriff around these parts and out into the county. Welcome to Pueblo. We've had a lot of traffic out this way recently. Some few are planning to stay. Most are moving on, Arizona-bound, some of them, or into the far hills and grasslands of this here Colorado. Some hoping to make it to California before all the gold is picked up off the streets. A few have been further west already and are heading back. Heading back to comfort and familiarity. Which camp would you folks be finding yourselves in?"

Gwyneth waited while Trent sought out an answer. He wasn't sure their intent was any business of the lawman. Thoughts that it was still a free country rattled through his mind before he adjusted his own attitude, in the interests of getting a friendly start in their chosen country.

"We're hoping to locate a ranch, Sheriff. Just heading to the land office to see what we can find out."

"Ranch, is it? Well, that's good. Good business, the cattle business. Doubles up on my reason for speaking to you though."

"How does that concern the law, sir?"

"Well, son, beyond keeping the peace in this here town and the outlying county, I have kind of appointed myself as advisor for newcomers. If'n you had told me you were intent on carrying on to the west, I would have wished you a good day and gone about my business. But with your intent to explore the country around in search of available grass, it might help to have an idea of what's possible and what the risks are. Where the trouble spots might be, you could say. Where the best possibilities lie.

"Now you take the country to the north. After the first little ways north and west, it's mountains. Mountains all the way into Utah. That's mostly a mining show. Seems to be three holes in the ground for every man that sets out with a pick and shovel over his shoulder. Rough land. You keep moving into the western mountains, you go far enough, it's Indian land. Friendly at times, those folks. At other times, you gotta watch them.

"Even further west, you come to the big hills. The Sangre de Cristo. Some say there's a couple of ways through. Others say there's not, that it's all up and down, vertical, don't ya know. Almighty pretty country in a way, but not all that welcoming. Cold up high. Snow on the caps all the year long. But the valleys, now, close by to here or further out, either one, that's a different tale. Grassed and well-watered in places, what I saw on my one ride out that way. Very little actually settled on, but a lot of it claimed, if you get my drift. Seems some men feel they can drive in a hundred skinny cows and a couple of bulls, call himself a rancher, claim every blade of grass in sight, then sit back and wait for nature to bless him with three or four calves a year for each of those cows. You have a Texas look about you, young fella. Perhaps you have some idea of what I'm trying to say."

Trent took a long look at the sheriff, then a shorter look at Gwyneth before eyeing the town's main street again, all the time wondering how to respond. His eyes fell on the livery stable. Cob and Daniel were working over the new team with a curry comb and brush. The team Abe had fought over would be getting their first trial, pulling the pup wagon. The hostler stood by. He appeared to be talking, making Trent wonder what Cob was learning from the old man.

Several wagons of different constructs were making their way slowly along the dirt of the town's main street. And the same rider he had seen earlier was nearing the end of the business section. The roughly dressed man from the bank was riding a handsome, paint gelding. He was on the opposite side of the road, but his actions were obvious and deliberate even from a distance, as he turned his head away after another leering glance at Gwyneth. Trent watched long enough to see him swing onto the westbound trail, apparently intent on leaving town.

The sheriff, dropping their other conversation uncompleted, followed Trent's glance and shuffled his feet, then cleared his throat. Trent still had not offered any information in answer to the sheriff's veiled question when the lawman said, "I'm seeing trouble in your eyes, fella, and wise you are to spot it."

"I'm listening, Sheriff."

"Well, now. You understand that a lawman has to be careful. Can't hold himself out in favor of one man over another. Has to hold his opinions close to his chest, I believe the saying is. But it's not gossiping to say that you appear to have taken note of that rider. Most men in from the frontier are neither good nor bad, but perhaps a bit of both from time to time. Mind you, in a country where the man rides for the brand or finds himself moving on—from his own desire for a peaceful life, or at the strong suggestion of the brand's owner, either one or the other—you have to assume that trouble for a part of the brand means trouble with the whole brand.

"That big fella riding the paint answers to the name Big Beef Cameron. B slash C brand. Drops the slash when talking about it. Holds out to the west of here and some to the south.

Nice, but remote valley out there. South side of the river, but further along to the west a good bit. Seems to have found what he was looking for before facing the really rough travel even further west. Good grazing out that way, and a-plenty for a small bunch. You want to grow to Texas size, you'll wish to find another part of the country to drive your stake in. That would mean considerable rough going, following the river and doing the best you can. It's said there's a couple of big valleys out that way. Biggest of them apparently opening right down into New Mexico. Ain't never been out that far my own self, nor expect to ever be. No real established trail. A little hard to reach, that country is. You'll work for what you get, but worth the trouble. Or so I'm told."

Gwyneth couldn't hold back a snicker, while Trent glanced back down the now-empty road. "Big Beef Cameron?"

The sheriff was holding back his own grin while saying, "You may well snicker, young lady, but if occasion should come your way, you'd best use his chosen name. He's been known to take exception. Mind you, I have no jurisdiction that far out. Different county."

Trent had no interest in names, strange or otherwise. Or the men who claimed them as their own. He'd ridden the trails with men who had assigned stranger names to themselves than Big Beef. His own interest was in grass and possibilities and little else.

"What can you tell us about grass and water, Sheriff? That's what we've come for and that's where our interests will continue to lie. Our group was figuring on following the Arkansas. At least as it allows for wagon passage. That's all the time admitting that the land office might point the way to something more suitable to our plans. Whoever or whatever this Big Beef fella is, is of little interest to me."

"And I hope it stays that way, Mr. Wycome. Big Beef, he swings a sizable lariat. Likes to think of the land as his own. Hoping on gaining a Texas-sized ranch on land that ain't up to it. I'm only suggesting that you scout out the area and choose carefully. Like as not you'll end up miles from him, and just as well if you do. Sooner or later, someone will take Big Beef down a notch or two, but it needn't be you. Not now, at least. Lots of good grass without going down that path.

"As for grass and water, both are available most everywhere in the hill country on the eastern flank of the Sangre de Cristo. You've got a rocky trail ahead of you to reach it. But others have done it. No reason to think you can't. Keep this in mind. The trail to those big valleys is on the north side of the river. The trail to the closer, but greener grass is on the south. Far as that goes, they're putting the narrow-gauge tracks through. Or at least talking about it as if it's a done deal. North. Mostly mining up there, but beef will follow. Slow, hard going, what with all the rocky country, but one day, by 'n' by, unless you choose to move further south, you'll be riding the cars, all the time thinking back to the adventure you experienced being among the first to move in with cattle. Folks will buy you drinks in the saloon just to hear your story."

"Not much they won't. Seldom touch the stuff. And I expect to be too busy for any of that."

"Regardless, you get to where you're going, you'll see soon enough what pleases you. Or what doesn't. I'll be getting on now, folks. I'm wishing you well. And as a final word of unasked-for advice, I would remind you that the Arkansas eventually comes to an end, or rightly said, the beginning, should you go that far. But that's not the only water out there. Lots of smaller runs. Pays to keep an open mind. Far as that goes, there's lots of land closer in that might bear looking into."

The sheriff had taken two or three steps away when he paused, then turned slowly back to Trent. "I see you wear a gun, Mr. Wycome. Are you a gunfighter?"

Hesitating, not liking the question, he asked himself what really makes a man a gunfighter. Is it protecting yourself as he had done on the first day away from home when he downed those rustlers, or at the river crossing on the last day on the trail, when he took out another? Or was the handle reserved for that very rare specimen of man who swaggers about, hoping to be challenged so they can demonstrate how fast or good they are at slinging lead? Amazed, as he had been times before at how fast thoughts can fly through a man's brain, he came back to the question.

"No, Sheriff, I'm not a gunfighter. I'm just a man fresh off the trail drives and hoping to have my own ranch. Mine and Gwyneth's. I carry a gun for protection only."

"Good day to you both."

With that, the sheriff turned and continued his walk. This time, he kept going.

AFTER A VISIT to the land office, at Gwyneth's urging, they returned to the main street and followed a sign that led them to a small apothecary shop. Upon entering, they were greeted by a quiet, "Be with you in a moment, folks."

Gwyneth responded with, "No rush," and they proceeded to examine the offerings on the shelves and within the glassed-in cabinets that separated the working area from the rest of the space. Trent's interests and curiosity were soon satisfied, demonstrated when he settled into a delicately carved oak chair.

Gwyneth continued to examine the items on offer until the chemist said, as if to himself, as he studied the compounded medicine he had just completed, "And that will do just fine." He brushed imaginary dust off his small apron and turned to see who had entered his establishment. "Morning, folks. What'll it be for you today?"

"Just some trail supplies," answered Gwyneth.

"On the road, are you?"

"We are. I'm a long way from holding myself out as a medical physician, but I've nursed for some time under a well-trained doctor. That was after experiencing some of the butchery taking place in the medical tents during the war. The doctor was kind enough to explain things to me as he worked through his procedures. I'll have to admit his work was mostly on injuries, from broken arms to horn gorings and the like, but there were enough illnesses to leave me with a rudimentary knowledge of treatments. Plus, of course, I've accompanied him on a number of births. I'd like to purchase some splints and rolls of bandage materials, as well as whatever you have of salves, ointments, and prepared medications. Your advice on what might be most helpful on the frontier where no professional assistance is available would be appreciated.

Trent was a bit mystified by the collection of items placed on the counter and then wrapped into a secure bundle, but Gwyneth paid for it all with her own money. He had come to trust her judgment, so he said nothing as he picked up the package and toted it across the street to the wagon where the purchases were carefully stowed. With their business in town completed, they mounted up and followed the wagon as Abe carefully moved the team out of town. Within a half mile, it was evident that Abe believed he had his fifty dollars' worth of horse flesh moving out ahead of him.

OVER BREAKFAST, on their last morning at Pueblo, Trent said, "I know the route we intend to follow has all been discussed, but Dad has that wagon pretty heavily loaded. I think heavier than what he wants to believe. Our information is that, for the first many miles, there's no shortage of good driving land within easy distance of the river, but the land shades upward as we approach further into those mountains.

"It's been upward ever since leaving Dodge, for that matter, but apparently, it becomes even more so. That means the teams will have a constant pull. The wagon will feel heavier the further we go. We may have to spend time searching out the best route and take more rest stops than we would prefer. According to the information provided by the land office and outlined on our map, we'll be swinging a bit further to the south, holding the river close on the north. We'll soon enough be into the hills. Hopefully, we'll be able to follow the tracks of previous travelers. And Daniel, we may ask you to scout out a route ahead when we leave the river. Now, if there's nothing I've forgotten, let's dump a pail of water on this fire and head to our new home."

Chapter Ten

A WEEK OUT FROM PUEBLO, THE TRAVELERS HAD gathered in the early morning shade of the sheltering cliff face they had camped under. They had been surprised the evening before to see three other close-by smokes rising into the evening sky. Daniel looked for a long minute before saying, "Indian don't make so much smoke. Indian, he'd be back in a fold of the hills cooking his meat over a fire he could put out with a single scoop of dirt. White men. Probably other travelers."

When the same three fires could be seen the next morning, they decided Daniel had been right. Abe offered his judgment. "Travelers. Same as us. And same as us, they figured to take a day of rest, Sunday or no, before facing those rocks we see ahead. Ain't seen no settlers along here, other than that one big outfit we passed on the other side of the river just to the west of Pueblo. Good-looking ranch with a fine house under construction and a well-planned-out ranch yard. Cattle were grazing the summer dry grass. Takes hard work and good planning to put all that together. Then there were some smaller outfits holding close to the river. And that trading post, but that was all miles back. We'll keep a watch just the same."

The day of rest turned into a washing day with enough time

left out for naps. Abe had gone over every inch of the harness. Following that, he had taken up most of the day crawling under the wagons looking for problems and tightening a bolt here and there.

Despite Abe's fussing, a welcome restfulness descended on the camp.

READY TO MOVE out the next morning, Cob and Daniel were brushing the horses, staying close enough to the camp to hear what was said as they planned their day. The gentle rain from the evening before had settled the dust and left a welcome freshness in the air.

Breakfast was completed, and most of the cleanup chores were behind them. It remained only to put out the fire, reload the wagon, and for the riders to saddle up and swing aboard.

Trent looked over the saddle he was tying in place, glancing from Cob to Daniel.

"Fella at the land office suggested we stay on this trail. Stay close to the river. By and by, we'll butt up against a good-sized stream flowing down from the southern mountains to join the Arkansas. Should be just a short way along here. His directions were to establish a trail heading mostly west with a southward lean to it. Word is that we'll find a suitable crossing spot before long. The news was that there's folks already settling in out this way, mostly tucked into the northern part of the valley. But there's supposedly room for more smaller outfits to the south. Mining to the far west, further into the mountains and north, back in the hills. Daniel, I'm going to ask you to stay back today. Drive the other wagon. Gwyneth and I will ride forward. Dad will pick a wagon trail from here and we'll find you at the end of the day. It won't hurt to have a change of pace for a day or two."

Everyone seemed satisfied with the day's plan until Abe hollered, "Hold up, y'all."

Every eye turned that way to see Abe, bent over, with the hind hoof of one of the team balanced over his own knee. "Ol Blue, he's gone and broke a shoe. Must have been earlier this morning. I checked them thoroughly yesterday. We can't move these wagons until I get that fixed."

With evident disappointment, everyone stood down. Abe unhitched the animal and tied him to the side of the wagon. He then proceeded to pull things out of the pup wagon. He had a sizable stack of goods on the ground when a woman's voice hollered, "Morn'n, folks. Me and mine is camped just over that there rise where you see the smoke. We're planning on one more day of rest before we tackle the uphill ahead of us. Thought I'd come over and say hello. Answer to the name of Clare."

They had seen three or four smokes the evening before but thought nothing of it. No one bothered to walk up the hill to meet the other travelers. There were travelers enough on the trail and there was no saying where a bunch moving together might have pulled off for reasons of their own. "Let 'em be," was Abe's single comment.

Helen turned toward the voice, hesitated only a moment, and said, "Morn'n to you. We was just going to break camp and make a day of it but c'mon in. Seems we're facing a change of plans."

"Problems?"

"You might say. Abe, that's my husband over there by the wagon, he just discovered a broken shoe on that gray. He'll get it fixed all right enough, but it'll take time. Heating a shoe over a campfire is no comparison to having a forge."

"Pshaw," the visitor said with a laugh, "there ain't no need for all that."

Clare hollered over to Abe. "Put all that stuff back where it came from and git yerself up ta the camp, just over that rise. Ask around till ye find my man. Howey Saint, by name. He'll be tickled to fire up his forge for you. Do the fitt'n too if'n you keep out of his way. Git that there job done in a tick of time."

Abe nodded his thanks, dropped the shoe blank he had set out into a sack, flung it over his shoulder, and led Blue, limping a bit with the one broken shoe, toward the still rising morning smoke. It took no time at all to locate the smithy and no time at all either to find that Howey Saint was a talker. Abe wasn't sure they'd ever get the shoe in place, but eventually Howey said, "All this here talkn's fine fella, but you got to leave me to my work now. Else I'll never git 'er done."

Abe chuckled under his breath and strolled away to leave the man to his smithing. Howey wasn't fast at his work, and he was easily distracted, but he did a fine job. Abe had to give him that. With the work done, Abe reached for the leather pocket-book he kept in the back pocket of his jeans. He was fishing out a few coins when Howey looked over and saw what he was doing.

"If'n you was figur'n on pass'n that over to me, I'd take that as an insult. Just so you know."

Abe grinned, letting the coins fall back into the little pocket sewn into the billfold. He offered a handshake instead of the payment, saying, "Sorry, Howey. Felt I had to offer. Like to pay my way. May never get the chance to look you in the eye again, what with all of us on the move. Can't promise to return the favor."

"More than just the one way to return the favor, ya git my mean'n."

Abe grinned wider in recognition of the meaning of the words. "You just take your time with the cleaning up and set in the shade for a bit. I'll lead this horse home and be back quick as a wink."

BACK AT THE CAMP, Abe was rustling in the back of the wagon when Trent walked up.

"What now, Dad?"

Abe turned with a bottle in his hand. Cautiously, he glanced around to see where his wife was.

"It's all clear, Dad. Mother is over with the ladies, preparing lunch."

Abe carefully settled the bottle under his belt, where his hide vest would cover it.

"Just got to return a favor, son."

Trent nodded and watched the older man slowly walk toward the other camp.

Chapter Eleven

With the shoeing complete, the half bottle stored carefully back where it came from, and the gray reharnessed, Abe was in a rush to make the most of the remains of the day. They had all known and discussed their plans before. There was no further talk except for the forever impatient Abe shouting, "Mother, let's get these teams to moving. These young folks can stand here and talk all day, but y'all and me, we've got miles to make."

Trent and Gwyneth moved ahead to scout out the trail, but they were soon back, after noting that the trail roughened to where they would be needed with the herd. Even at the slow pace set by the wagon, it was clear that the distance to the foothills was shortening by the hour. The ground they had covered was showing a decent growth of graze, with a mixture of sagebrush. But far ahead, even as the trail was becoming more challenging, the ground cover was greening as it rose into the foothills. And surrounding it, there was a good growth of trees. Trent found himself silently praying that the settlers would leave the forest intact, except, perhaps, for just the logs needed for buildings. There was something about the forest that sat right in Trent's mind. To log it off would remove something that couldn't be replaced.

As they were shouting the herd into a drive, a young rider dropped down the grade from the camp where Howey, the blacksmith, had re-shod Abe's horse. He was leading a second animal loaded down with a bedroll and camp-fixings by the look of the bundle. Without asking, he fell in behind and, following Cob's actions, helped gather and drive the herd. Cob and Daniel both took a study of the young man but saw no threat. He appeared to be just another traveler who had decided to lend a hand. The rider was dressed in well-worn clothing—canvas pants, a less-than-clean cotton shirt, topped with a hide vest. A hat that looked as if it might be older than the man who wore it completed the look. They wouldn't turn down the offered help, but they would keep a wary eye on him anyway.

Soon they were lining out, the wagons well out front, led by Abe, who had shown an uncanny sense of the ground ahead in previous days, leading the way. The herd followed last, with only Cob and Daniel on herd duty, both taking drag positions, allowing Trent and Gwyneth to take the point positions. The brush-lined trail was helping to hold the herd in a compact, forward-moving mass. The riders were all feeling the eagerness of the rested horses. With all appearing in order with the cattle, the young rider tipped his hat to Cob and Daniel as he eased past the herd, riding up beside Trent.

"Morning, sir. Mind if I ride along? Just for a while. I've been pushing my animals pretty hard this past week. Be good to slow to an easy walk for a few miles. Besides all that, I've been missing the sound of human voices."

Trent turned in the saddle enough to examine the man's horses, their packs, and the rider himself. The horses looked like quality, but the saddles and other gear were as worn as the man's hat. He took special note of the Colt .45 held in place in a scratched and faded holster by a loop of leather. The carbine stock he could see protruding from the saddle scabbard was equally scratched and abused. But the bit of metal showing above the scabbard, the hammer assembly, and part of the receiver appeared clean and serviceable. He turned his glance upward to take in the man. Good-looking fella. Pleasant smile on his face. Three-day growth of beard covered the sun-burned cheeks and chin. The rider's blue eyes were taking in Trent, even as he himself was being examined.

"You the rider we saw making a zig-zag trail down the big hill in back of the camps yesterday?"

"That would be me. Name's Eustice. If that might help your judgment. Eustice Ward. Up from East Texas. Tried ranching on a small scale. Starved out. Took a little help from the rustling riders of the biggest ranch in those parts to get the job done. But starving out on your own or with help amounts to the same thing. Give 'er up with just enough left to sell out and bankroll this trip west. No particular destination, although I've seen the place in my mind. Kind of like a vision, if that don't doesn't ruin your judgment of me. My folks tried to tell me I wasn't cut out to be a rancher. 'The Lord called you to lead folks in their spiritual battles,' is what they said, 'but you go ahead and try it your way first. Might be the only way you'll learn.'

"I was young and not put to listening like I should have been. Well, I tried. Failed, as I've just said. That's when I remembered my father's words. Neither of the folks survived the war, so I never got to repeat that conversation with them. When I rode home to say hello and bite the bullet, as they say, all I found was a rough-carved wood headstone and other folks holding down the place. Never did find out what killed them. Guerillas? Free lancers? Regulars? Who knows. Just like broke is broke, dead is dead. Cause don't really matter when it's all said and done. Well, you don't need to hear any more of that story. Anyway, I'm heading west. See if I'm really meant to be a preaching man. How much further west I don't really know. Figured to head to the town of my vision somewhere in ranching country. That way, if I fail again, I'll at least be able to get a job doing something I know."

Trent was silent for the count of thirty before he turned directly at the man, saying, "Eustice, you said?" Without waiting for confirmation, he carried on. "Not up to one man to tell another what the Lord has in mind for him, except perhaps a father. Could be a father has that right and privilege. Well, I wish you every success. I don't think you're going to find much for settlements up ahead, but I expect the country will grow. Fill up. Mostly miners there now is what I'm led to believe. Others will follow, given time. You got to be patient while the Lord does his part, drawing folks to the area."

"Folks like yourself you mean?"

"Could be. But we're for ranching, although my parents have the fixings for a trading post in those wagons up ahead. Might not be a town close by. New country. We all got a lot to see and learn. Might could be we'll start a town of our own,"

Eustice shared a wide grin with Trent as if the two were in some silent partnership.

Eustice bid Trent farewell before moving his animals into a slow trot, with his eye on the wagon ahead. *Best to get past them before the trail narrows down, as I've had been told it will. Might enjoy a visit with the wagon driver for just a bit. Might even join the man, rest my own animals, if he'd be lean'n toward shar'n his wagon seat for a while.*

Eustice was some surprised to see a woman holding the reins, guiding the wagon through the rocks and the occasional dip in the land with great skill. When he tipped his hat and said, "Morn'n, ma'am, I'm figuring that's your husband riding point on the herd. I've just been visiting with him. Nice fella. I'm guessing he's a good man."

"Well, you've got one thing right and one thing wrong. I suspect it's Trent you've been talking with. And yes, he's both a good man and my husband. But he's not leading the way this day. That honor goes to Abe. Abe's a good man too. Fact is, he's my father-in-law. You push on ahead to the other wagon, you'll find my mother-in-law holding the leathers. You'll see Abe somewhere up ahead, sorting out the best way west. And as far as visiting goes, Abe's a talker, and good talk it is. That is, as long as you don't talk about that war, he'll show you his good side. But don't go to pushing him against his grain."

"I'll be careful of that, ma'am."

Eustice moved ahead, approaching the lead wagon and Helen, holding down the spring seat, repeating almost word for word what he had just told Gwyneth. Helen listened, pushed her bonnet a bit further away from her eyes so she could see the rider more easily.

"You want to visit some, you tie that horse to the back of the wagon and come step up here. Going slow enough you should be able to catch up if you can move your feet at all."

IT CAME time to pull the herd to a stop and put out some lunch for the crew before Helen and Eustice had covered most of the subjects worth discussing. Abe, still leading from a half mile ahead, signaled a stop at the first small stream they had seen since setting out that morning.

They stretched the nooning to almost two hours to allow the cattle to drink their fill. Even though the land nearer the foothills showed much promise, looking on from afar, the morning's travel had taken them to a higher elevation where the grass was thinning out, being replaced by rocks and dry desert growth. According to the military map, there were still miles to go before travel got better. But there was enough water, following a larger creek, but the water flowed in the bottom of a small, steep-sided canyon. The plan was to cross over at the first opportunity. That opportunity came later that evening. Trent hollered, "It's getting late. We'll overnight here and find our way down in the morning. I'd rather be on the other side, but darkness will overtake us if we try it. We'll wait it out."

But the cattle were not about to wait. With the first smell of the spray rising from the tumbling water, there was no stopping the thirst-driven bunch. The leaders hesitantly eased over the lip of the trail but soon found themselves being pushed by those following. It became a mad scramble to the bottom. All the riders could do was move out of the way and watch, amazed that no animals were seriously hurt. With no real choice, the wagons were slipped over the edge. Abe had taken the reins from his wife. The steady team slipped most of the way, with their front hooves tearing out chunks of sod and side hill brush, but they did their jobs. At the bottom, where the creek-side was wide enough to allow the rig to come to a rest, Abe climbed down and showed his appreciation with soft talk and gentle strokes along their necks. "Good girl, Bess. You're the best, Blue."

Trent hollered at his father over the chaotic noise of the camp forming up, "If I'd have had a plan, Father, that wouldn't have been it."

EVERYONE KNEW that working the wagons out of the draw the stream ran through the following day was going to prove to be a monumental task. Also confronting them was the truth that overnighting in the bottom of the draw was a chancy thing. After a long study of the sky in every direction, Trent said, "I'm thinking we'll push the cattle up the south bank tonight. At least they'll be protected from any flash flood. There's no sign of rain in any direction. Holding the wagons here is a gamble, but I'm thinking it's a reasonable gamble. If we hold the cattle to a narrow path, they should break that bank down for us. Make the going easier for the wagons."

Everyone but Abe saddled up and, with much hollering and

smacking of rumps with doubled ropes, the cattle were moved off the water and, in twos and threes, driven up the slope and onto the grassed plain above. By the time they were done, the evening sunset had been taken over by darkness. But none of that altered Abe's thoughts, which he expressed in no uncertain terms. "Y'all can do what you want, but I'm taking these wagons out of here right now."

Abe had lit a lantern, which Helen was holding as high as she could while Abe worked over the horses. Trent had been so preoccupied with the cattle that he had not noticed what his father was doing. Finally staring through the gloom of the lantern light, he saw that the lead team was still in their place at the front of the large wagon. As Trent watched, Abe maneuvered the team and wagon until it was pointed at the trail the cattle had opened. He then stepped down and went to the new team that was harnessed and standing by. He had tied a double rope to each trace chain. Hollering up at Trent, he said, "Step down and catch these reins."

Trent took the long reins and, with his father hollering directions, gently drew the team across the shallow water and onto the slope.

"Now get them up there. Stop as soon as their feet are on level ground."

The volume of Abe's gravelly voice made him sound angry. Trent knew there was no anger in the words, only the determination to get a job done and done correctly.

With some scrambling and a good bit of slipping, the team made it to the top. As instructed, Trent held them still while Cob went to their heads, telling them what good horses they were.

Abe waded into the water to pick up the dragging ropes, flipping them this way and that until he had them untangled. He then walked them back, tying the ends to the single tree.

"Clear the way up there. Once we start pulling, there's no stopping. Now, slowly move forward. Take up the slack."

Working in the dark left much to the imagination, but with Cob on one rope and Daniel on the other and with much shouting between them and Abe, they soon had the setup ready.

Abe mounted the wagon seat and hollered, "Everyone out of the way," and laid the ends of the long reins onto the animals' backs. Trent urged the second team forward, keeping tension on the ropes, forcing the two teams to work as one. As the wagon started up the grade, there was a great clattering of boxes, tins, and what have you as the merchandise slid to the back, tumbling every which way. Helen made as if to rush to the wagon, but Abe shouted, "Keep back."

The pull for the dual teams took not much more than a minute, but there was some question about whether any of them had breathed during that minute. The darkness was all-encompassing except for the ring of pale light surrounding Helen, who still held the lantern on the stream edge.

The pattern was repeated for the pup wagon.

Abe clambered back down to the stream and, with some difficulty, and with the aid of both Trent and Gwyneth, got Helen up the slope. Abe then slid back down with the lantern. Waving the dim light in front of himself, he scoured the area in search of lost or dropped items. He finally said, "Trent, throw me the end of that rope. Help me out of here."

Standing on the level grassland, Abe said, "Let 'er rain. Now get yourselves some sleep. We're moving out early."

Eustice stayed over for an early breakfast before offering to stay with the travelers for another day, perhaps two. "I've taken a liking to y'all. You're workers, that's plain enough to see. Could be I'll learn something of trailing if y'all let me hang around."

≈

As if something had sprung up within Abe, he began taking more authority onto himself. Trent grinned at his enthusiasm, wondering where all that energy had been hiding throughout the years of their nomadic existence.

Ten days of difficult travel faced them after the ordeal at the creek. They lost track of how many boulders they had either pried or rolled out of the way. Twice, they had to double up the teams to conquer a steep slope. And once they had to create a log drag to hold the wagons against a runaway on a steep downward grade. With that challenge behind them, they were wearied beyond description as they went into camp on a drizzly, miserable evening. There was light forest in every direction, but nary a piece of dry firewood. Trent sawed and split several sections of logs to get at the dry wood inside the bark. By the time they were ready to settle in for the night, the only positive thing Trent could think to say to Gwyneth as they rolled out their blankets under the shelter of the branches of a large fir was, "At least the cattle are too tired to wander."

A short few miles the next morning presented them with a widening valley and a view of pale-green semi-desert grass and low, broken hills resting comfortably at the base of the larger foothills with the Sangre de Cristo hovering over it all.

"There she be," hollered Abe. "That's our new home. Danged if it ain't."

The cattle were pushed onto the flats and allowed to move over the grass and scatter at will. Abe was standing in the wagon, the reins hanging slack from his fingers as it slowly moved onto the large plain that lay before them. Helen picked up her skirts to prevent them from being tangled in the spokes of the wheel and half climbed, half jumped to the ground. Gwyneth rode up beside her and dismounted. Daniel, driving the pup wagon with the new team in harness, pulled up beside Abe, slowing to match the larger wagon's speed as he hollered, "Look'n good, brother. Could prove to be exactly what you've been on the lookout for."

The two women walked along behind the wagon, smiling and pointing out the many wonders nature had laid before them. Trent called his gelding to a halt while he studied the grass-covered plain before him. Unconsciously, and out of character for him, he stood in the stirrups, raised his arms to the heavens, and quietly said, "No man could ask for more."

The wagons sagged under the heavy loads Abe had selected. But freed from the entanglements of the past week, the team stepped out, virtually uncontrolled and unrestricted, with the reins hanging slack. In his glorying over the grassed plain, Abe was momentarily careless, failing to see a jagged rock half buried in the grass. When he picked it up in his peripheral vision, he jerked the team to the left. The front wheels cleared the obstruction, but the offside rear wheel struck, raised up, and then dropped. A sickening crack was enough evidence to let him know his carelessness had cost him a broken axle. Ears bent toward the troubling sound of wood grinding against wood. Slowly, he eased the wagon into the shade of some trees and stepped to the ground.

Without even looking, he knew he had a two-day job ahead of him, squaring a pine trunk smoothly on two sides and ripping it end for end to create matching planks that could be wrapped tightly to the broken axle, bolted into place, and then further secured with steel wire Abe had intended for resale. He shamefacedly pointed out the damage to Trent, who had no response. This was his father, after all. The respect gained as Abe guided the wagon unerringly from South Texas to the point they had finally reached far outweighed the current situation. Abe half turned away and then glanced back, his arms spread in frustration.

"We went through this past week clattering over hazards much worse than this little rock. I thought we were home free. Goes to show. Just goes to show."

The teams were turned loose to take full advantage of the plentiful grazing as if they understood that it was resting time.

Although others had, in earlier decades, completed longer, more arduous journeys, Trent and the rest were about at their limit—cattle, men, horses, and, of course, the hard-working women who guided the teams and took their turns herding cattle during the drive, while starting and ending their days over the fire, the big pots, and the grilling plate.

The wagons had been overloaded since the last purchase done in Pueblo. The fact that they held together to make it so close to their destination, while needing so little attention, was a credit to the strength of the oaken axles and the driving skills of both Abe and Helen.

They didn't have the material or the woodworking skills to make a whole new axle, but they could do a patch that would carry the empty wagon back to a Pueblo blacksmith who could complete the task, although the thought of fighting through those last miles again about took Abe's breath away. But until the axle was repaired, they would be moving into the valley without the wagon. They would face that question in the morning.

Cob, who had led the entourage onto the grass plain, rode a mile out onto the grass, turned to look back at the others, and let another loud hoot out of a dry throat, past heat and dust-cracked lips. Riding to within shouting distance of the others, he stood in his stirrups and waved his hat in the air. "Ain't she somethin'?" he shouted.

The sight of knee-high grass and a few scattered cabins and tents on the fringe of the plain to the north said anyone settling here would have neighbors, as well as graze for growing herds.

And for immediate need, the broad green meadows gave promise of at least a chance to rest and allow the animals to recover from their long walk, while Trent and Gwyneth searched through the distance to the western wall of rock for an unoccupied corner, a homeplace not yet claimed by others.

They had arrived with no one suffering serious injury or mishap. There was much to be thankful for. They had lost only a few cattle along the way. One had stumbled over a jagged rock and broken its leg, ending its days being butchered for meat. They suspected a couple of others may have wandered off during the dark of night, but they wouldn't know until they spread them out to graze, and they could take an accurate count. They had allowed for some losses in their planning, and so far, the shrinkage was below their estimate.

Looking over this highland plain across the distance, Trent and Gwyneth—searching out the land as they stood side by side, holding hands like the young lovers they, in fact, were— saw no end to the possibilities. A thinking and working man could establish himself almost anywhere that was not already claimed. Studying on one of the numerous small streams that leaked snowmelt down the cliff face, feeding it onto the grassland, Trent said, pointing across the valley, "That. That right there. That's what I saw in my mind's eye. Water. In small streams, to be sure. But judging by the snowcaps, the melting will never end, just one winter's buildup on top of the last one. Well, we'll ride over there by and by. For tonight, we'll hold here. We'll rest for a night or two. Explore some before we move further."

The cattle, after pausing at the stream, were soon spreading out over the grass. Cob turned to Daniel, saying, "Look at them. They're making themselves to home already."

Daniel responded, "Well, the Indian-half of me is still raring to ride over the next hill to see more land, but the white-half is ready for a rest. I do believe we just might find some shade in that fold of the hill alongside the stream."

Trent built a fire from some sticks and chunks of wood he scrounged from beneath the brush beside the wagon. Coffee was soon ready, and everyone huddled into the bit of afternoon shade, taking their ease. Gwyneth, becoming excited by the possibilities the land offered, looked over to Trent. "What's next?"

"Next, my dear, you and I are going to go for a ride. I was figuring to wait, but we've got some hours yet today I'd hate to waste. Just as soon as we drain that coffee pot and take our fill of the lunch leftovers, we'll leave the others here to set up a temporary camp while we do some exploring."

The newlyweds rode several miles, seeing only two other settlers along the way. Neither of them had anything like an established setup or a long-term home. Trent figured they hadn't arrived too much before his own bunch. They skirted two small bunches of cattle but no large herds.

They were riding west, with the almost barren hillsides on the north and east at their backs. Out on the flats to the south of them, the land greened up as far as they could see. The low hills defining the limits of the valley on the west were backed by higher, forest-covered hills. Beyond the few temporary camps hugging the northern edge of the valley, they saw no further homesites, no fire smoke, no riders. It was as if they were gazing at this big, beautiful country, just the two of them, seeing it for the first time since creation. They rode in silence, almost in awe at the space before them and the snow-topped mountains virtually all along the western horizon.

Trent turned his animal to the south, where the increased altitude of the valley floor allowed them a grand view of the country down that way. The view was limited only by a bluish haze which shrouded the far horizon. Gwyneth stopped her horse and studied her husband as he studied the land. She waited long enough to allow him to fill his mind with thoughts before she quietly asked, "What are you thinking?"

Trent stretched, stood in his stirrups for a moment and then settled back down. "I'm thinking it's partially what we've been looking for. Not all, but not bad either. As we've said several times along the way, the grass doesn't compare to the eastern states, by what you've told me of your homeland, but there's many a prosperous ranch in Texas built on land no better than this. And what are you seeing?"

"I'm seeing what you're seeing. You've described it well enough, and no, the growth doesn't compare to the east. I suppose we could have gone east if that was what we were looking for. But there's little land left for homesteading, and the money we have would soon be gone, making our road ahead considerably slower."

The one thing lacking where they rode was trees. The upland forest seemed to stop abruptly when the hillside flattened out and became the collection of slightly rolling flatlands they were riding on.

Trent suggested, "Let's swing over to that other side. I'd like to see that western flank up close. That hillside is green with tall enough trees, but we're a long distance from there. Can't tell if they're building logs or just rail-thin aspens that don't make for good lumber anyway."

Gwyneth smiled and answered, "I have always loved your enthusiasm, my dear, but you seem to have missed the fact that we have ridden a good distance and that the sun has already dropped below the mountain peaks. I'm thinking the other side of the valley will still be there come morning."

"So, it has," was Trent's grinning response as he glanced to the west, seeing the disappearing sun and the back-lit outline of the Sangre de Cristo. "Where would I be without you? Probably sleeping with a rock for a pillow, and on an empty stomach to boot."

THEY ARRIVED LATE at the dimly lit camp, guided the last couple of miles by the light of the dinner fire. In the distance, Trent could see the other men pushing the small herd toward that same fire. Gwyneth continued into camp while Trent urged his horse into a lope toward the herd. The light was nearly gone when he rode up beside Cob. Not bothering to wait for the question, Cob offered, "Took the herd to the better water. The stream out of those hills beside camp wasn't going to keep them satisfied. Anyway, we wanted to look at the grass and see the possibilities on that side."

Trent nodded, although it was too dark for Cob to see.

Left to themselves, they knew the cattle would eventually gravitate back to the lusher grasses and forested shade of the west side. Seeing no harm in it, they clustered the animals close to the wagons and then turned them loose before returning to camp in time for dinner with a glowing report of the possibilities.

"Cob, you and I will go out in the morning to take another look. Gwyneth could use a day of rest. Daniel and Dad can hold the cattle."

Without comment, Cob, lying comfortably in the grass with his head resting on his saddle, simply lifted his coffee mug in response.

Eustice, who had stayed with the group longer than he intended, had ridden out the evening before, claiming his interest in seeing what lay to the north. He arrived back just in time for a late cup and a report of what he'd seen. Trent pushed the report off to the morning. The women had already found their blankets, and the men wouldn't be many minutes behind.

Chapter Twelve

ABE, WHO DIDN'T PARTICULARLY CARE WHERE THEY set up their ranching operation, wanting only to get his trading post built and open, cautioned, "We won't get far stepping on other folks' toes or pushing ourselves onto claimed and used grass. Got to be careful of that. Of course, more than enough ranchers have gotten in the habit of claiming half the country as their own. I figure if the government or the homestead people got involved, they'd say grass must be used to have a legitimate claim to it. Of course, the government boys are a long way off. We'll have to be careful. We'll do better with friends for neighbors than we would with enemies."

The next morning, Cob asked, "Wonder where this gent calling himself Big Beef Cameron hangs his hat?"

"Don't know. It could be miles away or in some other area altogether. Sheriff indicated that he was out this way somewhere. Recommended us to leave him alone. Seemed like good advice."

Cob grinned in response. "Now be still a minute. I'm trying to remember if either of us ever heeded good advice."

With a slight smile on his face, Trent bent to give another tug on the latigo strap. He checked the leather for tautness,

tucked the end of the strap behind the rigging where it
wouldn't be in the way, then straightened himself out, studying
the men facing him.

"Well, I heeded the good advice of whatever voice it is that
sometimes speaks into my mind. Result is that there's a beautiful lady who rides beside me. Took my name and all. So that's
at least once. Could have been other times. Might think on that
if I find time after all my other thinking is done."

With that, he swung aboard his gelding, and with a nudge
of his heel, the animal stepped up beside Cob, who was already
mounted. Daniel, who had insisted on joining the day's search
and who, so far, had not bothered adding anything to the
conversation, dropped in behind. The duo left in camp watched
them ride off.

Trent knew from all the advice and gossip he had heard on
the trip west that while it was common for two men to partner
up in a new ranch effort, it was unusual to include an Indian.
That Daniel was half white changed nothing in the eyes of
most. Half Indian was as good as all Indian. But they had found
Daniel to be a good man, a good worker, and a good companion. They were all peaceful folks, Trent and those riding with
him. Peaceful when that was possible, but ready to do what had
to be done when the situation changed. He continued with the
thought that he and the others would take folks they met in the
valley at their word. Still, Trent, since leaving home, had
adopted the belief of the times that the best way to live a
peaceful life was to be ready, when called upon, to enforce peace
with distinctly unpeaceful means. Then he asked himself what
had turned his mind in that direction. He came to no real
conclusion.

After the months and years of tedious trail drives, Trent had
developed an itch to move on, to get where he was going, see the
new country. If he dared to think that through, he would probably concede that he was not so different from his father as he
liked to pretend. The drives had been for making and saving

money, although what he learned of cattle, horses, and men was invaluable. It seemed that from that first day he had left his folks on their little dairy operation, he had been dreaming of this day, dreaming and planning of this opportunity, as was his want. *Plan for what you hope to accomplish and then figure out a way to fulfill the plan.* And here he was, looking at land that would one day be filled with ranches and farms, but for now was available to homesteaders. He hadn't given the Spanish land grants a single thought. That they might force themselves on him was nowhere in his thinking.

They rode a bare five miles that day before crossing the valley to examine the surrounding, well-watered, treed area. Nature was difficult to understand, leaving one area bare rock while just a half mile away, lush forests graced the hillsides. Before them stood one such area. Pine, aspen, spruce and fir grew in abundance. None of the riders really knew one tree from the next, except for the aspen. But their main concern was satisfied. Here there were building logs and firewood in abundance.

THE NEXT DAY, Gwyneth joined Cob and Trent, determined to ride quickly over the route the men had already covered and then slow to where a more studious approach might bear fruit. Daniel had been asked to scout the small valleys leading off to the west, across the river, to look for Indian signs. He and Trent rode side by side, crossing the shallow river and onto the western grassland. Daniel left them at that point, going his own way.

Plodding along, at Gwyneth's pace, the impatient Trent, at the merest suggestion, would have put his heels to the gelding's flank and moved ahead at a good trot, giving in to temptation. But Gwyneth, with roving eyes, and a fascination for the low mountains that flanked the eastern horizon, and as the only one

with book learning, pointed out items of interest all along the
way, from the many tree-lined streams in the distance, to the
grass their futures would depend upon, a change of terrain here,
a different species of tree over there, and several times, subtle
changes in the rock structure lining the trail. Only once did she
notice a flower just coming into bloom, although she suspected
the grasslands might be awash in color in early spring.

The men could have pointed out things she had missed
seeing, things that were so natural to their eyes after the
hundreds of miles riding over every type of country that they
just took nature for granted. It wasn't that they didn't notice or
appreciate the changes in terrain or ground cover as they moved
along. It was more that their minds were on grass, shelter, and
water. Always water, because everything else was meaningless
without water. And when hard times came upon a situation,
water was the very essence of survival.

Gwyneth picked up the conversation with, "We will have so
much to learn about this high, semi-desert country. I picked up
a book on what to expect in the western lands. I've been reading
about snakes. Where I was raised, we had very few snakes, and
even fewer that were venomous. Here, if I have my information
accurately memorized, most of the snakes will bear watching."

"We're high up here though," replied Cob. "Might make
the difference."

Trent studied his young wife carefully, trying to read a
message into her comments on snakes. He could see nothing
particular, either way. He satisfied himself with, "For my part,
I'd just as soon Old Noah had closed up the door to the ark
while the snakes were still on the ramp."

"Noah didn't close the door. The Lord did that himself."

"Makes no never mind to my wishing. Someone let the
snakes on board, and here they are, growing meaner by the
year."

They pulled up in a shady spot beside a bare trickle of a
stream to eat their lunch and then continued to the south.

There was no trail or even hoof prints as a sign of others in the valley. One of the protruding rocky outcrops had been blocking their view to the south. They rode together around its end, and it was like the whole other world was exposed before them. Without a word, they all pulled to a halt, taking in the expanse their eyes beheld. Cob pulled up beside the lead riders.

Daniel, who had rejoined them at noon, stepped to the ground and squatted on his haunches, his elbows on his knees and his open hands held out before him. Trent thought he heard some low-voiced muttering, almost like a prayer but in a language, he had never heard before. As he rose to a standing position, Daniel lifted his right arm, with his hand open, face down, and silently swept it from side to side. His three companions watched in silent wonder. Again, there was the slight muttering sound. Daniel had gained influence from so many cultures growing up, and in his wanderings, he may have developed his own hand signs for Creator or for giving thanks. Trent could only guess, and he would never ask unless Daniel opened the subject himself.

The sight before them had struck each one differently. Cob had stood in his stirrups, as if the few inches of added height would provide more clarity as he gazed all around. Trent and Gwyneth had held their seats. Trent would have argued that he hadn't moved, but somehow, he found himself holding Gwyneth's hand.

The decision to move on was made by Trent's gelding, with a double nod of his head and a slight pressure on the bit. Trent slackened the reins and let the animal have his head. The others broke back into their previous formation, and they moved into the high mountain valley. The land close to the wall was rocky, with jagged, broken granite lying on the grassed open areas. The surrounding hills were rounded boulders or, at times, solid walls of multicolored granite—grays, light browns, darker browns, much of it covered in lichen where the occasional pine tree offered sheltering shade.

Away from the hills, what looked like an animal trail wandered in an erratic path through broken, jagged-edged granite. There was a bewildering variety of cacti, some in bloom. And away from the hills, a short way, grass. Enough grass for all the beef animals in the world. Or at least it appeared that way to the wandering riders. Grazing close to the upthrusts, an animal might pick up a cactus spine or two before they learned how to deal with the situation, but there was grass enough to make it worth whatever problems they would have to solve. With the multiple streams plus the occasional show of surface water, a man could establish a ranch almost anywhere.

As estimated, ten miles south of where they had camped the night before, hugging the base of the rising hills to the west, they soon began spotting B/C cattle. They rode on for another couple of miles, seeing only a total of perhaps three hundred animals, all scrubs in Trent's mind.

"Well, whatever else Big Beef Cameron is, he isn't a cattleman. Not one with any pride in what he's raising anyway. We saw enough of what the buyers were looking for at the rails to know these we're seeing are a poor lot and would command only a reluctant return from the buyers."

Without turning her eyes from the couple dozen multicolored animals on the gentle hillside they were skirting, Gwyneth said, "There's grass enough, but those poor beasts are all ribs and hide. Not fat enough on them to keep a soap maker happy, or to properly grease a pan. It's got me wondering if they lost their weight over the winter and haven't recovered it yet, or if this grass doesn't offer the nourishment they need."

The three men were silent long enough to think that over before Cob said, "Family ranch, the Sombrero, or Hat brand, down to the Texas hot country, we had some animals that never did fill out. Looked much like these. Pa, he finally rooted them out of the herd and shipped them off. Packing plants probably bought them for the hides, or maybe some tough beef to turn into sausage. You add enough spices and folks down south will eat anything. Them Mex's, they put a stew together they call Birria. Cook that tough beef until it's nearly falling apart. Could do the same with a boot or an old saddle. Stir it in with whatever potatoes and garden truck or such as they have available, add spice enough to spark a fire you'll carry with you into old age, if it don't kill you first.

"Had a cook one time on the Hat. Mex. Couldn't speak any more English than to tell Pa what supplies to bring back from town. Made a dish he called chili. Of course, that's what the peppers he grew are called too, so you get the idea.

"That was back before the war. The war years were tough on ranching. Not enough men left to care for the animals. Stock wandering where they chose. Not seeing man for years on end, they became independent and brutally mean. And wild? Let me tell you, they presented a chore rooting them out of any kind of cover, brush, cactus, whatever. And open, unused land everywhere. Rangy bulls, wild as coyotes, sniffing out every heifer in sight. The quality of the stock dropped off. Inbreeding and lack of care, I'm guessing.

"To look forward to a better day and better animals, they had to be cleaned out. Gathering them all up and driving them to the rails was the only solution. The bulls especially had to go. The only hope for quality was better bulls and good cows, carrying beef on their bones. On the Sombrero, with the war seemingly steering a path clear of the home area, Pa spent about the last two nickels he had bringing in upgraded bulls. The men were away at war or had ridden west to avoid the conflict. No one to hire. Made a lot of work for the family, keeping the cows and heifers clear of the wild stock that remained. More than one wandering bull, looking like a rack of bones, was laid out with a saddle gun.

"By the time I pulled out on my first trail drive, the newest calves were showing promise. Last letter I had, a few months ago, the new bulls were confirming their worth. Now Pa's taken to fencing his land. Some old Texas cattlemen are threatening to cut the fences, preserving the open range, but Pa, he's got a stubborn streak a mile wide. He left the details out of his letters, but my thinking is that he said something like, *Cutting my fence could prove to have a seriously negative impact on your personal well-being.*"

Gwyneth turned her eyes from Cob toward her husband and asked, "Are these animals we've brought along with us tough enough for this country, Trent? You've said they're a good breed, but this isn't the green hills of Illinois, as I keep repeating. I can see some challenges in this short grassland with its rocky areas, the occasional cactus, and its elevation, which points to the possibilities of hard winters."

"They're called Herefords. Apparently, that's a good breed for packing beef on their bones. They're not longhorns such as we're familiar with, but they're horned enough for their own protection. If we can hold them tight to the ranch headquarters and close to the two bulls we brought along, we should get a start anyway. And our steers should fill out nicely on this grass. We'll need some fences and good, solid corrals. We don't have the money for more than just the breeding animals we've got, so the herd will grow slowly. But I've held back a bit of money to bring in some more local calves for fattening, if we find any available. We should be able to make out."

They moved forward, heading south along the forested western edge of the valley, easing a bit further from the hills to get a broader perspective. As they were rounding a point of a pine-covered bit of hillside that nature had left jutting into the flatter land, they were startled by the whap and then the whining ricochet of a rifle bullet right in front of Trent's horse. He managed to hold the animal, but it was a near thing. All the horses were scrambling, as frightened as their riders. The shot was followed by a high-pitched voice hollering, "You're on B/C land. Trespassers ain't welcome. Turn and go back to where you came from."

There was nothing to see, but the sound of the voice left

little to wonder about. There was sparse cover, just the pine trunks, with the lower branches starting several feet from the ground. The shouter's location was apparent. The high-pitched voice identified him as a kid. He could only be hunkered behind the pines on the protruding rock. In turn, they had to assume the shooter had stayed where he was after triggering off that one shot, and that he could still see them. But it was too late to concern themselves with that.

They were scattered a bit with the plunging of the horses, but as each turned their horse to face the hillside, they had their saddle guns pointed and ready. There would now be four weapons facing the shooter. Trent glanced sideways to take in first Gwyneth, and then Cob and Daniel. He was about to place himself between the shooter and Gwyneth when he glanced over to see what Daniel was doing. But Daniel was nowhere to be seen. His horse was there, but the saddle was now empty.

Trying not to make his movements obvious, Trent turned his head just enough to be able to spot Daniel out of the corner of his eyes. He disappeared for a moment and then, there, behind that large pear plant. Crawling. Slithering. His movements steady, but slow. Cautious. He was moving toward the cover of the trees, maybe a hundred feet away. As he watched Daniel, Trent hollered, "Come out here and show yourself like a man. Any coward can hide in the brush and throw lead around. We're only riding through and offering no harm to you or the land. You had to know that before you pulled the trigger. Now show yourself. You shoot again, and you'd better believe this will be your last day on earth."

DANIEL WAS COVERING the last bit of distance. Suddenly, he rose to his knees and then his feet, so quickly it was like a single motion. Three quick, silent steps put him into the trees. Only seconds later, there was a startled yelp, followed by the command, "Stand and walk out there."

A kid, perhaps fourteen years old, showing the beginnings of the bulk Big Beef carried, slunk out of the bush with Daniel prodding him along with the kid's own rifle. There was an empty holster flapping against his right leg. Daniel held the rifle like a pistol, with his own carbine in his other hand. The kid's holster weapon was shoved behind Daniel's belt, at his back. Judging by looks and actions, this had to be one of Big Beef's offspring.

Daniel prodded the shooter until he was almost under the nose of Trent's horse before he said, "Now, Mr. Shooter, tell us what this is all about."

Showing a bit of returning bravado, the kid said, "It's about protecting our ranch. You wait till my father hears about your trespassing and how you've treated me. You'll be sorry you ever left town."

Trent said, "Not sure what town you're talking about, kid, but I'm going to make a guess that your father calls himself Big Beef Cameron. That would make you young Cameron. What's your name, kid?"

"Ty Cameron. And quit calling me kid. I ain't no kid."

Feeling that the next move should be up to Trent, Cob, Daniel, and even Gwyneth remained silent, waiting. Trent was studying the land around them, wondering if the kid was alone. Finally, he brought his eyes back toward the kid, Big Beef's son.

"Well, you're acting like a kid. A kid who could easily be dead right now. You shoot at a man, and he's just naturally bound to take exception, maybe express his feeling by scattering a little lead of his own. Didn't that father of yours teach you anything? I'm going to think of you as a kid until you show some maturity. So, we'll call you Kid Cameron.

"My name is Ty. Ty Cameron."

"Well, kid. That's a good enough name, but you ain't hardly growed into it yet. Not by a long shot. And speaking of shots, you listen, and you listen carefully. You ever take a shot at me or any of mine, we're going to shoot back. I don't remember the last time I missed a shot. And Cob here is a better shot than me. That's saying nothing about Mrs. Wycome here, she can outshoot all of us. And Daniel. Well, Daniel is a whole other situation. You want to fight shy of Daniel. Now, if you'll step onto that horse Daniel just brought down from wherever it was you had staked him out, you can ride out of here."

"I want my guns."

"Of course you do. But you see, there's a problem. These are adult guns. Meant for grown-ups. You're just a kid. You can't be trusted with guns."

"My father—"

"Your father is going to come up one son short if you don't shut up or if you ever pull a trigger against any of us again. You can have the guns. Kid guns. Daniel, give him the guns the way you think they'll be safe in the kid's hands."

Daniel, looking as if he would just as soon scalp the kid, lifted the carbine, resting it in his left palm while he slowly jacked each brass jacketed shell from the magazine, allowing them to fall as they would. He would probably argue that he wasn't particularly aiming for the large pear patch at his feet. But the shells were going to be a challenge to anyone wanting to retrieve them. Taking hold of the bridle cheek strap on the kid's horse, holding the animal steady, he shoved the long gun into its scabbard and pointed his finger. "You no touch." He then methodically moved his fingers from loop to loop on the wide leather belt the kid favored, lifting out each shell. These he dropped into the pear, along with the shells from the Colt. "You go home now."

Scowling, the kid turned his horse toward the hills, spurred it unmercifully, and was soon out of sight. Cob grinned at Trent. "That went well, wouldn't you say?"

Gwyneth gave each of the men a questioning look, nudged her gelding forward, and continued the ride. Watching her actions, Trent feared he hadn't heard the last of her opinions on the matter.

THEY RODE their horses into a sweat under the afternoon sun and finally, spotting a hollow in the western hills, turned in and dismounted. As the men were watering the horses from the pool at the base of a small stream, Gwyneth wandered around the hollow. To the north and west, were short, rocky hills. To the east was open country, clear to the purple-hazed hills in the far distance. To the south was a gentle, pine-covered slope protruding into the grassland, that would let in whatever warmth and light didn't get filtered out by the growth. She turned in a slow circle, taking in the size and slope of the hollow's floor. Then, pacing off the distance she felt was necessary for a cabin, she stood looking at Trent. She had made a decision. The distance demanded a raised voice to be heard against the slight wind that was rustling the grass and swaying the smaller trees and brush.

"I'll stand right here, and you can build a cabin around me. This is home."

Trent was shocked into immobility. He stood, reins in hand, and studied his wife. He had known her to be a determined woman and had seen no reason to question her. Up to this point. Cob and Daniel remained silent, figuring that was the shortest path to avoiding a family discussion.

Cob reached for Trent's horse. He was unsure if Trent even realized when he dropped the reins into Cob's hand. As he and Daniel led the animals into the shade and staked them on short ropes so they could pick at the hillside grass, Trent walked toward the immovable Gwyneth. He stood close but neither said nor did anything. Keeping his silence, he turned slowly in a ragged circle, studying every aspect of the hollow. A surface glance said he agreed with Gwyneth. It was a sheltered and lovely location comprising thirty or so ragged-edged acres. But lifetime decisions, about horses, cattle, women, or land cannot be made on shallow first looks.

He could see that Gwyneth was about to say something, but right at that moment, he didn't wish to hear it. Turning away, he much more slowly studied the location, finally deciding it would make a right fine home place. But, again, the final decision would have to be supported by quality range. There was no value at all if the nearby range, the range beyond their eyesight, wouldn't support the cattle he had planned out in his mind, even though he acknowledged that it was a long-term plan. For the small herd they had trailed in, there was enough grass, and more. But he couldn't make a living without more animals. There had to be room to grow.

Turning back to Gwyneth, he put his arm around her waist and urged her to take the few steps that would take them into the shade. Cob and Daniel were there, squatted on their heels, waiting for Trent's next move. It was soon to come.

"Fellas, I'd like it if one of you would ride off to the east, easing to the north, across this flat. The other could ride east, but more to the south. Take a study of the grass and water, if there is any. You both know what cattle need. I'll trust your judgment. We'll need a hay meadow too. You could watch for that. Gwyneth and I will ride south, staying close to these western hills. And marking out any other ranches trying for a foothold in the area. We'll meet back here this evening, make camp, and discuss the whole thing over dinner."

Looking first at Daniel and then at Cob, who both looked so comfortable he hated to ask them to move, he said, "That suit you?"

Cob glanced at Daniel, ground his cigarette out on a flat rock, rubbed the last of the heat from the tobacco with his work-hardened hand, and rose to his feet. Daniel was only a few seconds later coming to a standing position. Cob had just one comment. "Best we keep some estimate of distance. Longhorns will walk miles for feed and water. Those heavier breeds need a bit more pampering."

The two men were gone within a half-minute. Trent looked at Gwyneth and asked, "You up for more riding?"

"I thought I might stay right here and sort of plan out the site."

"Well, this time, Mrs. Wycome, you are being overruled. You are not staying here alone."

As he walked to where the horses were staked out, he was asking himself if he had ever spoken quite so firmly to her before. But knowing the risks of a new country, he pushed the concern out of his mind and readied the horses. Gwyneth flashed a wondering look at him when he passed her the reins, but she mounted with no discussion, and they headed south.

Chapter Thirteen

TRENT AND GWYNETH MADE A SLOW, ALMOST tediously painstaking ride south, searching out all the easily accessible pathways into the gentle western slopes, always looking for grass or water. Some of those slopes held enough grass to feed a small herd for a while. Trent's hope was that there might be flat lands among the upper hills or perhaps a hidden, grass valley or two in the highlands. The methodical Trent was visualizing the land spotted with cattle. His cattle.

Planning. Always planning. That was Trent. Those slopes that presented more challenge, or that would have to be examined on foot, were left to a later time. But Trent added to the time spent by periodically riding further out into the grassed flats, where he turned his mount back toward the hills. He would then sit in the saddle, giving careful study to the possibilities and the limitations of the land, as seen from the broader reach of a half mile of distance.

Gwyneth, in the meantime, stayed closer to the shady side-hills, studying the flora and fauna nature had offered the world. She had been noticing the tiny flowers, such as Brittlebush, Mexican Gold Poppy, Desert Marigold, Desert Paintbrush, Blue

Phacelia. Some were hugging the shady spots, others were flashing their full beauty in the sunshine. In one place, she noticed Broadleaf Stonecrop, a ground-hugging vine. She had no idea what any of them were named. Nor did she know if they were at the end of their blooming cycle or had most of it before them. She did know that there was more flowering growth here than there had been just a few miles to the north.

When possible, she bent from the saddle to pluck a sample, occasionally dismounting, picking small flowers, together with a few leaves from the rock crevasses that gave them shelter and, somehow, gaining sustenance in their rocky and sun-drenched world. She had no names to apply to them, but she intended to find out, searching out the wisdom of those who already called the area home, or perhaps finding a book that carried the information. She knew that wandering botanists had covered most of the west, leaving behind a wealth of information. *Perhaps*, she thought to herself, *someday I'll find a friendly Indian and quiz him, or her, about their names for the plants and trees.*

Leaving the bulk of the exploration to Trent, Gwyneth concentrated more on the matters that would help turn a rough cabin into a home. Although she was a self-assured young woman, normally well able to care for herself, she liked the gentle things of life, the colorful things, such as flowers that would help to set aside the drab grayness of a sun-blasted and quickly aging desert cabin. So, she picked flowers wherever she found them. These were not the larger, long stemmed, cultivated, garden grown flowers of her eastern youth but short, beautiful plants with smaller blooms that, for the most part, hugged the ground as if seeking shade from the shadow of the larger plants—the various cacti, the creosote bush, the Palo Verde or the desert willow, which also makes a show of its pink blooms in season, or the grand and showy Joshua trees.

She carefully wrapped the delicate blooms in a well-used piece of newspaper that part of their lunch had been packed in.

She dampened the paper with a dribble of water from her canteen and tucked it carefully into one saddlebag.

By the time ten miles had been covered at Trent's continuing, studiously slow pace, the afternoon was well advanced. When Gwyneth spotted a small stream, little more than a rivulet, really, she offered the first opinion since she had been overruled right after lunch.

"There's a bit of water. Probably the horses would do better for having a sip, and for sure I would."

"Under normal circumstances, my dear, you would have my full support. But from the vantage point that last ride onto the flat gave me, I'm thinking there might be an alternative. Let's step it up and see what's on the other side of this jutting rock."

Gwyneth saw a whole new Trent, a new husband. Although she had sincerely pledged her love privately, as well as before the young pastor who married them, this new self-assured Trent was bringing up new emotions, new feelings. While she still loved him and vowed, she always would, she was beginning to like him, as well. Strange, that the two feelings were so akin, but still, in some senses, miles apart. She was more than happy to live with the Trent she loved. Now she came to the realization that she could easily follow the Trent she was coming to like. And to trust his judgment.

It was a short, half-mile ride, first to the east to clear the lichen-covered but otherwise bare, rocky hillside, then a sharp turn to the south for the final couple of minutes it would take to open the view in that direction. Gwyneth could both smell and see the drifting smoke before she could see its origin. She had noticed that Trent was watching her out of his peripheral vision. He seemed to be holding back a grin of some kind. She pretended not to notice while she kept her eyes peeled to the land ahead of them, waiting impatiently for the last couple hundred yards of rock to be cleared. She was tempted to mention the smoke but held back, determined to discover the source for herself.

The two horses cleared the rock side by side. As the view opened ahead of them, both riders pulled to a stop. There, nestled into a corner of a tree-shrouded slope, was a building of some sort. Crudely made and, over time, added onto in three directions. And further away, by what would be perhaps a two-minute walk, another building, this one little more than a pole shelter, like an upside-down V, with a couple of small corrals close by and a house-sized stack of hay. Clearly, they were looking at what passed for a livery stable. But why here? And how did this exist, with the Indians not yet settled into the idea of losing their land to cattle ranchers, who were always on the lookout to relieve the owners of their horses?

As if in practiced unison, both riders turned their eyes back to the larger building. In the short few seconds since they had glanced away, a man had materialized under the covered walkway that appeared to be little more than a flimsy sun shield that just might take flight at the next windstorm. The man was hatless. His unruly mop of black hair telling of the need for a long overdue visit with a barber. Along with a more exacting study of the ramshackle building, Trent was giving close attention to the other structures close by. In addition to a small barn, a woodshed, and two outhouses, there was what appeared to be a cabin, showing another small wisp of smoke, as if it was signaling the final efforts of a dying fire.

A boy of perhaps ten or twelve summers was riding a stubborn pony that clearly had no intention of doing what the boy wanted. The lad was using his heels along with the tail ends of the reins, all to little avail. But he did raise enough forward motion to slowly disappear from sight behind the larger building. A sudden clang of hammer on steel caused the pair to glance again toward the livery shelter. No one was in sight, but the hammering persisted, so there was clearly someone doing a bit of blacksmithing.

They had been noticing wagon tracks along the trail they followed. None of the tracks had been recent.

"This might explain those wagon tracks we were following for a while."

"Let's ride down," suggested Gwyneth.

Trent took a long look around, turning a half circle on his saddle, first one way and then the other. That was followed by another study of the building and the man standing in the shade before he made up his mind.

"We'll keep our eyes open. We'll not let anyone get behind us."

With that, he slackened the reins, and the gelding stepped out. The ride into the settlement took little more than a long minute. The man in the shade didn't move. An unseen dog barked. The hammering ceased. The boy on the pony rounded the corner of the building, coming back into sight, and stopped, staring at the visitors. A woman emerged from the doorway and stood beside the man, shading her eyes with her left hand. She held something in her right hand, hanging down, covered by the folds of her skirts. All looked peaceful and welcoming, but Trent would be a while before he gave up his extra caution. And he would keep an eye on the woman's right hand.

Thinking first of the needs of the horses, Trent kept a wary eye on the man and woman but rode right on past, keeping some distance between them, heading for the shade of the livery. They saw no one until they stepped to the ground a few feet from a water trough. The wooden trough was new enough that it was still leaking a bit of the precious liquid from the seams between the planks. In time, the planks would swell to where it was holding the water without leaking.

"Howdy." A man wearing the broadest-brimmed hat Trent had ever seen, and who had stripped to the waist except for his bib overalls, was closing on them as he moved slowly through the barn. "There's water enough and welcome. Clean and cold from the pump. Dug and cased the well myself before I chose the site for this here barn. Figured it was easier to hold the horses near to the water than to forever be toting water the other direction, if you catch my meaning. Dug the well first, I did. Then built the barn. Third well I dug. First with water. You got any use for a dry hole in the ground, you can take either of the other two I spent a part of my life's days digging, and welcome.

"Traveling through or come to stay awhile? See the sights and relax in the bountiful surroundings of Conville, kind of settle in and avail yourselves of the luxury offered across the other side of town, kind of contemplate on life and things that matter?"

Trent couldn't hold back a grin as the talkative man prattled on. His response was, "Well, friend, you've laid out too many choices to expect a fast answer. We'll just take up your offer on the water first, then hire out a bit of shelter for these animals in your shaded barn, then think on the rest. All the time hoping that's all right with you, and in keeping with the general tenor of the village."

"Sounds just fine, young fella. And as far as the general tenor of the village goes, you'll find that when us residents of Conville aren't comfortable with one tenor, as you said, why, we'll just up and try another. Flexible, that's what we are. As happy one way as the other. The one rule we expect visitors to abide by is that you leave your weapon in its holster. This here is a sleepy little place, but we can wake up almighty sudden if one of us senses a threat."

"You'll find no threat in us, my friend. Water, shade for the animals, and coffee, if such should be available. That's our formula for peaceful cohabitation. A short rest for the wife and me and our animals, then a regretful parting as we head back to camp."

"Name's P.A. Angus, case you been wondering. I'm not telling what the P.A. stands for, and I'm not altogether sure how to spell Angus. Don't much matter though. I've not seen it spelled out in writing since the sad day I was given a paper that said I was now a soldier. Stuffed the paper in my pocket. Found a good use for it along the way, by 'n by. Fought when I had to, rested when I could. Didn't wait for my discharge paper. Them good ol boys on t'other side, look'n pretty as all get out in their blue uniforms, they staked me out as a prisoner, then sent me west to fight Indians. Didn't much care for the task, figuring we might do better if'n we were to try to get along. So, I discharged myself and jest kep riding west till I come upon this bit of paradise. I 'spect most everyone back east has forgotten me or at least given it up as a poor prospect, find'n no reason fer want'n me back."

When P.A. Angus stopped to take a breath, Trent offered their names and followed up with, "Doesn't hardly seem likely, calling you P.A. Angus. How do you like to be addressed?"

"Mostly the few folks that wander out this way know me as Smithy. I'll also answer if you call me P.A., or just about anything else that don't cast doubts on my ma and pa's marital arrangements."

Sensing they had just entered onto sensitive ground, Gwyneth said, "Why don't we walk over to the store, if that's what that building is, and see what the folks have on offer?"

"I'll walk along. It could be that in the excitement of welcoming cash customers, Ginny will lay her shotgun down and put out the welcome mat. It's a thin mat, but we're hoping for better times. Could use a cup of coffee my own self."

Trent and Gwyneth stepped back into the blazing heat, with every bone and sinew of their body rebelling at the rough treatment from saddle and sun. P.A. Angus strolled along beside them as if the sun's glare was a normal matter and as if he hadn't moved beyond a stroll since he had last sat a McClellan saddle.

As they approached the walkway cover, the smithy said, "Lay the shotgun down, Ginny, before you hurt yourself or someone else. I keep telling you you're going to have to work on your welcome if you ever expect to get rich in the supply business. Lay it down and say hello to these folks. This here is Trent

and Gwyneth Wycome, come to share this little corner of
paradise with us. Folks, this here is Griz Bailey. Griz and Ginny
run this here establishment. If'n we talk nice and don't ask too
many personal questions, it's possible we may be able to work a
cup of coffee into our visit."

Just as they were stepping into the shade of the overhang,
the kid on the spotted pony managed to heel the animal around
the corner again and along the front of the building, pulling up
close to the smithy. He sat there studying on Trent and
Gwyneth as if he hadn't seen a stranger in some time.

The smithy said, "Trace. I'll like it if you'd go call your
mother. You might be better off to walk, speed that gelding is
making."

The group moved into the dim interior of the store. Ginny
laid her shotgun on the counter, taking a careful look at Trent.
She relaxed visibly after her second look at Gwyneth. But she
still hadn't spoken. Neither had Griz, her husband, until he
said, "You folks take yourselves a seat. Anywhere you like."

There was a small home-built table with four chairs placed
evenly around it. Close by, leaning against the outside wall, was
a series of filled-out burlap sacks. Trent figured these would
hold grain for horse or chicken feed, or, perhaps, seed for the
couple of farmers who were trying to coax life out of the gravelly caliche-topped soil that was so common in the desert country. Beside the burlap sacks leaned a row of half a dozen white
cotton sacks. These would undoubtedly hold flour. All the
sacks, burlap and cotton alike, were indented on the top,
showing where folks had been using them for seating. Trent
turned away, reminding himself not to purchase flour from
these two. But all in all, even as skimpy as the stock on hand
was, it was still more than seemed logical or profitable to Trent,
in a country where there wasn't more than a smidgen of folks in
many a mile.

The canvas curtain hanging in the doorway opening rustled
and a woman entered, followed by the boy. The woman was

sunburned, her hair bleached by the constant rays. She was slim and attractive. P.A. Angus introduced her as Rose. The boy's name, he reminded them, was Trace.

Neither Gwyneth nor Trent had taken a seat yet. They were enjoying the standing after so many hours in the saddle. Gwyneth stepped forward with her hand extended.

"I'm pleased to meet you, Rose. My name is Gwyneth. And this is my husband, Trent. We're down this way today searching out the land."

"Y'all going to come ta ranch'n?"

Trent turned a bit to get a closer look at the boy who had spoken.

"We're planning to, young fella. Ain't picked a spot yet. This is our first day on the land. We hope to choose carefully. You got any advice on that, Trace?"

Trace glanced first at his father, then lifted his eyes to Trent. "You want my advice, you'll turn them horses around and go back to where the grass is greener and where it rains at least once in a while. And take me with you."

Trent grinned, shifting his eyes quickly between the lad's folks and then down at the pleading boy. "Are you saying you don't like it here?"

"Ain't nothing much to like. Snakes and spiders enough to do for the whole world. Nothing to do one day to t'other. No other folks around. You take your leave of the country, I'd sure enough go with you. I could earn my keep caring for the horses and such."

Trent smiled at those words and said, "Well, Trace, I kinda think your folks might have something to say about that. And anyway, we just got here. Might take a bit longer to decide for sure what we're going to do. But if we settle somewhere close by, you could come and visit from time to time. Mrs. Wycome would like that. Cabin can get mighty lonesome without a visitor now and then."

The smithy laid his hand on his son's shoulder and said,

"Trace ain't never lived anywhere else. Not that he was old enough to remember anyway. We keep telling him the land is starting to fill up and soon there'll be folks around so's we'll have to comb them out of our hair. Might could be we'll have a school and perhaps even a church, come by 'n by."

Still resting his outsized hand on his son's shoulder, he looked down at the boy and smiled saying, "How would it be if Griz were to invite you to ride along on the next trip to Pueblo. I'm thinking you could be a help with the loading of supplies and perhaps drive the team while Griz takes his afternoon siesta."

Trace was about to reply when Ginny spoke up, half shouting as if she was a bit hard of hearing, or thought everyone else might be, "That's all well and good, fool talk as it is, but I got this coffee ready. Made up some bread and buns yesterday. Rose, you pull that plate of buns out of the cold cabinet. The butter too. I've got some prickly pear jam around here somewhere. Sit down now, you folks. Make yerselvs ta home."

As they were enjoying the coffee and fresh buns, Trent, only out of curiosity, asked, "Good town name, Conville, how did you come about it?"

Griz was suddenly quieter than he had been, as if the question had opened thoughts best left buried. But he finally spoke.

"Con was the wife's brother and my best friend from my youth up. He was planning a new start, right along with the two of us. Hotshot punk of a kid gunman called him out in some flyspeck of a settlement in west Texas. Called him out just out of pure spite and misery, no purpose in it. Con, he was wearing a gun like all of us do, but he was no gunman. He was just turning to face the kid when the punk pulled his iron, and Con fell dead on the dirt trail. Well, I stood there in shock, but Gin, she's kind of a no-nonsense woman. The kid had no more than a few seconds to enjoy his victory before he was tossed into the air, falling to the dirt beside Con, most of his one shoulder and his head gone, while Ginny's shotgun leaked black smoke from the barrel, with the boom of the shot racketing off the couple of buildings in the settlement we never did hear a name for.

"We laid Con over his saddle and moved on a few miles before we found a pleasant little hollow in the hills to bury him. We left the kid where he lay. Come to settling in here, wasn't any real choice on a name. Conville she is, and Conville she'll stay."

It was a full, silent minute before conversation resumed.

Gwyneth was familiar with the larger, more cultivated stores of her hometown, and the more or less tamed, general supplies stores of Dodge, and even the small railway town where she and Trent had met. There, the stores were packed with every item a rancher or a homemaker might need. She had seen trail bosses park their wagons behind the store and load up with everything a camp cook required for the long trip back to Texas, loading the wagon until its springs were sagging.

Inside the store, there would inevitably be shelves weighed down with every kind of rough clothing, boots, leather goods, and such. On the free-standing shelves scattered aimlessly on the store's floor were childrens' and ladies' wear items, discreetly separating the ladies' must-haves from the more basic needs of the working men. Even from the ceiling, displays of supplies hung, suspended from hooks screwed into the wooden ceiling boards. On the walkway out front were barrels of shovels, axes, spare handles, and all manner of tools any hard-working farmer or rancher might need. And, of course, behind the counter was the inevitable range of firearms, short guns in the glassed-in counter itself, with rifles on the rack behind.

And the smells! How she had enjoyed the ever-present, collective odors of ground coffee, leather goods, cooking spices, peppers grown and shipped in from the southern lands, and many other food and camp needs. Not quite so pleasant was the odor of horse and cattle, dragged in on the boots of the riders, of unwashed bodies and sweat-soaked leather, of felt hats suffering from exposure to rain, sun, and wind.

Griz Bailey's little store was similar only in intent. His stock was sparse. The choices few. But in an alcove behind the service counter was a small wood-fired cook stove where Ginny had made the coffee. A few metal plates, a row of heavy crockery mugs, along with a bit of cutlery, suggested that a meal could be prepared and purchased if the rider had the time to allow Ginny to build a fire and gather a few eggs from the hen coop out back. It all left Gwyneth wondering where the store's few customers called home. They had seen no homesites on the ride south. If young Ty Cameron hadn't been skulking in the bush as they rode past, they could have believed the land to be empty.

Rose laid out the buns, butter, and jam, and then returned to the alcove to bring out five of the heavy mugs. She laid them out, placing one in front of her young son, saying, "You go fill the bottom half of that mug with milk from the jug in back."

His "Aw, Ma," was ignored, and the boy rose from the tree stump stool he was sitting on.

A HALF HOUR LATER, after explaining their need to return to the camp spot where the other two men would be expecting them and having dug out all the information on the country, P.A. Angus and the others seemed prepared to be parted with, Trent and Gwyneth rounded the lichen-covered boulders and moved out of sight of the tiny settlement. They had made a few small purchases in the store in the hopes of being seen as good neighbors. They rode in silence until Trent shook his head a bit, as if he had been trying to sort out his thoughts, before saying, "Strange doings that. I doubt the smith makes five dollars a month, and the store not much more. Makes a man wonder if there's something they're not saying or if they just choose to live the way they're living."

Gwyneth had been asking herself the same questions. "I'll be no help to you in trying to understand it. The boy might be the brightest of them all. He wants away from there at whatever cost."

That much talk seemed to satisfy their needs. They rode in silence until they rounded into the little cove to see that Daniel had a fire going while Cob was allowing himself a nap in a bit of late afternoon shade.

Chapter Fourteen

WITH THE ARRIVAL OF TRENT AND GWYNETH, DANIEL backed away from the fire, satisfying himself with a further hunt for dry wood that wouldn't need chopping. Trent unloaded the sacks carrying the food and utensils and then backed away himself. Gwyneth would take over the fire and the food preparation with Trent's voice echoing in her ears, "Call me if you need help." As she watched her husband disappear up a narrow gully in the search for more grass, she knew the offer to be well-intentioned, with little likelihood of it being fulfilled.

An hour later, the four land searchers were well fed, the dishes scrubbed, first with sand and then rinsed in the stream, the remaining food stored carefully away from marauding birds, insects, and the odd coyote that might risk the man smell in search of an opportunity to scrounge an easy meal. The fire was banked, allowing it to burn down, and the coffee ready. Taking care to avoid the needles that seemed to somehow show up on every living plant, Cob and Daniel were leaning against a couple of small trees. Trent and Gwyneth satisfied themselves with sitting cross-legged on their saddle blankets, their shoulders slumped in weariness. Each had a cup of coffee. Gwyneth was still trying to acquire a taste for the bitter beverage without the addition of either cream or sugar.

Cob spoke, saying, "You first, Trent. What did y'all find?"

That question led to an evening of information exchange about the land, discussing it all and storing it away in the backs of their minds, awaiting the findings of another day of travel. The discussion left Trent hopeful. There was grass in abundance in small areas among the higher, rocky ground cover. Grass, and to spare, if they managed to claim and hold enough land.

WITH THE HELP of the few supplies purchased on a second trip to the tumble-down edifice Griz Bailey had thrown together, the search for ranch land lasted almost another full week, during which they rode more miles than they had ever planned for. Daniel had left the others, determined to contact close-by Indians. At the suggestion that they may not be as friendly as he wished, he shrugged and replied, "If you don't see me again, you'll have your answer on that. Indians like to say this is a good day to die. The white half of me never quite understood that."

At the end of another week, they were running short of supplies and were weary of riding. Arriving back at the campsite, they settled in for one more night. Daniel hadn't returned. Leaving their half-Indian friend to his own plans, the early morning light led Trent, Gwyneth, and Cob on the shortest route possible back to the wagon and the herd.

Abe and Helen had been left with the wagon and the cattle, but on their arrival, Trent and the others were surprised and pleased to find that Eustice Ward had returned and settled into herding the grazing cattle in exchange for Helen's well-cooked food.

After telling them of their explorations, it seemed to take no time at all to convince Trent's parents to reload the partially repaired wagon in readiness for the slow move south toward Conville. They had a bit of trouble pinpointing their chosen location on the rudimentary maps the land office had supplied, but they finally marked an agreed-upon spot. They would register their claim on their next trip into Pueblo.

When they returned to the campsite in the morning, Daniel was sitting, lit pipe in hand, with a cooking-size fire working its way down to coals. Three Indians were relaxing around the fire.

"Good to see you, Daniel. You got any holes in you that weren't there before you went hunting Indians?"

"No, Trent, my worrying friend, no new holes. Might have made a friend or two. This here," he said as he pointed over to his left with his thumb, "is Wandering Eyes, a sub-chief of the Utes. And here, on the other side, is Walks A Lot, Wandering Eyes's son."

He stopped there as if the introductions were complete. But the girl sitting against a tree several feet away was looking on as if being ignored was a natural part of her life, although she didn't like it. Gwyneth spoke up. "And who is the beautiful young lady?"

"That's Likes The Night, sister to Walks A Lot and daughter to Wandering Eyes."

Lifting her attention from the men, Gwyneth smiled at the young Indian girl and asked, "And do you speak our language, Likes The Night?"

"I speak. I understand. My brother also understands but won't use the white man's words. He says it is not right for Ute to speak in a lesser tongue."

"Perhaps that is right for him. And perhaps if you will visit from time to time, I could learn something of the Ute tongue from you."

The girl simply smiled. Gwyneth completed the introductions of Trent and Cob and then turned to the just-arriving wagon. The herd was allowed to scatter along the small waterway. Eustice joined Abe and Helen as they walked into the camp. With no knowledge of Indian protocol, Gwyneth completed the rest of the introductions. The men didn't know whether to offer a handshake, speak, or simply nod. They settled for a nod.

In a growling, but quiet voice, Wandering Eyes turned his head to Daniel. "Woman much talk."

Daniel smiled in response. "Woman make good grub."

That bit of news brought another growl and a momentary glance at Gwyneth from the older man. Gwyneth exchanged slight smiles with Likes The Night.

When the trio of Indians had helped drink up two pots of coffee and a plate of bacon and beans each, they walked silently to their horses. With no further words, they mounted and left. Gwyneth took note of how easily and gracefully they mounted, no easy task without stirrups.

The entire camp then turned quizzical eyes on Daniel, leaving their unspoken questions hanging in the silence. He set his coffee mug on the flat rock containing the fire and casually said, "No new enemies. Maybe good friends to have if trouble comes. I'm hoping they'll come back. Maybe come for a visit. Bring a dressed-out deer as a gift. I took a fresh killed buck to their village. Took their measure and roughly counted their numbers. I can say they would be a bitter enemy. But they're leaving Cameron alone with his claim. And Griz and P.A. Angus. They simply seem to be mystified by the smithy and the supply shack. They might buy some coffee and flour if they ever figure out what a store is. Or they might just come and help themselves. My guess is that they take more to the hills than to these flats. And to others of their own kind rather than to strangers. We'll know, come by 'n by."

Abe climbed back onto the wagon seat and slapped the reins. "We'll just go down to this settlement. See if that smithy can be of any help with this broken axle." As the wagon started to move, with the half-repaired axle screaming as if it were in pain, he hollered to Helen, "You coming?"

"Nice of you to invite me." She said as she rose to her feet and stepped toward the wagon. Abe held his hand out for her and, before she was truly seated, hollered, "Hep up there, Blue. Step out, Bess." The wagon was soon out of sight around the point of land.

THE MEN SET OUT IMMEDIATELY, with axes and cross saws, to fell trees for a cabin and a shelter for Daniel and Cob. Abe and Helen would choose their own spot when they returned. They laid down a large gathering of trimmed tree trunks, ready to be dragged off the mountain slope to the building site as soon as Abe returned with the team.

A two-day absence seemed to make their return unnaturally delayed. Trent and Gwyneth saddled up and rode the few miles to Conville. There, they found Abe comfortably settled in on a ladder-back chair at the smithies and Helen delicately sipping tea with the women across the clearing. Trace had turned his pony loose, perhaps in the hope that it would wander off, and was riding Abe's big gelding, which he had brought down tied to the rear of the wagon in the hopes the smithy could find time to work on the wagon axle. He greeted Trent and Gwyneth with the first smile the young man had shown.

Trent pulled his horse to a stop, glanced over at Gwyneth with a grin. "Ain't hardly got the nerve to break up this little social gathering." Trent grinned at the two men in the smithy's shop. "Y'all gett'n anywhere with the fixing of that axle?"

"Got 'er about done. And a sweet job Mr. Angus made of it too. These here folks in Conville will prove to be valuable neighbors."

"That's good news. I was hoping to see you back in camp about this time."

"All things have their time and place, son. I think you can look for us about mid-morning tomorrow."

WITH THE SWEAT of the big team added to the men's efforts, the cabin was soon laid out with the foundation logs carefully resting on flat rocks gathered and snugged down in shallow holes dug out of the hard ground with the pick and shovel. Trent was the best with the adze. In preparation for the laying of logs, he was flattening two sides to create a tight fit. The men were prepared to charge ahead with the walls when Gwyneth called a halt. She approached the building site with a Mason canning jar half-filled with water. She passed the mysterious implement to Cob with the instructions, "Lay that on its side and let the water settle down. We'll see if that log is placed level."

Cob shrugged and did as he was told while Abe and Daniel stood silently by. Trent lay flat on his stomach and studied the water. By the way the liquid lay in the glass container, it was clearly obvious that the log lay on a slant. "Lift 'er up an inch on that end," he said, pointing to his right. The leveling slowed the initial work, but it put a smile on Gwyneth's face, and that was more important to the men than a few lost minutes.

By late summer, they had the cabin built with a crude stone fireplace and hearth gracing one side of what was to be the sitting room. It would serve for cooking until they managed to haul a metal kitchen stove in from the big city, which Trent had promised his wife would be their next priority. Gwyneth made the cabin as comfortable as possible, with the few things on hand, along with fixings she had bought and packed onto the wagon before leaving Pueblo, and the rough table and chairs crafted together by Trent and his father.

Cob and Daniel built a shelter for themselves and hung pieces of canvas shield over the window openings. In every spare minute, they would do the necessary bits and pieces to prepare the shelter for the winter that was fast approaching. It was time for the cattle to become their number one priority. That meant hay.

Trent, in his wanderings, had spotted an uphill flat that held enough curing grass to fill the immediate need. Abe had brought along two scythes and a number of hay forks, all in the hopes of reselling them. Trent pulled them out of the wagon, commenting, "Put them down to my name. Consider them sold. On credit."

Since the group had settled in, there had been a couple of travelers passing through, but no sign of Big Beef Cameron or any other rancher, which raised several questions in Trent's mind. As far as they had seen, the Mirrored W brand, along with Cob's Hat-2, were the only brands within their chosen location. But Cameron's brand was on those few they had seen on the trip south. Where he held the bulk of his herd continued to be a mystery. Not really caring, or having time to spare, no one had bothered to look for them.

After a long day of haying in the early fall heat, the boys descended the mountain trail, following the overloaded wagon down the steep grade from the hay grounds. By the time they had stacked the hay, cared for the horses and themselves, they were ready to take on a feed. It was a typical day on the Mirrored W Ranch. Helen had been busy arranging a double cot for herself and Abe in the rear of the log cabin.

Arrangements for the evening had been left to Gwyneth. She kept busy attending to the haunch of beef that had been slowly stewing in its own juices in the fireplace. The cast-iron pot she had secured in Pueblo was banked all around with coals from the morning's fire. At noon, she had dealt the final touches, garnishing the beef with spices, chilis, and a handful of wild onions Daniel had brought down from the hills on one of his rides. She then used the afternoon to get her bread baked, near enough a half bushel of potatoes peeled and laid around the beef in the big pot, along with a smaller pot of carrots, purchased in Pueblo but now showing the ravages of heat and time. She hoped to grow her own vegetables next summer.

Trace Angus, atop his father's big black gelding, had ridden up for a visit with Gwyneth. To his surprise, he rode right into an active afternoon of work. He balked at first, seeing potato peeling as women's work. But Gwyneth soon had him thinking otherwise. He stayed so late, enjoying the cowboys and their talk of faraway places and long rides, that he decided to stay over, rolling into a blanket Gwyneth gave him. Sleeping between two cowboys, Daniel and Eustice Ward, made it the best night of his life.

~

AND THEN, one cool fall day, Cameron, his son, and three riders showed up, riding right into the yard as if they owned the place. Trent, who had been having his breakfast, saw, through the open door, who the visitors were, belted on his short gun, and walked outside.

"You men get those animals out of the houseyard. Tie them to the corral and come in for coffee."

"Didn't come fer coffee."

"Well, you'll still need to get those animals away from the house. Do it now."

The last words left no room for doubt about Trent's intentions.

Trent had always been a bit on the raw-boned side, slim through the chest and body, painfully narrow of waist, but wide of shoulder with a gristly neck holding his head high, a head where the veins stuck out on his forehead, pulsing and throbbing. Wearing no shirt over his sleeveless underwear on this sunny morning, the veins on his shoulders, arms, and oversized hands attested to the fact that he was all sinew and muscle, with no excess fat seen anywhere. His sidearm hung where his hand could grab it with no movement to speak of. All that, together with his unflinching eyes, left no room for misunderstanding his meaning or his intent to follow through.

Cameron was trapped by those eyes. Eyes full of under-standing, determination, and grit based on years of experience with the men and animals in the cattle trade. He showed no intent toward backing up or giving in. Cameron saw all of this and had no doubt about what he faced.

Gwyneth stepped into the doorway with her carbine in her hands. She too had determination written all across her face. It was her face that had first attracted Cameron that day in the bank, months before. A face that would not be called beautiful, but attractive nonetheless. Appealing might be a stronger way of describing Cameron's private thoughts. Trent had thought of his wife's visage as pleasant. *Wholesome*, his mother called her daughter-in-law after they first met.

Cameron took this all in without a blink, steadying himself. If there was to be a competition of wills, he could be as stub-born as anyone else. He had no doubts about winning his way until he sensed two of his men backing their horses away. Then, another lifted the reins as the signal to his animal to step back. Cameron was left there alone except for his young son. No one had spoken since Trent had ordered them off the houseyard.

The silence held for a bare five seconds more before Trent said, "You're a fool, Cameron. You've got nothing to gain here and a son to lose. That, and your own life. Now, tie up and come in for coffee. We'd best be talking. Any fool can shoot. But there's never any gain. Or any way of calling the shots back."

"There's four of us and one of you."

"No, there's just me and you."

A voice from the side of the cabin spoke. "I figure I can back those others off some, Boss." Turning his attention to the other riders, who were already backing off, the voice said, "You boys, you're riding for this man and for the brand, I understand that.

But thirty a month is poor wages for dying. I'd think it over if I was you."

Gwyneth took a single step sideways, into the shelter of the doorway. Her rifle barrel protruded from the edge of the door opening.

"I can account for at least two before you fellas even catch your breaths. On the other hand, the coffee is hot, and I can make more if need be. There's biscuits left from breakfast, and I've got eggs. Would you rather have breakfast, or would you rather die on this beautiful morning?"

Cameron spoke to his crew without ever turning his head from his study of Trent. "You men are fired. Useless cowards. Take B/C wages but cower at the first challenge to the brand. I'll not have you around. Go roll your beds and hit the trail."

One man, a grizzled old timer, spat out words around a freshly rolled cigarette that he hadn't yet lit, "You got a big mouth, Cameron. Was a day I'd have called you out for those words. But you just ain't worth it. I'm no coward, and you ever aim that talk toward me again will be the last day of your life. But I ain't ever shot at no woman either. Ain't about to start this morning."

"That speaks for me too, Boss, only I'll not be leaving without you giving me my owings. I've seen no pay for the past three months now. I plan to collect."

Trent watched as Cameron's shoulders sagged, and he settled back a bit further into his saddle. He sat there in silence, as if he hadn't sorted out his next move. Trent spoke into the silence. "The offer still holds. Back out, tie off, and come for coffee. Either that or turn around and get gone."

Cameron backed his gelding until he had space between himself and the cabin. When he spoke, it was as if most of his confidence had been spirited away. He was struggling to hold what little presence and dignity he had left.

"I'm told your name is Wycome. Makes no difference to me what it is. What does make a difference to me is that you're on

my land. These hills and this plain off to the east are B/C lands.
You can leave, or I'll drive you off. That's all I've got to say. You
heed my words and find yourself another claim. This one is
took."

Trent grinned a bit at the foolish claim and took the two
steps to the ground, walking halfway to where the stubborn
rancher sat his horse.

"Mr. Cameron, I'd like nothing better than to live in peace.
Cob and me, that's Cob standing over there beside the cabin,
we came up the trail with herds more times than I care to
remember. Saved our money. Saved mine toward having a ranch
and a herd of my own. Cob, he already has a ranch, him and his
family, down to South Texas. Anything happens to Cob, you
can expect the Hat to ride up here. It's a long way, and their
anger and determination will grow with each mile. But they'll
come. They're welcome to whatever's left of the B/C after I'm
done with you. As for Daniel, who's sitting silent in the bush
over there with a rifle aimed at you, well, Daniel, he does his
own thing. And as far as my parents go, who also have you
under their weapons, there's just no end to the misery Pa can
arouse with that rifle, when pushed.

"Gwyneth and me, we have our ranch, all claimed and regis-
tered, and we're not moving. Cob and me, we hold the big herd
together. The Hereford animals belong to the Mirrored W,
that's Gwyneth and me. The Hat bunch belong to Cob. You
have no claim to this land. As far as that goes, I've not seen a
single animal of yours in the months we've been here. Saw a few
on the ride down here, but that was miles to the north. Haven't
seen your homeplace either.

"A rancher has to have animals on the land to have a claim.
Wouldn't know you were in the country except that kid son of
yours took a shot at me some time ago. Had the full right to
shoot back. Didn't. You go home, Mr. Cameron. Come back
any time you want, but come friendly. Bring Mrs. Cameron
with you. Gwyneth, she'd like to visit with another lady, time to

time. But for this one morning, this has been enough. I've got work to do."

Cameron sat still for another half minute before turning his animal and riding away. His son rode tight beside him. Whatever he had hoped to accomplish that morning was left undone. The crew waited another full minute before tipping their hats to Gwyneth, as they turned their mounts north and rode away. The grizzled old timer grinned and said, "Suppose you could heat that coffee up? I'd admire to take you up on your offer."

TRENT AND COB rode endlessly that fall and winter, holding the cattle to the land claimed by the Mirrored W, hoping the animals would learn where their home was and the life-giving water. With not a single foot of barbed wire anywhere in the county, there was a lot of room for the dumb beasts to roam, and get lost, or be driven off.

On the return from one of their rides, they arrived in the ranch yard in time to see Abe and Helen preparing the wagon for the trail. In preparing the wagon for haying, which was now completed for this one year, their stock of supplies had been carefully stacked under an oiled and waxed tarpaulin. But it was easy to see that a lot of it had been reloaded onto the big wagon.

"What's up, Dad? Going on to California or maybe heading back to Texas?"

"No such thing, son. We're going to get our trading post built and opened."

"Well now, that is news. Care to tell the rest of the story?"

"Not much to tell. Anyway, already told Gwyneth. You talk to her. We've got work to do before this day turns itself into night."

Mounting the wagon seat, as excited as a couple of kids, Abe soon had the team moving while Helen gripped the seat with all her strength, grinning like a schoolgirl. The pup wagon was left for another time.

Trent and Cob both turned to Gwyneth with expectation showing on their faces.

"They've bought out Griz and Ginny, over to Conville. Griz and Ginny, they've already packed up and moved out."

"Well, with Griz and Ginny gone, there's two fewer fools over to Conville. Can't imagine they ever made any money in that store. Nor do I imagine my folks will do any better. I'm not sure they really care either." Holding his thoughts to himself, he was grinning at the number of times he had seen his parents do things such as this.

"Their problem, not ours."

"Their problem, perhaps. Still my concern."

ONLY ONCE THAT fall did they see Cameron again, and that was in Conville. On a chilly late fall morning, Trent and Gwyneth rode the few miles to the tiny settlement. They were low on coffee and a couple of other items. They would combine the buying trip with a chance to visit. After putting their horses in a stall, out of the wind, and exchanging a few pleasant words with P.A. Angus, they strolled over to the store. They were determined to avoid questions about the business that were buried in their thoughts, it was none of their concern.

A half hour went past with coffee and mostly meaningless conversation, when Abe finally got around to saying, "Folks up from down south. Two ranch families come in together. Near enough bought me out of stock. Supplying for the winter months. Sold off the most of Griz's old stock. Folks said there's six or eight outfits in that south country now. Mostly small, but with big dreams, like all of us, I guess. Fella said most have come to near hiding themselves in the hollows of the hills. Have to look some to find them."

He no sooner had those words out of his mouth when the door, captured by the wind, crashed back against a couple of stacked wooden boxes of supplies before it rebounded, coming to a temporary rest against the leather-clad shoulder of the man who had pushed it in. Abe and Trent rose from their chairs as if gravity had suddenly ceased to be a factor. Abe had been caressing his Henry as they visited, polishing the brass till it gleamed. As his weight settled into a startled, upright position, his toes digging into the leather of his riding boots while his heels lifted, ready to charge forward, the Henry swung into position, and he squeezed the trigger.

A few ounces of lead punched a hole so close to the intruder's head that the startled man shouted and fell in fright, almost as if the hole was in his skull, rather in the wood of the door. Another man, much younger, screamed and jumped back out, clear of the door and sheltered by the half-high adobe wall. The crack of the 44-40 shot brought all surrounding noise to an end. Swirling gun smoke was the last evidence of the recent three seconds.

Trent retook his seat and reached to take hold of the Henry his father was still holding, not at all sure he could trust the old warrior's judgment. Abe pulled the weapon away from Trent's grasp. His glaring eyes were fixed on the unhappy man on the floor. The Henry was zeroed in on the target as if it might be required at any moment. The old skirmisher held the weapon tightly, ready for anything. But clearly, the incident was over, a combination of foolishness and misjudgment.

"That's enough, Dad, you've beaten off the threat. I believe the enemy would surrender, given half a chance."

Cameron pushed himself into an upright position while still sitting on the floor. "What in tarnation do you mean by that shooting, you old fool?"

"Old, am I? Fool, am I? Well, sprout, I'm old enough to take care of my own, people or property. I paid good money for this store. I'll not have just any wandering grub line-rider kicking the door off'n it's hinges. Now, are you just trying to get out of the wind or you here to do business? Need cash money if that's the case. No freeloaders here. And you can expect to pay for the damage to the door."

The frightened man struggled to his feet and turned toward the outside. He saw P.A. Angus standing in the doorway over at the livery. Beside him was Trace, his shifting glance moving from the doorway of the store to a man moving along the outer wall.

Cameron said, "Come in here, Ty."

"Best he don't be holding no firearm when he steps into view."

"Lean your rifle against the wall, Ty."

"And he can drop his belt rig on the ground, suppos'n he's wearing one."

"Do as the man says, Ty."

During the elapsed few seconds, the women had found refuge behind the wooden counter. That the sawn wood was no shelter at all where weapons were in play had not yet sunk into their reasoning. But they had time and presence of mind enough to arm themselves, Gwyneth with her belt weapon and Helen with her shotgun.

As Ty made his careful way into the building, Trent was keeping his eye on the visitor. Having difficulty holding back his mirth, Trent finally said, "Dad, you'd best know your customers, man and boy alike. This here is Mr. Big Beef Cameron. Owns all the land and water from here to yonder according to his reckoning. The young fellow that I believe you might have frightened out of a week's growth is Cameron Jr., otherwise known as Ty. He'll bear watching. Likes to shoot from cover. Ain't too particular who he shoots."

Cameron ignored Trent but tipped his hat to Gwyneth, holding studying eyes on her a moment too long for either Trent or Gwyneth's comfort. Trent thought, *that's going to lead to serious trouble sooner or later*. Helen wasn't fooled for even a moment. She struggled with the serious temptation to permanently put an end to Cameron's obvious desires but held off only with the strongest self-discipline.

Helen, more mindful of the constant need to take advantage of any business coming their way than her husband was, waited until the smoke cleared and everything appeared to have settled down, and said, "Mr. Cameron, have you come to do business, or did you think it was time you tried kicking down a door, just for fun perhaps? Or just to see, could you do it."

Very cautiously, never taking his eyes off Abe and his Henry, Cameron said, "Wind caught the door. Sorry about that. Where's Bailey?"

That was a question her husband would normally answer, expounding on the details and bragging about the obviously bright future of the trading post and the town of Conville. Helen gave him a few breaths' time, and when no response filled the hollow of soundlessness, she simply replied, "Mr. and Mrs. Bailey gathered up their earnings, adding it to the purchase price of the establishment, and went off to another venture. You're looking at the new owners. Now, again, are you here to do business or to test our metal?"

"Holding out a folded piece of white paper, Cameron said, "Ty, you take this list. Give it to the lady. Then you and I, we'll leave these folks to their own."

After loafing away an hour at the livery, Cameron returned for the supplies. He paid over the asked-for funds and slunk back to the livery, saddled up, and rode north.

Rose and Trace tapped lightly on the rear door, pushed it open, and laughingly asked, "Y'all got those shooting weapons under control? I've got a plate of tea biscuits to share over coffee, but I don't want to get shot delivering them."

"Come in, Rose. Abe's pretty well settled down. And Trent's taken his long gun away from him. Coffee and biscuits sound just about right."

Chapter Fifteen

THE WEEKS OF WINTER WORK settled into something nearing monotony. The cattle stayed close to the shelter of the forested hills, occasionally finding a trail that led them into good shelter. Although cattle don't do well on it, snow took the place of water, except when the men found a creek or stream where they could break the ice, making the water available to the animals. The work was reduced to little more than riding the perimeter of the ranch, pushing back any animal that showed signs of wandering.

The cabin and other shelters were forted-up against the ceaseless wind and the dropping temperatures, with chinking that closed the gaps between the logs and with extra layers of branches on the roofs. Needing lumber for further building projects, Trent experimented with splitting the larger log sections with his axe and a post maul, showing little success except with the few cedars he found among the pines and fir. His stack of split boards, which roughly resembled cut lumber, grew discouragingly slowly.

Daniel went off visiting shortly after Christmas. He was coy about Likes The Night's part in that decision. Eustice Ward, the would-be preaching man, had wandered around the country, locating settlers and extending them a welcome in the Lord's name. He showed up in Conville and at the ranch every now and then, usually looking skeletal, in need of food and rest.

The single time Gwyneth pointed out the obvious truth, that a man wishing to live a long, full life needed to learn to take care of himself, Eustice, through a grim smile, replied, "I doubt you can find the words to sort me out any better than Helen did, down to the store. Might just as well let 'er go." She followed his advice, but the plates of vittles she laid in front of him were noticeably well loaded.

The next morning, he joined Trent and Cob, who were busy working cattle every daylit hour. Gwyneth spent her days close to the warm cabin until calving time. Then she was called into service. Fortunately, most of the heifers, never knowing any better, managed to drop their calves without human assistance. The continuing cold concerned Trent and Cob, but there was nothing to be done about it.

"I really don't know how these newborns survive," commented Trent while describing the day's work to Gwyneth. Gwyneth had a smattering of knowledge about the importance of the calves' first intake of colostrum but didn't bother taking the discussion in that direction.

The winter weather had shown a constant fluctuation between reasonably warm and bitterly cold. Snowfall had been light, allowing the animals to search out their own feed, for the most part. Even so, most of the hard-wrought supplemental hay had been tossed over the fence to the waiting cattle, while there was still a good bit of winter left. The first days of warming winds couldn't have been more welcome. Nor could the assistance of Daniel, who showed up in camp with a pack horse and a wife. He left Likes The Night, whom he had taken to calling Night Light, to Gwyneth's smiling care and turned immediately to the cattle. The women could figure out the living arrangements. As far as that went, the Ute woman and the half-breed man were totally comfortable making camp in the bush.

Over the months of their ranching in the area, which they had come to call the county of Conville, although that name carried no legality that any government would recognize, there had been no call for Gwyneth's medical assistance. She balanced that reality with the companion reality that she could not have expected anyone to know her as a medicine woman, since there were so few settlers anywhere close by. Allowing these thoughts to work their way through her mind, she discarded the fact that on the one recent occasion they had met with Cameron, it was obvious from the items on the rancher's shopping list that there was a need back at the ranch. No one expected Cameron to stoop to asking for help from the new owners of the Conville store. His pride would not allow that to happen.

Chapter Sixteen

COME SPRING, THEY SORTED OUT THE OLDER Mirrored W steers and made up a herd to drive to Pueblo. A few light ones were held over for another summer of grazing. Trent had no long-term interest in anything but the Mirrored W and the cattle carrying the W brand that confirmed their ownership. Cob would make his own decisions on the others. The newborn calves needed two summers of good grazing to bring them to market weight. The shipping of the older, weightier steers would pay out enough to build a bank account sufficient for the needs of the ranch until their calving-feeding-shipping rotation was established.

Trent was content that the bunch he had sorted out would serve that cause. Cob also organized his herd, making up a drive of about three hundred market-ready animals. With the drive sorted and bunched a mile apart from the heifers and their calves, the two young men sat their saddles, rolling their smokes and looking over the group of keeper animals, enjoying the green grass of spring with their calves at their sides.

Cob grinned at his riding partner. "You've done well, my friend."

"You've taught me well."

The first of the red calves were showing great promise. They were of good size, robust and bright, ever curious and healthy as far as the men could tell.

Trent was fussing about leaving the herds in the care of just Abe, when he could be spared from the trading post, Eustice Ward, when he wasn't ministering to some far-flung ranch, or Daniel, whose penchant for wandering seemed to have slacked off since he brought Night Light into camp as his wife.

When that incident first forced itself upon the ranchers, there were several whispered conversations about what was commonly called *country marriages*, or *custom marriage*, and in white Christian communities, *common law marriage*.

Gwyneth, in a private moment, boldly put the question before Daniel, assuring him that the discussion did not mean disapproval. "Night Light is a lovely lady, Daniel. I am looking forward to learning her language as she is trying to learn more of ours. And, of course, you gained our respect long ago. But I'm sure you remember your childhood enough to know that Christian folks take these things quite seriously."

Daniel responded, "Of course. I have not forgotten any of that. But what you must remember is that all people have their habits and rituals that they take seriously. I gifted my second horse to Wandering Eyes, Night Light's father. That was not really an attempt to buy her, although a lot of whites see it that way. Giving the gelding was a token of my respect for the father and my promise to always care for the daughter. I also brought a good-sized buck, skinned and cleaned and ready for the cooking pot, to her mother. This also shows respect, in addition to my pledge to provide for Night Light.

"These things are their way of showing goodwill and the promise to care and provide for our home. Their medicine man, the holy man for the village, made some smoke and blew it in our faces. He then rattled some bone instruments and chanted something I couldn't understand. That's all a bit off center for me, but a Christian ceremony would not be understood by them, either. If you need assurance, just know that I love Night Light and she shows that she loves me, although the Ute habit is more toward demonstrating love than talking about it."

All Gwyneth could think to say in response was, "Thank you, Daniel. We all wish you many happy years."

As Daniel rode out to the herd, Trent was riding into camp after many hours in the saddle. He loosed his animal in the corral, removed the saddle and bridle, before giving him a good rubdown. He then caught and saddled another horse before turning for the cabin. Gwyneth greeted him with a hug and a question, the same question she asked every day, "How are they looking?"

The answer was also the same, "They'll do. They'll show well for the buyers, and they'll make our time worthwhile. But I need to do something. I'll probably be gone two, perhaps three days. I'm going to ride south, see if I can find where those half dozen small ranches are. The ones Dad heard about. I'm going to try to hire a couple of men. Get some help with the herd for while we're gone. And how would you feel about me sending Trace up to help around the camp? Split you some firewood, haul a bit of water, that kind of help. That is, if his folks approve."

"He'd love that," answered Gwyneth.

Less than three hours slid past before the maturing Trace rounded the point of land and dismounted at the tie rack beside the corral. He was riding Helen's saddle animal. A tied-down pannier contained a lumpy cargo of extra clothing and gear. He stepped to the ground and hollered, "Hello, the house."

The porch door swung wide, and Gwyneth stepped out. Behind her, Night Light hesitantly showed her face.

"Come in, Trace. It's been a while since we've seen you. Thanks for coming up. We need an extra man around here, what with the others planning on herding that bunch off to market."

Three days later, Gwyneth was standing in the open grassland, far enough out to see past the point of land. To the south, she could see the smoke that constantly rose from the kitchens that kept the two women busy, and another smaller, darker smoke that told her P.A. Angus had his forge lit. Between the smokes and where she stood, three shadowy images, showing tall and thin in the dwindling evening light, appeared to be rooted in the grassland, like trees she knew weren't there, although her logic and her wishes convinced her they were moving. Her one hope was that it was Trent and a couple of hired men.

The images, if they were her hoped-for husband and some much-needed help, were at least an hour away. Smiling to herself, she studied the hills beyond the grass, to the east. The distance wasn't far. No more than a good day's ride. With the sun clearing the daytime air, those hills were visible as individual rises, craggy and sharp, unwelcoming, holding little growth. But in the gloom of evening, the narrow valleys that separated the individual peaks disappeared, leaving little more than a serrated outline, showing dimly against the blackening sky. Only in the few places where there was lighter colored rock did the setting sun find something to reflect from, showing in places as if there were a small series of fires glowing in the night. She constantly found herself comparing this land with the eastern land of her birth and raising. The differences were stark but not forbidding.

Turning back to the south, Gwyneth again tried to position the riders and guess at their progress. The dinner of venison stew was prepared and was slowly cooking, sitting on the hearth with red-hot coals banked around it. She warmed internally as she thought of Trace riding into camp the day before with his first deer kill. Both the women answered his holler. While Gwyneth was busy congratulating the maturing young man, Night Light was taking a more practical study of the situation. Even before Trace dismounted, Night Light was untying the deer and was showing signs of hoisting it onto her shoulder. "I clean," she said, smiling at Trace.

Stunned for a moment, not sure what approach to take, finally Trace said, "You don't have to do that. I'll do it."

The truth was that he had intended to gut the animal in the field but had no real confidence in his knowledge of the matter, although his father had shown him more than once.

"Woman's work."

Again, Trace was silent. Finally, he managed, "I'll help. You can teach me. It's men's work in our culture."

Night Light offered no answer, simply balancing the load over her shoulder and walking away as if it weighed nothing at all. Trace put his horse up and followed in her footsteps.

Happy to be building memories to hold over time, Gwyneth slowly made her way back to the cabin, needing to have coffee ready for when the men arrived. It took only a few steps for the point of land to block the view to the south. She then turned her eyes to the cabin, the rough-built horse shed, and the bunk house Daniel and Cob had thrown together. Cob was its only tenant now. Daniel and Night Light had built their own shelter a short walk up the draw behind the cabin.

Gwyneth seemed to never get enough of the view to the west. The low, forested hills defining the perimeter of the valley they had claimed, backed by the larger foothills and then by the tall Sangre de Cristo showing here and there the remnant of last winter's snow, reminding her of the feather-light touch of the early fall snows, the promise, at that time, of things to come. Those things, the struggles as well as the joys of camp fellowship, warm fires, and the knowledge that the animals were packing on the beef, in spite of the cold, had come and were now gone, leaving a sense of satisfaction and of a job well done among the settlers.

Gwyneth was busy at the fire when Trent pointed his horse around that same neck of land with two young men riding close behind. Trace was the first to see them. Raising his young voice to be heard over the distance and above the clop of the horses, he hollered, "This is it, fellas. You're home. Take a load off and put your animals in the corral. Water in the trough. They'll find it. Welcome to the Mirrored W."

Trent was tired but not too tired to grin at the young man, pleased at how he had settled in and was making himself useful around the place. He was further pleased when he dismounted, noticing how raked out and orderly the corral and the surrounding area was. He would have to be sure to commend Trace. Taking on work that wasn't assigned but that clearly needed doing was a sign of growing maturity. But more importantly for right then, his comely young wife was standing on the porch, a stew ladle in her hand, but forgotten, as she twisted her hands in her apron. Her smile of welcome was at least as bright as he had hoped it would be. Trent, turning his long-held social teachings aside for this one time, thought, *I can introduce the new men later.*

As they were sitting on the porch that evening, letting the venison stew and fresh bread settle, talking of what had been done toward their goal, and what the next few weeks, as the animals were delivered to market, would bring, Trent said, I'll be gone all of tomorrow. I'll leave it to Cob to get the new men settled into their jobs. I feel the need to ride up to the Cameron place."

That brought a raised eyebrow and a quizzical look from Gwyneth. Before she could properly phrase her question, Trent said, "It's a far distance to Pueblo. And driving a herd, we'll cover that distance at a slow pace. Seems neighborly to let Cameron know what we're doing. It wouldn't slow us down, not to speak of anyway, to fold a few head from the B/C into the gather if he wanted to ship. Or perhaps there's some shopping Mrs. Cameron particularly has in mind. I thought I'd ask anyhow."

"Wycome, you're a good man. Sometimes I think this country doesn't deserve you. I'll go with you."

"Now wait a minute."

THE RIDE TO THE B/C was somewhat experimental. Cameron had moved into the uplands behind the bordering row of hills, leaving no clear trace of their seldom and widely spaced comings and goings. And no sign welcomed anyone to the B/C Ranch. The few B/C cattle that somehow managed to wander onto the flats and mingle with Trent's or Cob's animals were soon separated from the others and pushed back to the north, closer to their home grass. They were never there for long before a B/C rider pushed them along, never coming near the W herd or attempting to make friendly talk. They were pushed around another point of land before turning them into the hills, leaving Trent still wondering where the main trail to the B/C was. There was no possibility of maneuvering a wagon over the trace they would be riding.

Trent and Gwyneth were riding north the next morning with Trent silently working through the three or four possible trails showing signs of use by livestock, any one of which might lead to the ranch headquarters, when he abruptly said, "Could be right. Could be just a wrong guess. But we'll take to the opening into the hills where the Cameron kid took a shot at us, way back, on our first venture down this way."

Gwyneth responded, "And if he's skulking around again with that rifle in his hands?"

"Then I may have to have a serious discussion with him."

Trent slowed to a bare walking speed as they approached the trail. Speaking to Gwyneth, he said, "You fall in behind. Stay four or five horse lengths back. Leave your rifle in the scabbard but have your belt gun close to hand. If you have to protect yourself, don't hesitate."

Gwyneth's response was to wordlessly lift the rifle a few inches free of the scabbard and then drop it, assuring its readiness, and to lift the leather hammer loop off the Smith and Wesson #2 Army .32 pistol Trent had bought for her in Pueblo. Satisfied that she would be under no threat she couldn't deal with, she nodded to Trent and flashed a hand gesture that meant *move on*.

The first sign that the kid had taken up his chosen post was the clicking of a hammer being eased into firing mode, followed by the rustling of shod hooves and the whinny of a horse. The animal was offering a welcome, even if no one else was on hand to do the same. Trent stopped abruptly and scanned the woods. Gwyneth's animal hesitated for three steps before pulling up tight against the lead animal, the one he had been following.

Gwyneth's quiet "Whoa" settled the gelding. Trent had been holding his carbine flat along the top of his right leg, where it was quickly on hand to point and shoot.

Seeing nobody, but knowing the rifle did not cock itself, and the welcoming horse would have no reason to be in the brush except it had brought a rider down that way, Trent was cautious. But tiring of the foolish game, he quietly said, "Stay," to Gwyneth before lifting his voice a bit. "Kid, if you want to live to see lunch time, you'll lay that rifle down and stand up where I can see you."

When that order brought no response beyond the shuffling of booted feet in the dry grass and leaves left over from the fall dye-off, he spurred his own ride in the ribs. The animal moved forward with a startled jump, moving up the slope of the hillside before turning into the brush as his rider directed him.

Trent hoped the move would force the kid, if he was truly hidden in the foliage, to twist from his grotto in order to keep his sight on the charging horse.

There was much snapping of dried and weathered branches breaking, more whinnying from the tethered horse, which Trent could now see, and the thud of hooves stomping through the fallen leaves, striking the rocky ground below. The kid, having no idea what to do and thinking only of escape, gave out a frightened yelp before rising to full height and running for his horse.

Trent caught him with three quick leaps of his horse. Before the kid could reach out for his own animal, Trent lifted his right foot from the stirrup and laid the flat of his boot hard against the runner's shoulders. The young man screamed, whether in fear or pain would have been difficult to gauge, and fell in a heap, barely missing the hooves of his own frightened horse, losing his grip on the weapon as he fell.

Trent pulled to a stop, lowering his carbine toward the flailing kid. "Don't you move, kid. Not until I tell you."

A slow count of five or six went past while the kid lay still, fearfully looking up at his assailant. Anyone who had never been in that position could not understand how big and ugly the bore of Trent's rifle was at that moment. Gwyneth took the opportunity to ride into the show, being careful not to get in her husband's way as he held the kid under the threat of his carbine.

There was no accounting for what might happen when guns were drawn, intentionally or accidentally, a fact Trent was well aware of. But the confrontation had started. It was time to finish it. With all the authority he could put into his voice, he said, "Okay, kid. Sit up and slither away from the horse. No, don't reach for the rifle. Now, stand up, facing away from me."

The kid glanced over his shoulder before rising to a standing position. Clearly, he was startled to see Gwyneth staring down at him. From somewhere, he remembered his little bit of teaching. He touched his right hand to his hat and said, "Ma'am," before rising.

Trent allowed the kid a moment to gain his balance, then instructed, "Pick up the rifle with one hand. By the barrel. One hand. Turn it so's the barrel is facing the ground. Good. Now back up and pass it to me. Don't turn around."

When those instructions were followed, Trent said, "Now, release your belt gun and hang it over your saddle. Good. Now untie the animal and lead it to me."

The kid was pouting and seething with anger and embarrassment, but he did as he was told. When the horse was alongside Trent's, he leaned over far enough to pick up the belt gun rig. He checked the loads and then draped it over his legs, resting easy with the Colt's butt close to hand. He dropped his own carbine into the scabbard and kept the kid's rifle in his right hand. A quick partial drop of the lever showed the shiny brass of a cartridge ready for firing. He carefully eased the hammer to the safe position before saying, "Now walk. Lead the horse. We're going to the ranch."

A SLOW, uphill quarter mile walk brought them over the top of the rocky rise that outlined a green, teardrop-shaped valley leading away from the ranch yard and into a natural rock enclosure of tree-lined hills. The green freshness of the layout suggested ample water whose source could be either from flowing streams or an ample supply of groundwater, shallow enough that the grass is able to pull it up through its root system. Trent and Gwyneth drew to a stop, allowing the walker to proceed to the corral, where he tied his animal after calling, "Pa. Pa. Where you at, Pa?"

The house door opened, and Cameron stepped outside. He said nothing at all, as he stared at his son. The boy just pointed at Trent and walked into the small barn, seemingly turning his back on all that had just happened. Cameron slowly turned to face his visitors, saying nothing for a short moment. Finally, hands on his hips, his right hand dangerously close to his holstered Colt, he said, "Mostly don't welcome visitors."

"Well, Mr. Cameron, we already figured that out. But we're not here to visit. We've come on a bit of business. But before we address that, we'd best talk about your boy. This is twice now that he's been staked out in the brush with a loaded rifle. The next time might get him killed."

A woman who must have been listening from the doorway stepped into view. Her attention was not on Trent or Gwyneth. Or her husband. Cameron stood sullen and silent while the woman, skittering as only a slight-built person can do, made her way to the barn, a short hundred yards away. She disappeared into the dim interior, returning to the yard within seconds, in complete control of the kid, who was taller than her by a head, with a twist of his ear. Trent sat his saddle in silent amusement, watching the drama in the ranch yard. Gwyneth held her own thoughts, while Cameron barely hid his anger.

"We didn't ride up here to talk about the kid, Cameron. We've come to talk cattle, but the kid thrust himself into our plans. That's the second time. This time, I managed to roust him out of the nook he had hidden himself in before he decided to pull the trigger on a weapon he isn't mature enough to handle."

In the silence that followed, Trent lifted the carbine with his left hand while he stared down the Cameron trio standing silently on the door stoop. With exaggerated slowness and precision, Trent jacked one shell out of the gun, letting it fall to the ground. Never turning his eyes from the target of his unspoken message, he jacked another shell to the ground. One by one, painfully slowly, he dropped the lever, as shell after shell disappeared into the stubby, sun-browned grass at his horse's feet.

When he had counted ten shells, the mechanism came up empty. He jacked the lever once more, almost like an exclamation point, and taking the weapon in his right hand, his fingers wrapped tightly around the mechanism, thrust it forward, and then releasing it, allowing it to gently glide through the air, not as a threat but as a show that his point was made, and the empty gun held no more threat.

Cameron easily caught the weapon. Lowering his hand, he held it at arm's length alongside his leg. He was seething with anger, but he held his silence, figuring his time would come.

While the silence held, Trent lifted the Colt from the belt apparatus and repeated the previous actions, emptying the shells one by one. With that completed, he replaced the gun in the belt holster, rolled the belt tightly, and gently tossed it to Cameron. "The next time the kid takes shelter with a weapon, against me or anyone from the Mirrored W, you'll be digging a grave."

Mrs. Cameron studied her son for a moment, gave his ear an additional twist, which brought the response, "Ow, Ma," and thrust him off the stoop. "I'm sure I heard your father telling you this morning to get yourself down to work with Blackie."

"I hate working with Blackie."

"That's because he makes you actually work. Now go."

The kid pushed just his fingers into the top of his jeans pockets and, with hunched shoulders, moved slowly to where he had tied off his horse.

Trent, knowing the time had come, or it would never come, said, "Now, can we talk business?"

"I look after my own business affairs."

"Well, I do too, so far as that goes. But we're all pretty isolated out here. I'd hoped we might find a benefit in doing some things together."

"I ain't interested, but I'll listen to what you have in mind."

Trent figured that was the best he was going to get, so he proceeded with, "We're taking a small bunch to market over to

Pueblo. Be gone maybe two weeks. Wouldn't be much more of a burden if you wanted to throw in some of yours that are market-ready. So long as they're branded, there's no chance of a mix-up. I'd charge you a small driving fee and either bring back the proceeds to you here or make a deposit at the bank for you. Whatever you wish. We're driving down to the settlement this afternoon. That's my folks who own the trading post. They're coming with us, team and wagons. The post is about sold out and it needs stocking up. We're leaving from there tomorrow morning early. But if you wanted to do a small gather, we'd hold off one day, no more."

Gwyneth waited for a moment of silence before saying, "I hear a baby crying, Mrs. Cameron. May I come and see it while the men talk?"

"You'll be staying out of the house," was the gruff command from Cameron. Neither Gwyneth nor Mrs. Cameron made a comment. Mrs. Cameron, looking embarrassed, turned and walked into her home. While the men talked deals and possibilities, Gwyneth listened to the happenings with mother and child. Soon the crying stopped. But surprisingly, three more little ones shyly poked their heads out of the door before bashfully gathering on the stoop, competing with one another for the front view of the visitors. The kids looked healthy enough, even in their well-worn and soiled clothing, and the mop of curly hair crowning each one. But the whole of it left Gwyneth wondering at the age difference between the older boy and this new batch of children.

Cameron's loud voice commanded the space, saying, "I'll take a chance this one time. But if you don't hold up your end, I'll have something to say about it. I can have a hundred head picked out by evening. Drive them down to the settlement tomorrow."

"You do that, and we'll take them to market for you, doing the very best we can against Indians and rustlers, with no promises. You'll be paying us six dollars the head."

Cameron replied, "I'll be riding along, me and the boy, so it's no extra work for you."

"That would change the deal some. You bring your own shelter and bedrolls. We'll do the feeding. You'll do your share of the work. Your cost will be two dollars the head."

"Ain't paying no such thing. I'll be caring for my own animals. Ain't about to pay for what I can do myself."

Trent was wearying of the whole matter, but he put out his final offer.

"We work together, one helping the other. Two dollars the head. Meals and extra protection in the event it's needed. Up to you. Suit yourself. We don't need you or your animals. Just trying to be neighborly."

Trent turned his horse and his back on his difficult neighbor and was about to leave when Mrs. Cameron came from the house carrying a blanket-wrapped baby. She took the few steps to where Gwyneth sat her horse and held the child out for Gwyneth to see, folding the blanket back just a bit to expose the tiny face. She was not smiling with pride as most young mothers would be. Gwyneth saw a totally different look on her face but couldn't sort out its meaning.

Tucked under the blanket was a folded paper. Mrs. Cameron made a point of bringing the paper to Gwyneth's attention by tapping her finger on it as she passed the child up to her. Gwyneth took the paper between two fingers before reaching for the child, with a concerned look on her face.

As she unwrapped the blanket a bit further and held the child more closely, Trent could see her concern blossom into something more. The moment hung silently, only to be broken when Gwyneth said, "Why, Mrs. Cameron, this child is not well. Have you taken note of her hot forehead and her heavy breathing?"

"I've taken note. No mother could miss that. But there's no doctor ready to help out here, so we just do what we think best.

What we know to do, which isn't much, has already been done."

Trent turned his horse back around to face the Camerons. "My wife here, she's near enough a doctor. Nurse anyway, with more experience than many a small-town doctor. I'd advise you to listen to her. You'll not be wanting to lose a child."

Gwyneth gripped the paper again and tucked it into her jacket pocket without making a point of it and opened the blanket further. As the paper slipped from her hands into the pocket, it opened just enough for something heavy to slip from the folds. She looked at Mrs. Cameron and then down to where her fingers were still gripping the paper. A quick glance showed her two ten-dollar gold pieces. As she slipped her hand out of the pocket, she locked eyes with the baby's mother. The woman's pleading eyes said, *Please say nothing.*

Gwyneth laid the back of her hand on the baby's forehead and then gently onto its chest, not bothering to remove the cloth it was wrapped in. She surmised by the facial features that the baby was a girl. After wrapping the baby back up snuggly, still tucked into the fold of her arm, she said as kindly as she could, "Mrs. Cameron, your little girl is very ill. I feel sure in suggesting that she has pneumonia."

The weary and worried ranch woman almost squeaked out the plaintive words, "Can you help her?"

There was a long pause, with the two women studying on each other, before Gwyneth said, "You'd have to bring her down to our cabin. I have some simple medicines. There might be something we can do."

With that, she turned to Mr. Cameron. "Have you made a final decision on Trent's offer?"

"There's no decision to make. I'll not be paying others to do my work. I'll look after myself."

Cameron would normally feel duty-bound to challenge Gwyneth's next words, but, giving way to the woman, he heard her say, "Fine then. Go and saddle a horse for your wife. A gentle horse. And another for those three children. One they can all sit on." She emphasized the last few words with a pointed finger. She then turned back to Mrs. Cameron, saying, "You go get yourself ready, you and the children. Bring enough clothing and what have you for several days. And hurry along now."

Wrapping up her instructions, she said, "Mr. Cameron, when you get those horses ready and your wife and kids mounted, you get yourself down to wherever your older son is working with this Blackie I heard mentioned. If I'm to stay and care for the baby, I'll not be going on the drive. That will leave one wagon driver short. Your son can fill that gap. If you could give him an attitude adjustment and see that he has no hidden guns before you send him off, that would be helpful. Now, Trent and I will be taking the baby down to the cabin. I'm hoping it's not too late. Hurry along now. There's no time to lose."

HOLDING to a steady but sluggish pace for the sake of the child, it was the full of an hour before the cabin came in view. The smoke from the chimney was a welcome sight, as was the fact that Daniel and Night Light were standing side by side on the small porch watching them ride in. Gwyneth, grasping the saddle horn tightly, swung her leg over and carefully dropped to the ground, still holding the child. To Night Light's unasked question, she, with a nod of her head, invited the Indian girl to join her inside.

LEAVING the child to the women, Trent got busy putting the last of the trail supplies together, then turned the extra horses out of the corral and pushed them onto the grazing land where they would join with the cattle already there. With a simple, circular wave of his extended arm, he, with the help of the hired riders, had the cattle moving south. In a short three hours, they would rendezvous at Conville. The remainder of the day would be spent getting the wagons prepped for the trip. P.A. Angus had already checked the shoes on the team and gave them a thorough look-over before he declared them fit for the long pull to Pueblo.

Abe muttered under his breath, "Knew that before that pup went and got his hands dirty doing the job that didn't need doing. Charged me fifty cents to tell me what I already knew."

Helen somehow managed to hear the quiet muttering. She just as quietly responded, "Abe, you watch your tongue. Mr. Angus is a good man and a good smithy. And he's become a friend. We don't want any foolish words to come between us."

Abe, not given to taking the easy way out of any situation where there was a possibility of doing otherwise, simply turned his back. As he walked away, he thought, *Ain't heard no foolish words except'n from the smithy.*

BACK AT THE CABIN, Night Light hovered close as Gwyneth undressed the baby, holding her close to the fire, although it was warm in the cabin.

"Very sick. This baby," commented the Ute girl.

Gwyneth nodded her head. "Very sick indeed. Could you get me another pan of warm water, please. The baby will feel better if we can get her cleaned up. Then we'll decide what to do."

With the last of the washing completed, Gwyneth wrapped the child in a warm, dry cotton cloth, material she had purchased and brought along on the way west to be made into diapers in the event that the need should arise. Since it had become sadly clear that she and Trent would not be needing them, she would use them for whatever purposes arose. As she was doing all of this, she was going through in her mind the little bit she knew about pneumonia and very young children.

Having come to a conclusion on what she might do with the items at her disposal, she said to Night Light, "We will keep her warm, but not too hot. I have a small supply of horehound leaves. We will make a mild tea. The child is too young to drink, but we can dribble a small amount of the tea into her mouth. In some cases, with older children, it has been known to loosen the congestion and allow the child to cough up some of the mucus from her lungs. That would ease her breathing. And I have powdered mustard. I can make a mild plaster for her chest.

"Mustard is very strong though. I must be careful. I wish we had some way of making steam that she could breathe in. Perhaps when I complete the plaster, I can get a pot of water simmering at the edge of the fire. We don't need much steam. Just enough for the child to drag in along with her breathing."

Night Light, struggling with the many words she didn't understand, somehow caught Gwyneth's meaning. Jumping to her feet, she rushed out the door, leaving no explanation behind her.

Somehow, Night Light and Daniel had found a mix of words that allowed them to communicate in a way both understood. After a couple of quick sentences from Night Light, Daniel turned toward the pile of stove wood stacked for cooking and the cool nights that would come soon enough. Ignoring the axe, he picked up a smaller hatchet and began splitting wood into smaller pieces, which he gathered up and carried to the side of the cabin. Within a few minutes, there was an eager flame biting into the split wood. Daniel then laid on several heavier pieces of wood, creating a bit of a platform.

Night Light had already gathered a dozen shattered pieces of granite, brushing off the dirt and bits of growth clinging to them. Daniel picked them up one by one and set them on the wood where the ready flames would heat them through.

With that done, Night Light disappeared into the brush. She soon returned with several long, flexible willow branches. She began building a small sweat lodge by embedding the ends of a half dozen branches into the unyielding ground. She banked those up with rocks and loose dirt, knowing the slight penetration accomplished would not hold them in place. Slowly, carefully, massaging the wands with one hand while she bent the other end toward the ground, she repeated the process, leaving her with an arched bow four feet wide and about two feet at the peak. Busily she repeated the process, wand after wand.

When she was done, Daniel, looking on from his place by the fire, smiled at the ingenuity of the woman. She returned the smile but added *blanket*, embellishing the point with her hands, outlining the idea of a cover. Daniel, with a smile growing on his lips, jumped to his feet and rushed to the small shed they had built to keep saddles, tools, etc., from the weather. When he returned, he had a piece of canvas in his hands. Together, the young couple covered the small hut, holding the edges of the canvas tight to the willow stems by piling rocks and soil along the edge, while leaving the front flap loose.

Night Light brought a pan of water from the stream and dribbled a few drops onto the heating rocks. A satisfactory rise of steam brought a smile to her face. She jumped to her feet and rushed to the cabin door. "Bring baby," she said to Gwyneth.

Returning to the small hut, she ushered Gwyneth in, taking the baby from her hands. When Gwyneth was seated, following the Indian girl's directions, she was passed the child. With the use of two sticks of split firewood, she transferred the hot rocks into the canvas-covered lodge. She dribbled water over the rocks, and as the steam filled the space, she smiled. "You hold baby. Face open. Water smoke come. Is good."

Gwyneth figured out that the Indian girl didn't know the word for steam.

Daniel, trying to keep one step ahead of his wife's thinking, was gathering more wood for the fire and more rocks to heat.

Night Light was squatting in front of the lodge, holding the canvas high enough for fresh air to enter while still capturing most of the steam. As the rocks cooled and the steam production faltered, Daniel had more rocks ready. And so, the process was repeated until Gwyneth, first massaging the tiny chest and very lightly tapping the girl's back, hoping she would cough out some of the mucus clogging her lungs and causing her problems, finally said, "I believe that is enough for now. Daniel, please bring me a dry towel and a dry blanket."

Chapter Seventeen

TRENT LOOKED TO THE NORTH WHEN HE HEARD THE bellowing of cattle. The last word from Cameron was that he was turning down the deal. But the big man riding point on a small herd was clearly his difficult neighbor. Somehow, finding another way to frustrate Trent, Cameron was leading double, and then some, the agreed to one hundred head. There were three riders. One was certainly Cameron himself. Taking up the flank, drag combination in the small bunch on one side of the herd was a black-bearded man riding a solid black gelding. He was dressed in black, wore a black hat, and showed the abundant, but straggly ends of black hair, dropping out of his hat and falling below the top of his shirt collar. The opposite flank, drag position was covered by the kid, whose name Trent remembered as Ty.

Deciding not to mention that Cameron's last words were a refusal of the offer, Trent and Cob rode out together to show where to bed down the herd.

"That's considerably more than one hundred head, Cameron."

"Suppose it is. But I'm sending Ty along. I was told he would be needed to drive a wagon. That's fine, but if he's needed with the herd, you'll find him a help. Good rider and knows more about cattle than you might first suppose. Do him good to get away from the ranch for a while too. You'll make out. Don't take many men to make a drive once they're trail-broke. My count is two hundred thirty-seven head. Brought along a small remuda too. You'll be needing horses."

"All right, Cameron. The horses could be a help. But two things. First, the kid causes any trouble, he gets sent home, no matter where we are. Second, your cost goes back to six dollars the head. The kid in no way replaces you on the drive, no matter how much you think he knows. Take it or leave it."

"Figured that's what you'd say. I'll go along with the cost, but I'm leaving Ty's welfare in your hands."

"You get your animals settled down while I go talk to the kid."

Cameron and Blackie turned for home, leaving no farewell or good riding wishes behind them.

Chapter Eighteen

BACK AT CAMP, WHEN THE TOWEL WAS PASSED INTO the sweat lodge, Gwyneth found herself looking into the eyes of Mrs. Cameron, the child's mother, who was on her knees so she could peer into the small tent. Those eyes were dull with concern, red rimmed with weeping and loss of sleep, but somehow there was hope showing through as well. Gwyneth removed the damp blanket from the child and dried her with the fresh towel. She looked at Mrs. Cameron and said, "We've done what we can do here. We may repeat the treatment, but for now, you take the child and wrap her in the dry blanket. Take her inside out of the wind. Then we'll see what else may be done."

Gwyneth dried as best she could before going into the cabin to find fresh clothing for herself, with the intention of making her way to the creek for a quick bath. She paused long enough on the way to kneel beside the three older children who had created seats for themselves out of the split and stacked firewood, asking each of them for their name.

A little boy, perhaps three years old, piped up with, "Me Bobby. Me twee," he said, holding out three fingers.

When Gwyneth looked at the girl, she offered, very properly, and with a bit of an inflection, "My name is Greta. I am five years old."

The oldest of the three kids reluctantly answered Gwyneth's stare with, "Samuel." No age information was offered. Gwyneth thought silently that the boy was already taking after his father.

Entering the cabin, she had been immediately struck by the pungent, almost overwhelming odor emanating from the big soup pot nestled among the coals in the fireplace. A slow steam was rising as the lid lifted slightly with each escaping puff of steam. Gwyneth commented, "I don't know what you have in the pot, Night Light, or when you found time to put it together, but it smells good. Strong, but good. A little of that should help the baby get right up and walk out of here."

Daniel chuckled, "I asked her what was in it but all she would say was, 'Is good.' I checked, just to be sure, but the dog is all right, sniffing out the new horses last I saw."

Night Light, showing little humor at the comment, said, "No dog. No for baby. Flower from hill." Meaning herbs she had picked from among the growth behind the cabin.

Gwyneth said, with a bit of a grimace, "Well, I'm happy for the dog. For myself as well, so far as that goes." She slipped behind the curtain that was walling off the sleeping area and found another towel and some dry clothing. She glanced in the small mirror they had created so carefully and carried all the way from Dodge. A single glance was enough to tell her that she would have to deal with her hair another time. First came the baby's health. But the baby was in her mother's arms at the moment, taking on some nourishment and leaving Gwyneth time for her bath.

Daniel had stood quickly, ready to leave the cabin as Mrs. Cameron was quite openly preparing to nurse the child.

Just as Daniel reached the doorway, Gwyneth stopped him with, "Daniel, I'm going up to the creek for a bath. I'm taking my Colt. You might want to advise Trace of that fact."

Daniel didn't even turn around as he answered, "Ma'am, I

guarantee you'll come to believe that both the boy and I have ridden off hunting strays or whatever. You'll see nothing of us until you clang the iron for feeding time."

Gwyneth privately smiled at their friend's turn of words and glanced back at Mrs. Cameron. Night Light thought nothing at all about the process. She had seen the same activity many times in the village and took it as quite natural.

Gwyneth, reluctant to leave her patient, even for a short while, asked, "How is she, Mrs. Cameron?"

"I don't want to give in to wishful thinking, but I do believe she is breathing somewhat easier. But you mustn't go on calling me Mrs. Cameron. My name is Betty. I don't live by foolish formalities. Betty will do just fine. I've heard you called Gwyneth. May I call you by that name?"

"Of course you can. I'm not much on the formalities either."

"Well, Gwyneth, I can't thank you enough for being here and being willing to help. If I had known about the steam idea, I could have done much the same with a pot of boiling water and a blanket as a hood." After a moment's hesitation, she quietly said, "There's just so much I don't know."

"You could use a pot of steaming water. Most would have done that. But after trying Night Light's way, I'm thinking the steam from the heated rocks is a bit cooler, less likely to scald the child's lungs. Now, if you can get her to rest, it might be best to leave her for a bit."

To herself only, Gwyneth said, "These girls start into married life so young. What they didn't learn from their mothers, they have to learn for themselves. Sometimes it's a difficult process."

Chapter Nineteen

THE AFTERNOON AT THE VILLAGE WAS SPENT RIDING among Cameron's cattle, looking for anything that might cause problems on the drive. The spare horses were driven into P.A. Angus's corral, where he would check their feet and legs. One small paint was pulled out and isolated in another corral. The smithy called Trent over. "Take a look at this."

Lifting first one hind leg and then the other, he lightly scraped and poked at each frog. "Wouldn't get two days of hard riding out'a this one before you'd come up with a limping animal. Best leave him here. I'll see what I can do."

A light slap on the shoulder from Trent, followed by, "You're a good man," was thanks enough for the smithy.

THE SUN WAS BARELY BREAKING the grip of night the next morning when Abe's glance took in the overall picture. Just the evening before, almost at the last minute, one of the newly arrived settlers' wives rode into town offering to drive the pup wagon. Abe gladly accepted. That would put the kid back on horseback and back with the herd. Now, there she was, holding off to the side just a bit, waiting to take up her position behind Helen's rig.

Abe rode to within shouting distance, looking at his wife, who was proudly settled on the wagon seat. "Best give them a nudge, Mother. You're leading this parade. And it's time to move them. I'll be out front a half mile scouting trail, but no one back there would be able to see me. It's you the cattle will home in..."

Helen had little patience for her sometimes long-winded husband. His last words were drowned out with "Hi-yup, you horses. Git a move on, ye."

Cob rode over to where Ty waited for the herd to take the trail. He would be riding flank, at least until the herd was trail-broken. "Ty, I need you to listen up. And you listen good. You get just the one chance. Trent was bound to take your weapons from you, knowing you're not mature enough to use them wisely. I told him I'd talk to you. You'll keep the weapons. But if you even lift that Colt from the leather, there had better be a serious threat. Something like Indians bent on trouble, or rustlers or such. Anything less, I'll be wanting to see that weapon seated snuggly in the leather. The same with the carbine. We're all armed and all for the same reason. That single reason is to keep both man and animals safe and alive. Do you understand?"

The belligerent grimace on Ty's face showed itself for just a flash of time before he thought better of his first response. The truth was that he would put up with almost anything to get away from the B/C, if only for a few weeks. Falling under the impatient hand of his father and the overbearing nature of Blackie had been pushing him near his breaking point. Doing well on this trail drive might change some opinions about him. "I understand. I'll go along."

"See that you do, and all should go well. We're not expecting trouble, but a fella just can't never know for sure. Keep your eyes open and your mind on the cattle. But scan the surroundings time to time too. If you have questions, ask any one of us. We've all done this over more miles and more days than we like to remember."

The herd was shouted into movement and Cob hurried back to his flank position on the side opposite Ty.

TRENT HAD MET no travelers who had come this way except Herv Driscol and Thomas Verhune, the two settlers who had signed on for the drive, overcoming the need to work on their homesteads and care for their families, in the prospect of gaining a month's wages. North or south, the land was the same either way, although the view was different. The real test wouldn't come until they reached the end of the valley. By then, it would be too late to reverse course.

With Abe riding far ahead, Trent had little choice but to trust the man who had raised him. He had said nothing on the subject, but privately had been thinking of the changes that had come over his father. He seemed to have gained purpose in life. An attribute that hadn't been obvious in previous years. Perhaps he could even claim a direction for the latter half of his life. Certainly, he had made little or no money with what he termed his trading post in the gathering of shacks they referred to as Conville, following the lead of Griz Bailey, from whom he had purchased the squat building, along with the few supplies the trader had on hand. Clearly it wasn't financial success that had settled his parents down to where they had shown no interest at all in moving on as they had done so often before. Trent liked the changes, but the reasons behind them would remain a mystery.

The southern ranchers and their horses worked harder than they ever thought would be necessary in order to keep the cattle from straying off toward some inlet leading into the low hills.

Much to Trent's surprise, Ty Cameron was shaping up,

showing some responsibility and priding himself on the fact that he had lost no animals in their first few days on the trail. Once, he had even been trusted to ride opposite Thomas Verhune, sharing responsibility for a three-hour stint of night herding. Trent had said no words of praise, figuring the kid was doing only what he was being paid to do, but Cob took note. The first accolade of praise the kid had ever received, at home or anywhere else, was when Cob smiled and nodded to him at the end of the day. He found himself sitting taller in the saddle and thinking better of himself even after just that single tip of Cob's hat.

Chapter Twenty

MUCH TO THE CREW'S SURPRISE, THE ROUGH PASSAGE was short and not particularly difficult. And the opportunity to turn back to the east came quickly. Within less than one week, after skirting a long, well-constructed, north-to-south fence and easing around a large sheep outfit, they came to the Arkansas River. The river, as well as the continuing fence, now turned to head east, led them easily toward Pueblo. The cattle were separated and sold off. The banking was completed, and the men turned loose to visit a bath house and one of the several restaurants, with their pay jingling in their pockets.

Abe and Helen backed their wagons up to the loading dock behind the emporium and set themselves to serious shopping.

Gwyneth had passed Mrs. Cameron's note and coins off to Helen, along with a list from herself. Abe grumbled a bit when Helen left him to himself while she walked down the sidewalk looking for the ladies' store and the apothecary. The personal and medical items on the list didn't require discussion with Abe or anyone else.

The sale of the animals and the banking went smoothly. The shopping took less than one afternoon. By evening of the first day in town, everyone had satisfied themselves with hot baths, a restaurant dinner, and a rest for the teams. Ty Cameron had walked every street and glanced in every store window, as if he had never seen such wonders before. He said nothing to Trent or anyone else, but his churning mind had come to a conclusion. He had to escape the confines of the B/C Ranch.

As the newly rising sun was breaking the night's hold on the territory, the travelers, a couple of them still picking their teeth after their café breakfasts, gathered at the big barn. Abe and Ty Cameron were working over the teams. Abe watched the boy who, even on this short trip, was showing more of the manliness he would need to survive and prosper in the new land. He said nothing, but Ty had sensed his watching and was pleased when no raised voice came his way, criticizing his every move. It was so unlike the homeplace where either Blackie or Ty's own father were constantly making his life a misery.

Helen arrived with another armload of purchases. As she placed them in the wagon, three books slipped in a fan shape from her grasp, falling to the barn floor. Ty moved quickly to pick them up and brush them off on his pant leg before passing them back.

"Abe and I like to read, Ty. I'm constantly looking for new books. I traded some we had read several times in exchange for these. We may have a couple back home that you would enjoy. What kind of stories do you like?"

The response was so slow in coming that Helen was sorry she had asked. But being into the conversation that far, she decided to complete it. "I know it's a personal question, Ty, but can you read?"

"No ma'am. I ain't never learned. Pa and I, we lived alone, batching, he called it, after my ma died. There was no time for learning. And then when Pa came down with a new wife, I was sort of left on my own. Anyway, Pa, he can make out some words and he says that's enough for any rancher. Says if a man can read the numbers on a check from the cattle buyer, there's no need for more."

Helen bit her lip a bit while she studied on an answer to the sad statement. She finally said, "There's no herd to mind on the way home. If you'd like, you could come sit on the wagon with me. I'd be glad to get you started on your letters."

Ty offered no answer.

ON THE RIDE TO PUEBLO, Ty had taken careful notice of the large ranch they were passing. Miles upon miles of four-strand barbed wire enclosing the high-country semi-desert grass. There were but few cattle within sight, but those that were showed the best of breeding. When the ranch headquarters came into view, everyone's eyes turned that way. Abe, sitting the spring seat on the big wagon, hollered to Helen, who was carefully guiding the pup wagon along the trail, traveling side by side with her husband, "Seen this outfit from across the river on the way out. Best I've ever laid eyes on. Sign over the gate says *Bar-M*."

On the return trip, Ty rode close to Trent and said, "I'll catch up before nightfall. I'm going to ride in. Take me a look around. Maybe ask some questions."

Before Trent could inquire further, the boy was gone. When he rode up to the dinner fire a few hours later, he offered no information on his afternoon, but it was clear to Trent that the kid was deep into new thoughts.

Chapter Twenty-One

WITH THE CREW AWAY, GWYNETH WAS LEFT WITH A baby that still needed much care, but with fewer mouths to feed. Betty Cameron took over most of the cooking while Night Light and Gwyneth fussed over the child. On the third day after Night Light first built the steam tent, Betty was nursing the baby while she studied the telling signs of sickness so evident earlier on. In a quiet voice, she whispered to Gwyneth, "I believe you've done it. The child is much better. Her fever is gone and she's breathing much easier. I don't know how I will ever thank you. Or pay you. I'm thinking if you can put up with us one more day, we'll keep a careful eye on the wee one. If she's holding her own, we'll head home in the morning. Mr. Cameron will be tired of his own cooking before this time."

"I'm sure we'll find some way to tolerate your presence." Smiling widely, breaking the seriousness of the mood that had been set through the talk of the child, Gwyneth added, "There's no need for payment. Don't give it a single thought. Earning a bit of income may come later, but not now. I'm hoping someday to be able to hang out my shingle for medical assistance. I have no right to the title of doctor, but even good nursing is more than many settlements in the west can expect.

We'll have to see how the ranch goes before I can make that decision."

"If you were to give me the right to comment, Gwyneth, I'd say the west is full of ranchers hoping to make it big. Some will make it. Most won't. One ranch more or less won't make a pinch of difference, but one good nurse would have a dramatic effect on the area. And with Night Light putting in her knowledge, you'd be the talk of the whole countryside."

Gwyneth added nothing to the statement.

THE TRAVELERS RETURNED and life looked to be ready to settle back to normal. Trent waited until the morning after their arrival to ride up to the B/C. He found Cameron sitting in the morning sun with a cup of coffee. The children were playing in the yard while Mrs. Cameron cleaned up the breakfast doings. Trent tied off a good distance from the house. He walked up to Cameron, who hadn't bothered to greet him in any way, with two pieces of paper in his hand.

Using Cameron's lack of a greeting as the norm, Trent said, "Got your accounting here. Best you should take a look at it while I'm here to answer questions. We got a good price all the way around. No animals lost along the way." Digging into his vest pocket, he pulled out an envelope. "Made your bank deposit and brought out the cash you asked for."

He passed the envelope and took a step back, waiting. Cameron opened the envelope first, counting out the few bills, then the five larger coins, completing the counting with his eyes glued to the smaller coins. Saying nothing at all, he pocketed the cash.

Betty Cameron came to the door smiling. "Good morning, Mr. Wycome. I thought I heard voices out here."

"Good morning, Mrs. Cameron. How's that baby holding out?"

"Fit as a fiddle, thanks to your wife and that Indian girl, Night Light. I'm very thankful."

There was no indication of thankfulness from Cameron, for the treatment of the baby or the sale of the cattle.

Cameron was very slowly studying the papers, running his fingers along each line as he read. The startling thought came to Trent, *That's why Ty can't read. He's had no one to teach him. Cameron himself can't read but poorly.*

As the silence in the yard hung on while Cameron studied the papers, Ty came up from the barn leading a calf. He paused a distance from the actual yard and tied the animal to the fence. Stepping closer, he said, "Mr. Wycome, I owe you my thanks. Thanks for not shooting me when you had the right, and then for taking me on the drive. Pa has been covering my wages, paying with a calf each spring. This one here is four months. I weaned her a bit early, but she's taken to grazing, with a pail of milk every once in a while. I want you to take her down to Mrs. Wycome. Payment for what she done for the baby."

The yard fell to silence as the generous offer from the young man settled on the scene. Finally, Cameron growled under his breath, almost silently, before saying, "Never grow yourself much of a herd giving away your calves."

Mrs. Cameron, shocked at both the offer as well as her husband's response, bravely said, "That will be enough of that talk, Mr. Cameron. We certainly owe Mrs. Wycome something for her efforts. I offered before but she wouldn't hear of it."

Glancing from her husband to her adopted son, she said, "That's a very generous offer, Ty. But it's not truly a debt for you to pay. It's your father's debt."

Cameron kept studying the papers, saying nothing.

Trent, trying to stay clear of a family situation, said, "I doubt that Gwyneth was expecting any pay. But if you feel strongly about it, Ty, it would be best if you were to bring the calf down yourself."

Trent was more disgusted than ever with his arrogant neighbor. All he wanted now was to remount and ride down the hill. "I'll be leaving you now Cameron. You'll find the papers in order. We did what we contracted to do with the cattle. Ty stepped right up and played the man, earning his keep, and probably a bit more."

Having the last word, Cameron lowered the papers onto his knees. "You were mighty well paid for the bit of trouble my animals caused you."

Bravely, Betty Cameron said, "I guess I'm the only one who will say thank you, Mr. Wycome. So, thank you. Those animals were eating valuable grass when they were already at full weight. The ranch is better off without them, and the bank account is better off too. Thank you again. You and your fine wife are a credit to the countryside."

With a nod, Trent untied his horse and was gone.

Two DAYS LATER, Ty rode into the yard with the calf following on the end of a rope lead. His saddle was loaded up with a bedroll and camp necessaries. Gwyneth, expecting the visit after Trent's report on his return from the B/C, had decided that she would accept the calf. The young man who had finally shown the beginnings of maturity on the long trip to Pueblo would be deeply hurt if his payment on behalf of his stepmother and the baby were refused.

Gwyneth welcomed Ty to the ranch yard, making no mention of the calf. Ty made an awkward presentation of his reason for the visit, with Gwyneth graciously thanking him, assuring him that no payment had been expected. She quickly changed the subject, saying, "You look to be loaded down for the trail."

"I'm riding back to the Pueblo area. That big ranch, the Bar-M, they offered that if I got back in time for fall roundup, they most likely would have a month's work for me. The ranch is all fenced, so it would just be dealing with their own animals, but as long as it's a paying job, it matters not to me. I'll probably just be helping around and seeing to the fire for the cook, and such, but I'm looking forward to it."

"You watch out for yourself on the trail, Ty. And work hard. Perhaps they'll find a need for you over the winter."

THE SUMMER MOVED ALONG, with fall encroaching on the pleasant days, until one morning, there was a nip in the air. Just a warning of what would soon be upon them. Two more families had settled onto the grass south of Conville. One homestead was filed to the north. Abe and Helen were doing better business than anyone had predicted.

Word of the nursing care available at the Mirrored W had traveled the valley. Gwyneth was kept busy treating the ailments common on the frontier—scrapes, cuts that had become infected, broken bones, and the birthing of children. Trace Angus, growing into his maturity, was hired on to guide and protect Gwyneth as she traveled to the far-flung ranches.

Night Light and Daniel, now fully settled in at the Mirrored W, welcomed their first child. When Gwyneth carried that news down to Conville on a shopping trip to Abe's store, Helen said, "House ain't really a home without a baby in the crib." It was an insensitive statement that caused Gwyneth to tip her eyes to the floor with a quiet, "I suppose you're right," as her response.

Helen was all set to talk about grandchildren until Abe, showing more wisdom than he was usually given credit for, asked, "You got any more coffee over there, Helen?" The awkward moment passed after a bit more silence.

The truth was that Gwyneth herself had wondered about her situation. So little was known in the medical world, and the subject so awkward to talk about that silence, vain wishing, and embarrassment reigned. Privately, Gwyneth had times of deep sadness that not even Trent knew about. What Trent's thoughts on the subject were would never be known.

SUMMER BECAME winter and repeated itself until the Mirrored W was now three years old and fully established. Conville, which everyone knew would one day dry up and blow away, was now home to two additional businesses, one small saloon, and one ranch supply store carrying rolls of barbed wire, ready-cut fence posts, hay mowers, and a small selection of plows and cultivators for those settlers determined to break open the land for farming. Trent laughed, saying to Gwyneth, "Mostly wishful thinking, if you were to be interested in my opinion."

As Gwyneth was about to run her iron around the steel triangle hanging from the porch roof, calling the stragglers in for lunch, she was amazed to have a stagecoach running full tilt around the point of rock to the north of the Mirrored W buildings. Seeing the ranch, the bewhiskered driver pulled back on the reins, calling to the sweating horses, "Whoa, whoa, ye rangy varmints."

As the stage rocked on its leather suspension, with a couple of curious passengers poking their heads out the window, the driver called out, "Hello the house. Didn't expect to see you here. Didn't know there was any fixed ranches down this way. What ranch is this?"

Gwyneth, still carrying the iron bar in her hands while swishing dust from her face, strolling toward the rig, answered, "This is the Mirrored W. I'm Gwyneth Wycome. My husband, Trent, and I are settled in here. Where on earth did you come from? We've seen no other coach down this way. Where are you headed for?"

"Names Buster, ma'am, Jehu of this here rig. Down from

Bessie Creek, up north. Since the rails are run through and carrying people to their own promised land, the stage company figured they'd best be on hand to carry folks to where they wish to go. For a fee, don't ya know. Headed to some place named Conville and further south after that. Ya have any idea where that there metropolis might be?"

Gwyneth hid a grin as she explained where the village was. Buster came back with, "I'll be on my way then, ma'am. Got some mail fer ta drop off at the store. Hop'n ta maybe scrounge a bit of lunch fer myself and the pay'n passengers. Cain't stop every trip, ma'am, but I'll be sure ta wave, kinda lett'n ya know thet there's life on the other side a this here big pasture."

The jehu hollered the team into action, but before they had taken more than just a couple of steps, he hauled them down again.

"Been told there's a medical lady down this way, ma'am. By the looks of what has to be bandages, and a couple of blankets washed and drying on that line over there, chances are you might be her." He didn't wait for the answer.

With the news spread through the grapevine as well as along the stage route, Gwyneth was busier than ever with her medical work. A two-room structure had been erected on the property for a clinic. The increase in medical traffic was credited to the stagecoach, new to the area but now running regularly. There were a handful of folks, miners mostly, thinking of home as Bessie Creek, the elaborate name a half-canvas general store had named itself, taking the opportunity since it was the first and only establishment in what the confident owner promised himself would one day be a thriving settlement.

Chapter Twenty-Two

TRENT CONTINUED TO PLAN. THE GROWING BANK balance in the Pueblo bank confirmed the soundness of his plans. With that growing financial base, his plans were looking more and more as if they just might turn into reality. In his mind, as clear as if they already existed, were new ranch buildings—a warm home housing his precious wife and welcoming the children yet to come, a barn adequate for a growing ranch, corrals, a good and steady water supply. In total, the Mirrored W would be a ranch others would admire and envy.

The one thing that he failed to plan for, and that took him completely by surprise, was being dead.

It had come about on a warm, spring afternoon as he and Cob Fleming, his friend and partner, were sorting out the Mirrored W herd. Trent's cows calved early in the year. He liked to wean the calves off their mothers before the heat of summer overtook them. Free of their calves, the cows were free to roam.

Some of the cows had found their way to an uphill pasture heavy with good grass, but surrounded by flattened layers of shale rock, cactus, and rough tree growth. Lest they get lost, Trent was determined to guide them back to the main bunch.

He was riding a green broke three-year-old gelding that he

had ridden a couple of times before. The animal had impressed Trent with the beginnings of cattle sense, seeming to understand what was expected of him.

Cob had warned him the animal was rattle-brained, a calculation Daniel agreed with, but Trent, ever mindful of costs and waste, couldn't imagine parting with a working horse before it was given every chance to prove itself.

The gelding had tried to toss saddle and rider both, the first few times Trent had worked with him, back in the big corral on the homeplace. But that tendency was to be expected and seemed to mellow out with time, and Trent was satisfied that he had a good animal, one worth his time to train and trust. The bit of youthful skittishness left in the gelding didn't bother the experienced rider. The odd crow-hop or sudden stop was taken as a training opportunity. But that all changed suddenly as Trent pointed the animal toward a pair of yearlings that were breaking from the gathered herd, heading for the shade of the brush that bordered the range.

Trent spurred the gelding into a slow lope in their direction. He responded immediately and homed in on the escaping cows. But then the unexpected happened. A half-starved, scruffy-looking coyote that had been skulking around the herd unseen burst from the brush right in front of Trent's ride. The gelding shied and flew into a tantrum. Cob, watching from a quarter mile away, was impressed with the way Trent remained poised in the saddle, seemingly in control. It appeared to be nothing more than a situation that could happen to any ranch rider at any time.

Then the trotting yearlings, not liking the looks of the coyote, turned, facing him in challenge, with their horned heads lowered in his direction. The coyote, sensing a threat to his well-being, made a startled about turn and ran between the legs of Trent's ride. That brought out every bit of fear and rebellion the gelding had been holding back. The ride was wild and fantastic and short, lasting only another few seconds.

To Cob's dismay, and it can be logically assumed to Trent's dismay also, the rider lost one stirrup and then began to lose his seat. Another burst of equine fear brought about a situation that Trent was unable to overcome. He and the animal parted. Trent made an ungraceful flip through the air before landing on the grassy range he had such plans for, and didn't move.

Cob kicked his own gelding into a run, pulling up beside Trent's body. The so hopeful and happily married owner of the Mirrored W lay there with his neck and head at an impossible angle. Trent Wycome would ride no more. He would never father a son. He would never make another plan.

Chapter Twenty-Three

COB SAW IMMEDIATELY THAT THERE WAS NOTHING TO be done for his friend. With the crises over, the gelding had settled down and stood, quietly pulling grass from the fringe of the brush. Cob rode over and stepped to the ground. The gelding stood unquestioning while Cob picked up the reins and reached for the saddle girth. The tie strap was soon loosened, and the saddle dropped to the ground. Cob wrapped the reins around his own saddle horn to hold the three-year-old from wandering off. He left the two horses while he carried the saddle over to where Trent had fallen. He gently laid the leather over the dead man's face to hold off the varmints and returned to the horses. He led the gelding to a bare five acres of cap rock just a short ten-minute ride from where the wreck had occurred.

This time when he stepped to the ground, he was reaching for his Winchester, as well as internally, for all the determination and fortitude he could muster. An unpleasant few seconds lay ahead of him. A few seconds that he would think back on and remember in the early morning darkness of the bunk house, and hate. But there was no avoiding what had to be done. No one was going to ride a killer horse. Making what was, to his mind, the only decision available to him, and preferring not to dwell on his actions, he led the gelding away from the grassed edge and onto the rocks.

Stepping to the front of the horse, Cob lifted the carbine in a single smooth motion, picked the spot he wanted between the animal's eyes, and squeezed the trigger. The gelding dropped with barely a quiver. Cob wriggled the bridle off, having to force the bit from between clenched teeth, and remounted his own ride. He headed directly for the Mirrored W headquarters, where he would have to break the sad news to Gwyneth, Trent's wife, now his widow.

Chapter Twenty-Four

DANIEL, FROM THE SHADED INTERIOR OF THE BARN, and Gwyneth, enjoying the morning sun, fussing over her medical supplies and rolling bandage material, standing at a table she had placed in the front yard, saw the arriving Cob riding alone. His posture in the saddle and the strained look on his face seemed to be sending a signal, a message. A strong sense of foreboding fell over both onlookers. Daniel leaned his hay fork against the stall partition and stepped into the light. Gwyneth stood stock still, the bandage material forgotten in her hand.

Cob slowed his animal to a walk and then pulled him to a stand at the hitch post. He missed seeing Daniel, but as he stepped to the ground, he silently laid his eyes on Gwyneth. Clearly, his presence alone and the trouble his eyes exposed told her all she really needed to know. She dropped the bundle she was rolling and lifted her hands to her mouth, uttering the single word, "What?"

Cob had always kept a respectful distance from Gwyneth, respectful of both her own dignity and his strong sense of moral correctness. But the truth had been gnawing at him since even before the wedding vows had joined Trent with the lovely young woman. He had often wondered if Gwyneth sensed his love for her. He hoped not. Especially at this time. With every bit of self-control at his possession, he would continue to hide those feelings now, at the most difficult time he had ever faced.

"Been an accident, Gwyneth. It's not good."

Gwyneth stood as a statue, a jumble of thoughts running through her mind. Finally, the truth being sorted out of Cob's few words, she staggered as if she was about to fall. She wasn't the fainting type. If she had ever been, her medical training and experience had put an end to that impulse. But she did back up a couple of steps and sag onto the porch stairs.

If Trent was injured, Cob would have rushed in, hollering for her to grab her medical supplies while he saddled a horse for her. But Cob had been in no hurry. The message was as clear as if it had been written in the clouds.

Daniel had stepped into the yard with a question. "Was it that rattle-brained horse?"

Cob turned from Gwyneth to answer the question. "None other. I shot the brute after. Should have shot him a year ago. You want to hitch up the wagon, Daniel?"

Cob stood shuffling his feet as if he didn't know what to do or say. Well, the fact was that he really didn't know what to do or say. Finally, desperate to fill the air with some kind of sound, he said, "You stay here with Night Light, Gwyneth. Leave the rest to Daniel and me."

"No. I'm coming with you. I'll ride the wagon with Daniel. You lead the way."

Gwyneth held her emotions in check as they rode up to the accident site, and even as Cob lifted the saddle from Trent's face. But her excruciating heart pain broke through as the men lifted Trent into the wagon. Gwyneth climbed in, sitting cross-legged, lifting Trent's head onto her lap. She folded her hands reverently, laying them on her husband's chest, bowed her head, and wept bitterly. Looking on, Cob wondered if she was weeping or praying. Perhaps it would amount to the same thing. In any case, her need to be alone was evident. Cob remounted while Daniel climbed quietly to the wagon seat and picked up the reins. Daniel held to a slow pace on the ride back to the ranch, funeral procession slow.

WHEN TRENT WAS LAID out on his own bed, the bed he and Gwyneth would never again share, the men stepped silently out of the cabin, toward the barn. Cob quietly said, "Daniel, bring Night Light down here. There's nothing for her to do, but it might help if she put the coffee on and then just quietly sat by. You hang in here. I'll ride down to the store. Abe and Helen need the news as soon as possible."

THE AFTERNOON STAGE through Conville carried the news south, and on the return trip the next morning, carried that same news to the northern settlers and the few people who were forming up the new town of Bessie Creek, on the railway right of way. The jehu, Buster, took it as a solemn duty to spread the word. The hard-working Trent was well-liked throughout the valley. Buster announced an unauthorized run of the stage for daybreak the next morning. He would deal with the company officials later.

P.A. Angus, Rose and Trace, who had reached his early teens in age, and was showing responsibilities in all he did, rode to the Mirrored W for the funeral. They were joined on the trail by two of the three ranching families that had settled close by. The stage pulled into the yard just short of noon. Buster held the team to a controlled walk as he came near. The doors eased open and eight people, five men and three women, all dressed in their go-to-meeting clothes, stepped to the ground. Last to arrive at the Mirrored W was Eustice

Ward, just dismounting as Gwyneth stepped out of the house. He took the few steps from the hitch rail to the porch, removing his hat and holding it in his left hand as he approached.

"Gwyneth, I just heard this morning. I'm glad I got here in time. There are no words to express my sorrow, although that sorrow will pale in comparison to what has been laid on your heart and life. You know you can ask anything. Anything at all. If it's within my power, it's yours."

"Thank you, Eustice. I've asked Cob to say a few words. Perhaps mentioning their years together on the trail and such. But I'd be pleased, and I know Trent would heartily approve if you could read from your Bible and send Trent off with a few words."

"You honor me, Gwyneth. I'd be happy to do that."

Gwyneth had asked Daniel and Night Light to climb the grade behind the cabin and find a spot for the burial. "A happy place. I've heard you talking about happy places, Night Light. Use your own judgment. Perhaps someplace on the slope where the ground catches the morning sun."

Daniel and Cob worked together to dig the grave, fighting rock most of the way. P. A. Angus, the smithy from Conville, used his gifted hands to craft a casket, working six handles into the box, the product of his skills with the forge, to make carrying the body easier.

When the time came, Daniel and Cob took the two front handles, one on each side, while Buster and P.A. Angus took the center places. Trace and Ty, the two young men whose lives had been changed by the arrival of the Mirrored W, took the rear handles. Abe started to step forward, but Gwyneth gripped his arm, holding him back. "Not this time, Dad."

Abe sucked in a deep breath, seemingly lost in grief and misery.

The climb was not easy. Night Light had insisted on a spot some distance from the cabin. When they arrived, Gwyneth sent a sad smile toward the Indian girl, with a simple, "Lovely place, Night Light."

With a nod from Gwyneth, Cob took off his hat, passing it to Daniel to hold. He then took the hat he had been carrying in his hand, Trent's hat, and placed it atop the casket. Straightening to his full height, trying to recall the words he had rehearsed in his mind, he scanned the crowd before speaking. "Met Trent in South Texas, not much more than a mostly grown kid, lost in the world and looking for his way."

From there, he told their story, briefly but honestly, saying how he had seen Trent grow from a student of the cattle industry to become a teacher, teaching by example. Five minutes later, he closed with, "This is a man I will miss. The ranchers of the valley will miss him, but most of all, Gwyneth, Abe, and Helen will miss him. I wish him God's blessings in eternity."

Seamlessly, Eustice Ward took one step forward and opened his Bible. "Come unto me, all ye that labor and are heavy laden, and I will give you rest. Take my yoke upon you and learn of me, for I am meek and lowly in heart: and ye shall find rest unto your souls."

He spoke of the promise of eternity for those who knew and loved the Lord, finishing by saying, "I have spent enough time with Trent to be able to say with confidence that he fit that description. And I can also say with confidence that God's promises are true. Look to Him. He will give your hearts rest in your grief."

He picked up a handful of soil and let it run through his fingers onto the top of the casket, while he prayed a short, meaningful prayer.

As the gathering started to break up, Night Light, dressed in a beautiful hand-tanned-and-decorated buck hide dress, stepped onto a clear spot beside the grave. Two men were picking up shovels. The grave filling would begin as soon as the others moved out of sight. Not waiting for anyone else, Night

Light moved her moccasined feet in a slight rhythmic shuffle, with her hands hanging loosely down. Along with the shuffle came a quiet hum, which soon developed into a sing-song series of musical notes. There were no words, just the beautiful, high-pitched, soulful sounds. The shuffling gained in rhythm and complexity as the singing continued.

Gwyneth had started to walk away, but the chanting drew her to a stop. She turned to find the music's source. When her eyes fell on Night Light, she stood as if rooted to the spot, enchanted by what her Ute friend was doing. The two men laid down their shovels and stepped back. Daniel, remembering death songs from a couple of the tribes he had lived with, joined his wife but didn't touch her or in any way break her rhythm. It took a few seconds for him to fit his feet to the chant, but before long, the two of them were sending their friend off in the way they knew best. Gwyneth and the remainder of the group finally turned to the long walk down the hill, leaving their Indian friends alone.

Two of the ladies from the south ranches had stayed at the cabin, preparing food they had brought with them. They would welcome the family and mourners with this tribute of service.

Chapter Twenty-Five

AFTER THE FUNERAL ABE APPROACHED GWYNETH with the logical question about her future. She had simply answered, "Not today, Dad. I'll ride down to see you when I'm ready."

Two days later, she tied her mount at the railing in front of the small trading post. Helen was there almost immediately to greet her and, unnecessarily, steady her elbow as she dismounted. With their arms locked together, the two women sought the shade of the building's overhang. When they were settled in homemade chairs, Abe joined them, with a simple, "Hot for riding."

Weary from sorrow and lack of sleep and not in the frame of mind for long discussions, Gwyneth stated simply, "I'll be staying on for a while, at least. I've talked with Cob and Daniel. They're both prepared to stick it out while the future unfolds itself, for a while anyway, perhaps a year. The two boys will stay on too. The clinic is needed in the valley. I'd feel guilty leaving now. The rest will just have to work itself out."

After the thirty seconds of silence that followed that simple proclamation, Abe, catching the slight nod from Helen, answered, "We were hoping you'd say that. We've made a few quick decisions in our lives, but this is the time for serious consideration. That takes more than a day or two to work it all out. This little pretend village ain't about to grow into no metropolis, but we'll stick it out as long as you will."

TY AND TRACE were riding together on a warm morning one week after the funeral. With Daniel keeping busy around the ranch headquarters, breaking and training horses, and keeping the place well repaired, Cob had assigned the afternoon and evening watch to himself, and the early morning until noon shift to the young men.

There was little competition for the grass, but as the valley was discovered and new ranches established, that push for graze was bound to come. The first push came from an expected source, and a bit earlier than anyone had anticipated. About mid-morning, the sounds of cattle bawling and the shouts of drovers drew Ty and Trace to the north end of the Mirrored W claim. They sat their saddles in wonder as they watched a herd tumbling out of the treed hillside trail, being pushed by riders from the B/C ranch, Ty's family holding.

Leading the bunch was Cameron himself, followed by Blackie and the one other rider the ranch had recently hired. The B/C had grazed a few animals in the valley in times past, testing the fortitude of Trent and the Mirrored W, but never a bunch like this one. Silently, Ty thought, *that's most of the entire herd*. Still, he expected his father to turn the bunch to the north, onto grass no one had yet claimed. When he did the opposite, turning to the south, Trace was mystified, and Ty was startled. The intent of the B/C was obvious. Also obvious was the responsibility tied to the job the two boys had taken on.

Ty, his emotions all astir, lifted his Winchester from his scabbard alongside his right leg. Trace looked on, wondering what was to come next. His silent query was answered when Ty lifted the carbine to his shoulder and fired a single shot, too high to hit anything but not by much. As the sound racketed through the hillside, Cameron drew to a sudden stop. The cattle kept moving.

"Stay back. Stay back," Ty shouted, waving his weapon. The Mirrored W riders and the B/C riders were really too far apart for the shout to be meaningful, but the shot and the arm waving bolstered the message. Ty could see Blackie lifting his weapon. That frightened him. In his mind, Blackie was a maverick, unpredictable and uncontrollable, mean from top to bottom.

When Ty started to ride forward, Trace could see nothing to do but ride along. He, too, had his carbine in his hand. He admitted his fear to himself, wondering if Ty was as frightened, but he rode forward anyway.

Coming closer, Ty shouted, "Hold those animals back. Turn them away. There's no grass here for you. This is Mirrored W grass."

Cameron rode a bit forward. He was practically foaming at the mouth with anger. "Women can't hold homesteads nor grass. We're taking over."

"Not likely," Ty hollered at his father. "You have no right, and I'm being paid to stop you. Now turn off."

"You'd shoot your own father? Shoot animals that could be yours one day?"

"I'll do my job. And you can tell Blackie to pouch that weapon. If he makes a threat with it, I'll sure enough shoot him dead and take pleasure in the doing of it. Now turn those animals back."

The single shot had been heard back at the ranch headquarters. The thunder of hooves coming up behind him told Ty that Cob and Daniel had heard and were coming. Cob arrived at a full gallop, with Daniel close behind. The two men rode right past Ty and Trace, closing in on Cameron. They pulled to a stop with their guns drawn and pointed in the right direction.

"Cameron, you're a fool. This graze is spoken for. You know that full well. And now you're pushing your herd onto taken grass and running it over your own son in the doing of it. Turn them back, or I'll shoot you and that other rider over there and turn them back myself. You have just no time at all to think it over. Turn them back and don't ever again think you can push the Mirrored W off its graze."

Cowed and seeing the lopsidedness of any potential fight, Cameron turned to the side as he pushed his carbine back into the leather. He made a point of riding past Ty, spitting out, "You're not my son anymore. Stay off the B/C."

DINNER TIME that evening was quieter than usual, with everyone thinking of the challenge earlier in the day. The only decisive words came from Cob. "Ty, I'm going to have you ride the south border tomorrow. Trace can hold the north. And Trace, you stay back, in among the cattle, using them for shelter should there be any challenge. Neither of you are to fight off aggression. A couple of warning shots into the air will bring us running from the ranch. Don't you be playing the heroes."

Life was quiet for the next week, with the B/C herd back on their home range and with no sign of anyone bringing a challenge. That changed with a shot from the brush on the side hill beside where Trace was riding. That the shooter was serious and not just trying to frighten someone was shown when the grazing steer Trace was sitting his horse beside flinched and bawled, breaking into a short run before again coming to a halt. In the few seconds it took Trace to sort out his options, he could see a flow of blood running down the steer's left hindquarter. The shot from the brush was low and off target by about two feet, a reasonably close hit from the distance and considering the drop in elevation from the shooter's stance.

Both Trace and Ty had taken to riding with their saddle

guns held across their laps. Trace, never having been shot at
before, was frightened. But men hired on for a job of work in
this frontier country didn't run from a threat unless they
wanted to be labeled as a kid, or worse, a coward. Holding his
rifle high, away from the cattle, he stepped to the ground,
squeezing between a big red and white mottled steer and his
horse. He laid his rifle across the saddle, pointed in the general
direction of the source of the shot as he studied the distance for
a sight of the shooter.

He saw nothing until a man he was able to identify, even
from a distance, as Blackie, stepped from behind a small, bushy
tree and fired off another round. This one took leather off the
side of the saddle horn, much too close for Trace's liking. He
ducked instinctively, mechanically, but soon regained his position. Almost automatically, he zeroed in on the shooter and, for
the first time in his young life, sent deadly lead in the direction
of another human. To his surprise and his considerable conster-
nation, Blackie dropped his weapon, folded his arms across his
belly, and collapsed to the ground. Trace stared in fright at what
he had done. Having no idea what his next move should be, he
stood frozen to the turf, waiting to see if Blackie would again
rise to his feet. He didn't.

True to what Cob had said, the shots alerted the men at the
ranch. The thunder of horses in a belly to the ground run
alerted Trace to the arrival of Cob, Daniel, and Eustice, who
had shown up back on the Mirrored W a couple of days before.
Trace was back in the saddle, working his way out of the herd.
When the riders were within shouting distance, Trace caught
their attention with a bellow, waving them to the side where
Blackie had been. The men pulled to a stop and waited for
Trace. When he managed to work his way out of the swarm of
cattle, he rode over to Cob and wordlessly pointed to the hillside. "B-B-Blackie," was all he was able to get out in an emotion-
laden mutter until he finally managed, "I'm thinking he
believed he was looking at Ty. Mistook me for him."

With a quizzical look, Cob turned to the shrub-covered hill-side. "Up there?"

Instead of answering, Trace turned his riding animal in that direction and slowly approached the spot where Blackie had fallen. Cob and Daniel followed. Eustice stayed behind, watching for the approach of any other challenge. At the base of a small rise that was too much for the horses, Trace dismounted and climbed on foot. Cob followed him. Daniel stood guard. At a small, level spot in the brush, Blackie lay where he had fallen. His arms were still wrapped around his middle. His shirt and sleeves were soaked in blood. His unseeing eyes were open. His lips were sealed in a grimace. He was most certainly dead.

Trace looked at the dead man for only a short few seconds before he dropped his gun and lunged for the brush, slinking out of sight behind a large tree. From where he stood, Cob could easily hear the young man losing his breakfast. The gagging and wrenching almost made Cob ill. But to break the hold the ugly sight held on the moment, Cob hollered for Daniel to come up. Cob then started a search for Blackie's horse, finding the animal just a few yards back in the brush. He untied him and led him to where Blackie lay. Together, Cob and Daniel lifted the body to the saddle and tied it securely with Blackie's own saddle rope. Trace reappeared about that time. He had nothing he wished to say, although an avalanche of mixed words and thoughts rambled through his mind.

Cob led the loaded-down horse along the slope until he found an easy way to approach level ground at the bottom. Daniel laid his hand on Trace's shoulder, saying nothing, and slid down the embankment to where their horses had been left. When they were all together again, Cob said, "Trace, you go back to the house. Daniel will stand in for you here."

"Not a chance, Cob. I took on a job of work and I'll see it through to the end. I'm feeling pretty mixed up in my mind about what's happened but that won't stop me from doing my job."

Cob seemed to hesitate as he considered those words, but finally he stepped into his saddle. "You're young yet, Trace, but you'll do."

Daniel rode back to the camp. Cob led the burdened horse to the trail that led to the B/C. Eustice stayed, keeping Trace company with the herd.

COB TOPPED the hill outlining the B/C ranch yard. Silently, he tied the horse to the corral. In response to Cob's shout, Cameron stepped from the barn. His look was ugly as his eyes fell on the man folded over the saddle. On the doorstep of the house, Betty Cameron was shooshing the young children back inside.

If Cameron was moved by the death of one of his riders, he covered that emotion up with anger. Barely looking at Cob, he spat out a single word, "Ty?"

"No. Ty's at the south line. Your son was spared this ugliness. I'm not sure you'll ever learn, Cameron, but this should at least be a lesson to you. The Mirrored W wants to live in peace. But that don't mean we'll tolerate any foolishness from you or the likes of this." He was pointing his thumb over his shoulder toward the dead man when he said the words.

He turned and rode out of the yard with his back to Cameron, tipping his hat to Betty as he rode past the house.

Chapter Twenty-Six

COB AND GWYNETH RODE TO CONVILLE WITH TRACE.
Instead of riding to the livery as they usually did, they tied off in
front of the small cabin the Angus family called home. Cob
turned and walked to the livery to alert Angus that he was
needed at the house.

The fact and style of the visit were unusual. Rose Angus
sensed trouble immediately. She came to the door but didn't
invite the visitors or her son to enter. In her concern, she had
forgotten the social niceties of welcoming guests. Angus
followed Cob as they walked quickly across the sun-blazed yard.
Questions were swirling in his mind. It had been agreed on the
ride down that Cob would tell the story, keeping it short and
precise. As he talked, Trace stepped back and, half sitting,
leaned his weight on the tie rack, as if he couldn't stand on his
own strength. The final words of the story were met with total
silence.

Angus turned his head from Cob and studied his son.
Rose shuffled her feet while she stared at the short wooden
walk along the front of the cabin. Gwyneth unknowingly
held her breath, wishing someone, anyone, would say
something.

The silent spell was broken by Angus. He stepped to Trace and put his arm around his shoulder. "You all right, son?"

"I am now, Pa. Wasn't yesterday."

"It's a hard land, Trace. Better than that war so many of us got tangled up in, but still hard. Can you say honestly that you had no choice? That you were protecting your own or someone else's life?"

In answer, Trace pointed to the torn leather on his saddle. "Came that close to not being here, Pa. And back at the ranch, there's a fresh-killed beef I was riding alongside that wasn't going to live with a bullet buried deep in his haunch."

Angus nodded and looked to his wife. She finally fought off her shock and took the few steps that allowed her to hug her son. At her first touch, Trace reeled back a bit, feeling he was past having his mother treat him like a baby. But he soon enough gave in, placing his arm around her shoulder in response.

Cob placed his hat back on his head and untied his reins. "We'll be getting back, folks. Come the end, we'll all look back and wish that many things in life hadn't happened, but that changes nothing. You stay here, Trace. Take a day or two to rest up and sit up to your mother's table. We'll expect you back on the third morning."

Gwyneth passed Trace an envelope with his pay in it. There was no need for words, but her smiling look was enough for Trace to know nothing had changed in her eyes.

BETTY HAD COME DOWN to visit a time or two after the event with the sick baby. Gwyneth enjoyed the visits and wished they would come more often. But after the shooting, nothing was seen of Betty and the children, or the B/C riders.

There was no sight of Cameron himself for several weeks. When he did arrive, it was by stage, and he was in no condition

to even know what was happening. The herd had been driven
to another part of the claimed graze. There were just a few cattle
dotting the grass where the stage normally traveled. The few
animals that were there were scattered in every direction by the
shouts of Buster as he drove his rig at top speed through the
grazing animals. He pulled to a violent stop, with the horses
rearing back as he tugged the reins. He was shouting Gwyneth's
name even before the rig ceased rocking. Daniel heard the
shouts and ran out of the yard. "What ya got, Buster?"

"Got a dy'n man, that's what I got. Git yerself some help
and yard this here fella up ta the house. If'n Gwyneth caint fix
his sorry butt, no one can, so best ya git er done right soon.
Been some time on the road. That time and the jostling about
didn't do him one bit of good I'm thinking."

Trace and Ty were in the yard. Daniel called them to come
on the run. Gwyneth showed herself on the front stoop in time
to hear Daniel holler, "Got a job of work here for you, boss."

"What is it?"

"I don't know neither what nor who. But I know a bullet
wound when I see it."

At Daniel's direction, Trace took one arm and shoulder. Ty
took the other. Daniel climbed into the stage and grabbed the
feet and legs. It wasn't until the wounded man was clear of the
rig that Ty looked at his face.

"Pa. That's Pa."

"Well, bring him in here. Let's get a look."

Buster followed the men as they carried Cameron to the
crude but solid table Trace had built for Gwyneth to use in her
work. Gwyneth asked, "What happened?"

"Near as I kin tell, this here fella opened his fool mouth
when he should have known better. There's a rough bunch
taken to hanging around Bessie Creek this last while. Claim'n to
be miners. Keep talk'n about the gold fields. Southerners.
Shouting their dislike fer anyone who might have worn the
blue. Thought all that nonsense had passed from us, but those

fellas put the lie to that. Cameron, he never did have no more sense than it takes to come in from the rain. Way, I heard it, Cameron, he made out to be tough when he ain't no such a thing. One threat led to another. Anyway, give Cameron credit for trying. Foolish stupid, if'n ya take my meaning, but he tried. This here in front of y'all is the result. His Colt, if'n anyone should care, was left lying in the grass back up to the Creek."

In spite of the troubles and hard feelings, Cameron was still Ty's father, and those links are near impossible to break. The young man approached the surgery table as Gwyneth and Night Light were stripping off his clothing, using scissors and a sharp knife. The long handles the man wore were stiff with filth, accumulated before the cloth was soaked in blood. The women continued as if they hadn't noticed. When the man was lying naked in the sun, Gwyneth draped a towel across his middle. Night Light kicked the filthy rags to one side, ready for the burning pit.

The removal of the clothing revealed three bullet holes— one in his upper leg, one through his right shoulder, and one through his middle, just above the hip bone. They had all bled freely before the body's natural clotting system stemmed the flow. The bullet in the shoulder had gone right on through, making Gwyneth's job much easier. But there were no exit wounds for either of the other shots.

Ty had been around Gwyneth enough as she sewed people up to know he had to keep out of the way. He stood at his father's head, tentatively stroking his long hair off his forehead. He winced and shrank back a bit when Gwyneth washed the wounds with hot water and strong soap. The cleansing opened the wounds again. Watered-down blood ran freely, but it couldn't be helped. The wounds had to be cleansed. Cameron tossed his head and moaned a bit at the rough treatment. Night Light, who took circumstances as they came, was more direct in her assessment of the wounded man.

"He not dead yet."

"No, Night Light, He's not dead yet, and we'll try to see that he avoids that outcome. It will depend on where this bullet went and what organs were in its way."

Ty said to no one in particular, "I should go get Ma."

Cob answered, "Eustice has already gone. You set by."

Buster mumbled something about having to get the stage back and climbed to his high seat. Ty and Cob both walked over and thanked the man. Ty expanded his thanks with, "You find out what the charge is for the trip, Buster, the ranch will cover the cost."

"Thanks, son. I don't know as there will be a charge, but I'll let you know."

THE AFTERNOON WAS FAR GONE when Gwyneth leaned back, with her hands taking a grip on her hip bones. From that posture, she worked her spine in all directions, trying to gain a comfortable upright position. She had a grim look on her face.

The Indian girl simply washed her hands once more and walked away. Daniel walked with her, holding his hand on her shoulder. She needed to change her blood-spattered dress, and she could hear her baby crying for attention. Daniel smiled at her. "You are a good woman." The two didn't often show emotion, but this time, the weary Night Light leaned into him so he could hold her more tightly.

Betty Cameron arrived with the four children. She'd had enough time to settle her nerves since Eustice had outlined the situation to her. She turned the children loose to play and walked to where her husband lay under a clean sheet.

As tired as she was, Gwyneth rose from the rocking chair Trent had brought home from Pueblo for her and approached Betty. "I don't have any good news for you, Betty. There're three wounds. Two are no particular problem and I haven't bothered with them yet. But the third, the shot through his belly, hit critical organs, including his intestines. Much damage was done. I tried to clean the cavity out, but the leakage was more than I could deal with. He bled a lot on the stage ride, and he's bled more here. Between the loss of blood and the infection that is sure to follow the wounding, I'm afraid this is one battle he's going to lose, Betty. I don't believe he could be saved if he was in a modern hospital. There's little worse than a belly wound."

"Thanks for all your help, Gwyneth. Should I try to take him home?"

"There isn't time to take him home. He's not likely to live through the evening. If you wish to go home with the children, you can leave him here with us. We'll bring him up to the ranch later."

Betty's words were quiet but genuine. "He don't amount to much, Gwyneth. But I took him as my husband, and I'll not turn away from that. I'll hang in till the end."

TY TOOK OVER THE RANCH, firing the two hard cases Cameron had hired, replacing them with two young Texas riders who were exploring the country. Buster, on one of his regular trips through the valley, had mentioned to the riders that there was a need for help on the B/C. For the first time in the history of the ranch, there was laughter at the dinner table and smiles and giggling from the children as they were thriving on the teaching and teasing of the riders. It was almost as if their father had never existed.

Chapter Twenty-Seven

BESSIE CREEK, BUILT ALONG THE NARROW-GAUGE rails, continued to grow. Like any new town with strangers arriving almost daily and with little in the way of law, troubles were bound to show themselves. The differences of opinion ranged from shouting and fist fights to shooting affairs. The arrival of a lawyer did nothing at all to advance the desire for peace. The appointing of a town marshal brought a temporary peace, but the undercurrents of discontent were still there. The marshal lasted one month before he gave it up, bought a ticket on the train, and disappeared from Bessie Creek.

Other services, from blacksmithing to a small newspaper, to a ladies' wear store, had arrived and were showing signs of settling in. But no one, drunk or sober, admitted to being a medical man. In its place, the news about Gwyneth's nursing assistance was spreading from one end of the valley to the other, much more quickly than she had ever imagined it would.

The population was still not large, even with Bessie Creek growing with almost every stop of the trains. Three or four potential settlers had arrived in Conville with an eye to making a home there and offering services in one craft or another. It didn't take long for them to figure out that the tiny settlement was at its peak and would never grow beyond what was already there.

Anyone looking at Conville with an honest eye would know that no one was making a living. Abe and Helen didn't particularly care about that. They were no longer young. Struggle and business adventure held no real attraction for them, not like it had in the past, in any case. They asked for little from life, and what they did ask for was always on hand.

What kept P.A. Angus there was another question altogether. The mystery was solved over a cup of tea one afternoon, with Helen and Rose sitting in the shade, visiting. With little new ever happening in Conville, the conversations tended to become repetitious. It was that lack of conversational topics that prompted Helen to say, "You know that we came here to be beside our son and his wife. Now, with Trent gone, we're not sure what to do. It would help if we knew what Gwyneth's plans were. Nevertheless, we can wait. We have nowhere else calling our names. We're content to give Gwyneth the time she needs. But you have a growing boy, quickly becoming a man. What do you see in your future? There's sure no future in this six-shack excuse for a town. We haven't seen a customer in over a week. I don't see as how it's any different over at Mr. Angus's livery."

There was a long pause, with Rose studying her friend. The truth had been begging for release for so long, something just had to give. Was this the time? Finally, she spoke. "Helen, if you repeat this, you could kill a good man and cause untold sadness and misery for Trace and me. The truth is that Angus is, more or less, hiding, hoping the memory of a shooting will fade into the distance.

"We were well established in a nice town down in central Texas. Angus was well thought of. Everyone brought their blacksmithing to him. We were doing well. Trace was just a little fella, and we hoped to have more children. It all changed with the arrival of a crew of returning trail drovers. They got liquored up and decided to tree the town. At least that's what they called it. It amounted to the boys racing their horses along the street, onto the boardwalks, and into the saloon and a couple of other stores, terrifying dogs, women, and children along the way.

"For the first few minutes, they were content with shouting their foolish rebel yells, but it wasn't long before they drew their handguns and began shooting at the stars. The sheriff was over-powered and helpless. I had left Trace with a friend while I did some shopping. To pick up my son, I had to cross the road. I shouldn't have done it, but I picked up my skirts and ran, thinking it wasn't far, and I could make it before the drunken riders returned. Only thing was, when they saw me, they got even more excited, thinking riding me down would be great sport.

"There's no doubt it was the liquor working on their minds that loosened their good judgment. Three of them turned around and spurred their horses my way, shooting and yelling. I'm sure it was an accident, but one of them hit me and sent me flying onto the road. My scream attracted Angus. He ran from the livery, lifting his Colt. Angus was always very good with his hands, and handling a weapon was no different. In four shots, two riders lay dying and two others had lead in them. Four shots that changed our lives. Changed them in another way too. I was hurt pretty badly, with the result that we will never have another child.

"The law didn't blame Angus, but the other riders did. They rode back to their home ranch and returned with the rest of the crew, six in all. Their one goal was to kill my husband and finish treeing the town. Angus shot another of them before the sheriff gathered up enough men to control the situation. But that didn't really end it either. The men rode home vowing to return yet again. Angus decided to let things cool for a while and here we are."

Helen studied her friend, trying to think of some

comforting words. The result was silence. There was just nothing in Helen's experience that would generate the words that were needed. The two ladies, almost in unison, drained their teacups.

Helen rose to her feet, paused, took a step, and paused again. She didn't find the exact words she wanted, but she settled for, "Abe changed after his years in the war. He came home harder and tougher than when he rode away. Prepared to do things he would have shied away from before. And with the firm belief that some things can't be avoided. If Mr. Angus were to ask him, Abe would say, 'Be prepared, do what you can at the time, and be ready to face the future when it arrives.'

"Abe's not much on hiding. He won't talk about it, but there were a couple of situations he had to deal with back in Texas. Situations that resulted in gunfire. That we still walk this earth, and the others do not is really all you need to know about that. We'll still stay here, or somewhere in the area for Gwyneth, Rose, but I see nothing in this foolish excuse for a town for you and Mr. Angus. Let alone for Trace."

The comment was probably the closest Helen ever came to offering advice.

NOT LONG AFTER that tea-lubricated conversation, Abe and Helen stacked the remaining stock from their trading post onto the two wagons, along with all their personal possessions. After a tearful farewell with the Angus family, they pointed their teams to the north. It would only be a short journey, just up to the Mirrored W buildings. Their arrival was a surprise to Gwyneth.

"This looks serious," she said as her in-laws arrived. "Do you wish to tell me where you're going?"

With a grin, Abe answered, "We done already arrived."

"Okay, well, you're welcome, of course, but a bit more information may help me understand."

The explanation was held off until they were all sitting at the homemade table on the small, covered porch. Gwyneth brought out the coffee while Helen walked back to the wagon and returned with a cloth-covered pan of fresh buns in one hand, the final delicacy produced from the stone oven in the shanty at Conville, and a jar of preserved berry jam purchased in Pueblo, for resale in the trading post.

As Abe stirred his coffee, he began his explanation. "Gwyneth, from the very first day we stopped here, we knew Conville was a joke. There never will be a town here that amounts to anything. No water beyond the one well, no trees, no shade, no customers. It's a foolish place to open a store. But the building was free, or almost free anyway, and we needed to be someplace while you and Trent worked out your futures. Since then, things have changed. Trent is gone. Cameron is gone, not that that's of much concern. There's a new town growing to the north just a few miles. It came time for us to make some decisions. If we're going to make those decisions along with you, it's best we be here, where we can talk and where I might be of some help on the ranch."

Gwyneth, unsure herself of her future, was almost afraid to answer the open question. She and Trent had gambled on the west, staking their limited wealth and their futures on the prosperity, the promise of the grass. They had struggled through a miserable trip west, along with their travel companions, seeking their own promised lands. They knew the grass in their semi-arid valley didn't compare to some they had driven over on the way west, but that other grass was already claimed and used by ranchers large and small. Still, this corner of the world they had chosen for themselves would suffice for the smaller, specialized ranch they had finally settled on.

Having witnessed the troubles that could descend on a large ranch, from the weather to the unpredictable market prices, to rustlers who felt the big brands were fair game, to the constant need for new riders, as the restless ones took their pay and moved on, the attraction of size as the primary goal started to dim.

Trent, being a planning man, along with Gwyneth, who was gifted at seeing and sorting conflicting possibilities, was forced to change his mind. The final evidence was the prices offered by the cattle brokers at the buying stations. Scrubs and long-legged, rangy animals, more bone than meat, like the ones that made up a large portion of the trail herds, and the ones Cameron's B/C was still attempting to work into a profitable herd, received a discouragingly low price compared to the heavier, beefier breeds. Trent was wise enough to take it as a lesson learned and adjust his thinking.

Since taking on the new thoughts, Trent had said over and over, *"The money is in quality, not quantity."* To that end, they had bought bulls that would show their benefit as generations of calves were grown to breeding age, to produce offspring that would fetch a premium in the eastern market. After their brief time in the valley, they had shipped their first beef-sized steers from those bulls. The deposit in the Pueblo bank supported all the decisions Trent had made. But Trent was no longer there to enjoy his success. Gwyneth admitted to herself that she had held on at the Mirrored W mostly out of indecision. It was always easier to do nothing, but was it also better? The question had cost many an hour of sleep in her lonely cabin. In her lonely bed.

Looking at Abe and Helen and knowing their readiness to help in whatever she did, Gwyneth responded to their arrival at the ranch with, "You're quite correct. Decisions have to be made. I'm afraid I'm a bit lost in the mire of the whole thing right now. I welcome your thoughts. Do you have ideas we can use for a beginning of our discussion, Abe?"

Gwyneth had started out in marriage referring to Trent's

parents as Father and Mother. Abe and Helen put a stop to the formality before it became ingrained.

"Gwyneth, you know I have no problem coming up with ideas. The better question I have always reluctantly had to face was, *which of those ideas was worth following*? It would probably be easier for us to adapt to your thoughts than the other way around. We're not concerned about a future right now. We only wish to see to your happiness and do what we can to make that happen."

"If it were only that easy, Abe. My mind has been in a whirl ever since we lost Trent. Each day, I simply do what has to be done, with the odd few nursing situations that come my way. One thing I can tell you is that I have little interest in ranching. Ranching by myself is what I mean to say. I have much to thank ranching for, of course. Between Trent's trail drives and our cattle sales since that time, I find myself with sufficient finances. But that hasn't helped me see the future any more clearly."

Helen spoke for the first time, "Perhaps we should just keep our eyes and hearts open for a while. Perhaps it will be that the Lord will give us all insight."

"I'd sure like that insight to settle in before the winter winds start to blow," was Abe's unhelpful response.

THE WARM DAYS of summer were filled with riding, haying, and preparation for winter. Gwyneth and Night Light mounted their saddles, keeping the herd within sight, as the men sharpened the scythes and took to the hay meadow. Riding herd on a bunch of contented cattle that have no desire to be anywhere but right where they were left time for dreaming. Gwyneth found herself spending more and more time with her eyes glued to the Sangre de Cristo, with their snow-and-ice-covered peaks glowing like the brightest lantern as, together with the sun, they saluted the summer days.

Often, when away from the others, she would weep, thinking of Trent and the promises that remained unfulfilled, and would ever remain that way. *Where are you, Trent? I need you. I'm lost in life, and in this big country. Oh, Trent, I loved you so. Why did the Lord take you from me? And what am I to do?*

Praying. Weeping. Wondering. Nothing brought Gwyneth any assurance or direction. In discussion with Helen, that good woman said, "Sometimes our direction can come from others or from the circumstances we find ourselves in. It's not often the Lord will speak to us directly. He speaks through His written word and through faithful friends. Even, sometimes through harsh circumstances or through strangers. We have to be listening and watching and be prepared."

As always, Gwyneth had nothing to add, but she let the words soak into her memory, seeking the truth in them. So, it shocked her a week later when Eustice Ward, who hadn't been seen for a couple of months, rode to where she was herding cattle. He pulled up beside her, kicked his feet out of the stirrups, leaned back and stretched, with his hand on his gelding's rump. "I'm getting soft, Gwyneth. Don't spend enough time in the saddle anymore to stay in working condition. How are you doing? The men all decided to lie abed today, leaving you and Night Light with the work?" His always bright smile took the edge off the question.

"No, just haying time. Anyway, I have little or nothing to do at the ranch. Helen does all the cooking. This suits me just fine, sitting out here in the sun. Where have you been for the past while? Still riding your circuit?"

"Pretty short circuit, but yes. I have a small church started up at the Creek. Shows some promise. Decided I hadn't been down this way for too long. Neither here nor down to Conville or to the ranches to the south. What do you mean, 'Helen does the cooking?' They given up with the trading post?"

When Gwyneth explained all that had happened, Eustice

responded, "I doubt as anyone was really fooling themselves on Conville. The saloon lasted what, one month?"

Kicking her gelding awake, Gwyneth broke away as a bunch-quitting steer started trotting to the east. He wasn't serious about it though, and with the first approach of the knowledgeable horse, it turned back into the herd. As easy as it was, the horse could have done the job without Gwyneth's direction. She was soon back visiting with Eustice.

"Mind if I ask about your plans, Gwyneth?"

The answer to that question opened a long conversation that took them through lunchtime and into early afternoon. The earnest Eustice, who was showing the truth of his father's early advice that he was marked out to spend his life spreading the Word, came close to duplicating Helen's thoughts on making decisions. Gwyneth said nothing, but she listened intently. When Cob rode out to relieve Gwyneth, Eustice bid her farewell and stayed for a visit with Cob. Gwyneth rode past Night Light, saying, "Come. It's time we see what's left on the stove. And your babies are going to be wondering where their mama is."

ANOTHER FALL TURNED to another winter, followed by the much-welcomed spring.

Chapter Twenty-Eight

IN THE TOTAL VACUUM OF ALTERNATIVE MEDICAL help, Gwyneth's name was being spoken far and wide in the valley, and a little beyond, as some settlers were staking out claims along the rails, but still close to Bessie Creek. A rancher from the south end of the valley somehow managed to take a nasty slice out of his foot while he was splitting firewood. By the time he finally relented and allowed the neighbor to help him into the buggy, the wound was swollen and festering, while the man himself was becoming delirious.

Alone, he would have died, but his wife made the long ride to the neighboring ranch in a plea for help. Gwyneth scolded him in a friendly manner and teased a bit, mentioning how even the toughest working man was no match for a sharp axe. She cleaned and re-opened the wound, allowing her access to the infection, raising a weeping howl from her patient when she poured a stream of disinfectant over the damaged flesh.

"Sir, we're going to leave this open to the air for this night. We'll check for infection again in the morning. Don't you be putting any weight on it, and don't get it dirty."

He rested that night but insisted he couldn't be away from the ranch any longer and that he was feeling much better.

Hoping a few stitches or a tight bandage would be enough to get him back on the road home, he allowed Gwyneth to clean the wound again. She studied the damage, straightened up, and looked at the patient. "Mister, if you go home today, you'll be dead in a week. I can't make it plainer than that. We have not beaten the infection, and we're not going to for a few days. If you'll stay here and allow me to do what I can do, within a week, we should have it healed to where a few stitches are all you'll need. The alternative is infection leading to gangrene and then a miserable death. It's your choice."

The rancher had a mighty struggle between the known needs of family and ranch and the nurse's statement. But finally, caution won out. Eight days later, he limped from the horse Cob had lent him and hugged his wife, waiting by the front yard gate. With nothing more said, Cob took up the reins of the second animal and headed home.

Gwyneth knew these settlers were hard-pressed for money. Before he left for home, she accepted the single dollar the man offered, along with his profuse thanks.

"Hard way to make a living, Gwyneth."

She turned, still holding the single dollar coin in her hand, to smile at Abe. "You're right again, Abe. But if I had asked for more, the man would have been seriously embarrassed. None of these settlers seem to have any cash money. Whatever cash money they had to start with is tied up in cattle or other necessities. I suspect you're still holding some of their tabs from the store."

When Abe didn't deny the statement, she passed her father-in-law the dollar. "You know I don't really need this, Abe. Take it and apply it to that fellas tab. It would be a kindness to the man."

~

HER NURSING CONTINUED to be needed only on a periodic basis. There seemed to be little chance of making a living income from it, but with the ranch prospering, Gwyneth didn't particularly care.

Only rarely did Gwyneth ride along on the weekly shopping trip to Bessie Creek. She came this day because she wanted to pick out a new dress for herself, perhaps more than one if the small store had a stock she liked. Abe had come along, handling the reins as the ranch wagon rocked its way over the rough terrain. He would make the purchases that would keep the ranch fed and well supplied.

While Gwyneth wasn't well known in Bessie Creek, Abe and his wagon were recognized and greeted. They had been in town less than an hour when a local lady hunted Abe down, searching first in the small saloon but finding him at the general store. The door to the store slammed open, banging against the display shelving before rebounding to a half-closed position. The excited woman burst into the conversation Abe was holding with Emory Radcliff, standing behind his counter, holding out a new rifle for Abe to examine. Both men knew there would be no sale on the weapon that day, but Abe's mind would mull and work over the thought and perhaps one day he would say, *let me have that new Winchester, Emory.*

"Sir. Sir. Am I correct to believe you're from that there Mirrored W Ranch down south? Seems I've seen you and that wagon before, or had you pointed out to me as being from where the nurse lives."

Abe slowly turned to face the questioner. Without directly addressing the question, he asked one of his own. "What can I do for you, ma'am?"

"It's the nurse we need. Did she happen to come to town with you?"

"I believe you could find her at the ladies' store."

It seemed the door might be torn off its hinges in the woman's rush to find Gwyneth.

There were three customers in the dress store when the rushing woman entered, again breaking into the ongoing conversations. "Mrs. Wycome, come quickly."

Gwyneth turned to see a stressed and flustered woman holding the door open as if to ease and hurry the nurse's movements."

"What's the problem, ma'am?"

"My neighbor has been trying for hours to give birth. There's no sign of movement, and the poor woman is about done in with pain and fatigue. A couple of friends are there, but no one knows what to do. I saw your ranch wagon come into town a while ago and hoped you had come in with it. Please come. Anything you can do to help will be better than what any of us knows to do."

Gwyneth passed the dress she had been looking at to the clerk. "Set this aside for me, please. I'll be back for it."

Gwyneth picked up the medical bag she carried wherever she went and followed the woman to a small house on the outskirts of the village. She stepped inside to silence, except for a slight whimpering arising from the narrow cot that sat along the back wall of the two-room shanty. She stepped that way and bent to gain a closer look at the young woman lying there.

She was shocked by the sight of the poor woman. Although she was covered with a clean sheet, when Gwyneth lifted the cover off, she saw that the bed sheet and the nightgown the woman was dressed in were both soaked with sweat from the sweat pouring off her. After the hours of waiting in labor and tolerating the pain, she appeared to be beyond more pain-induced screaming. Silently, Gwyneth thought, *poor woman is close to exhaustion, if not to death.*

Gwyneth had not faced an unnatural birth before on her own, but she had stood by as the much more experienced doctor she had worked under back in Kansas dealt with something similar. He had at that time explained to Gwyneth that the complications the situation presented were serious indeed, and that the risk to both mother and child were extreme. That truth was proven with the loss of the baby.

Later, after all that could be done was done, when the weeping mother and the unsettled father were left on their own to grieve, the doctor explained to Gwyneth how the time it took for the remote settlers to reach town, plus the lurching and bumping of the wagon over the rough trail, with the frantic husband came close to ruining his team with the all-out effort to reach help, had contributed to the situation. As difficult as it had been to make the decision, the doctor had seen no real choice but to concentrate on the life of the mother, even though he knew he would lose a good deal of sleep in the coming days, questioning his own judgment.

No doctor wants to face the survivors with the news that they have lost a loved one. And who can understand the loss of a child but one who has suffered that loss themselves, so the doctor wouldn't play down the death or try to explain it beyond saying that the child was entangled in the umbilical cord, greatly complicating the birth effort. Gwyneth had to pray that Addy's baby would escape that particular problem.

The helpful neighbors had hot water ready and a stack of folded, freshly washed towels. Gwyneth had them place a bedsheet and a couple of large towels in the oven to warm. After thoroughly scrubbing her hands up to the elbows, Gwyneth pushed the soaked sheet aside and sat on the edge of the bed. Not addressing her question to anyone in particular, she asked, "What's this lady's name?"

"Addy. Addy Quinlan."

"If you can hear me, Addy, please try to relax. Allow your muscles to relax as well. It will help in what you and I are going to do together. Opposing me will make it more difficult for both of us. My name is Gwyneth. I live on a ranch south of here just a little bit. I'm not a doctor, but I've been nursing for many years, and I've seen more than just a few babies successfully born. I'm going to do everything possible to help you bring this child into the world and into your life. Do you understand what I'm saying, Addy?"

There was no audible response, simply two half sobs accompanied by breath drawn in through tightly clenched teeth.

Quietly, with a soft, gentle voice she hoped exuded a confidence she didn't altogether feel, Gwyneth said, "All right, Addy, first we're going to have you raise your hips and back so I can slide a pillow under you. That will make your position easier for the baby and you, both."

Addy, with the assistance of a neighbor-lady who was standing by, managed, with her heels dug into the mattress, to lift, and then lift just a bit more, while the cushion was put into place. With that done, Gwyneth more closely examined the birth canal, pleased when she saw and felt the advanced dilation, but concerned when her fingers touched the child's bum rather than the hair of its head as she would have in a normal birth. That left her wondering how much to tell the woman. With the baby already entered into the birth canal, it was far too late to turn him. There was nothing to be done but push on.

Gwyneth could sense the tension in the two neighbors who had come to help but were now simply watching. Other than keeping a pot of hot water on hand, along with the clean cotton pads Gwyneth had supplied, there was little for them to do.

"Good job, Addy. We're well underway. Now I'm going to massage your tummy to encourage your baby. To wake him up in case he's decided to take a nap."

Addy actually smiled just a bit at the thought of her baby going to sleep.

Gwyneth continued, "We must make him feel welcome in the world. We'll be very gentle. At the same time, I'm going to use the fingers of my other hand to adjust him a bit from the inside. All I can do is perhaps lift a bit to ease his passage. I believe this baby is ready to be born, and your body is prepared to allow its passage. We just have to slowly ease him out a bit at a time."

Gwyneth immediately went to work, pushing aside her own emotions and fears. For once, she was thankful for her small hands. What confronted her would have been torture for the woman if a doctor with larger hands had performed it. Working with just the tips of her fingers, she slightly lifted the child, more to encourage movement than to move him herself. All the while, she was gently massaging Addy's enlarged stomach with her other hand. With slow, careful movements, she lifted and eased the baby, ever so little, worrying about the child being tangled in the umbilical cord, but with no way to prevent it.

The process was long and grueling, punctuated by more pain-induced gasps and a few screams. But Gwyneth persisted, steady and focused. Finally, the baby moved just a bit. Talking all the time to Addy, she timed her slight finger movements to Addy's rhythmic contractions.

The baby seemed to almost be settled into his position at the entry to the birth canal, but once he moved just a slight bit, he got the idea, showing slightly more movement. And so the process continued, with Addy feeling a bit of excitement at the idea of birthing her own child, mixed into the fatigue and pain of the process. Finally, there was significant movement. Gwyneth retracted her hand as the body moved down, holding, but not pulling the child. Now she took a finger grip on one leg, waiting for the next contraction that she believed would force the head out. Her guess was wrong by two closely spaced contractions.

With a final push followed by another groan of pain, Gwyneth found herself holding a living and squirming little boy. As if the child had been waiting for the opportunity to announce himself, with no help or encouragement from Gwyneth, he let out a loud cry. The room filled with spontaneous smiles and cries of joy.

Without severing the umbilical cord, Gwyneth wrapped the

baby in a warm towel one of the women had ready and laid him on his mother's breast. The two neighbor ladies worked together to wrap mother and baby in the warmed bed sheet.

As the neighbor ladies complimented Addy on her fine, strong boy, trying to cheer her up and help her forget the struggle, Gwyneth did what she could for the mother, including administering several stitches where necessary.

Later, there would be a thorough cleansing for both the baby and the mom, followed by a change of bedding, which Gwyneth would leave to the attending neighbors while she cleaned herself up. Addy was finally at rest, smiling through her discomfort while gently stroking her firstborn as he settled against her breast.

Looking down at Addy, Gwyneth thought she had never seen anyone so totally consumed.

At last, the husband was called in. The nervous young man walked almost on tiptoe to the side of the bed. He bent and lifted the covering off the baby just long enough to run the back of his rough hand over the baby's cheek. With a grin on his face, he turned to his wife. He finally found enough courage to sweep some hair off her brow before picking up a clean cloth to wipe the perspiration away. The mom managed a weak half-smile in return for her husband's touch and, in a gasping whisper, asked, "The baby?"

"They tell me it's a boy. A fine, big, healthy son. But the doctor also tells me how badly you need rest. You rest now. I'll be close by."

Gwyneth didn't bother explaining to the father that she wasn't a trained doctor, simply a nurse. She had said it at the start. That would have to suffice. With all that had gone on in the past couple of hours, she didn't figure it would matter to the bewildered father. Or to anyone else, for that matter.

Chapter Twenty-Nine

GWYNETH'S BIRTHING SKILLS WERE PROBABLY BEING exaggerated as the news of Addy Quinlan's difficult pregnancy was being spread throughout the valley. But the truth was that she was being called on more often than she would have predicted. For a small population, there were surprising numbers of babies being added to the young families who had taken up residence at Bessie Creek and throughout the valley.

Her immediate concern was her lack of supplies. She sent a letter to the apothecary shop in Pueblo listing her critical needs and then adding, *Please send me whatever else you have available that may be of help, especially disinfectants.* She enclosed a well-wrapped twenty-dollar gold piece, held out from her original purse from when they had first come west. The small payments received for her services had totaled just slightly more than those twenty dollars.

"You're not going to get rich very quickly that way," Cob said as he pocketed the envelope. He would make the ride to the Creek for the specific purpose of mailing the letter, although he assured Gwyneth that he had other matters to attend to in town. Gwyneth saw through his ruse but decided to say nothing.

A FEW DAYS LATER, Trace rode over to where Cob and Daniel were minding the herd. "Gotta tell you something, fellas. Got a message for y'all from my father. I'm not altogether happy with the way this is being done, but I get no say in the matter. The message is this: 'We're pulling out.' Ma said Helen would understand. Folks don't want no goodbyes. Just said to tell you thanks. Thanks for everything. And I'll add my thanks along with that. You men settling down here changed everything for me. You treated me as older than I really was and gave me men's work when I was just a kid.

"And that wagon trip to Pueblo was something I'll never forget. Folks were all packed up last evening. The wagon and team are already on the trail. They'll be an hour away by this time. I'll have to lift this horse to a good lope to catch up. They're hoping to get through the mountains before snowfall. Yearning to make California by spring. Pass our thanks on to Gwyneth, please. And to Abe and Helen too. And Night Light. You're all good folks. We're wishing you good times ahead."

With that, leaving no time for comment or question, the young man spun his gelding in a tight circle and spurred him into a lope. Daniel and Cob watched him ride away. Neither could immediately find the words to express their thoughts.

When the news was relayed into camp, Gwyneth looked troubled, but had nothing to say except, "I wish them well."

Abe, never showing much emotion, suggested, "I expect what Angus hated most to leave behind was that well he dug. He sure did set store by that water well. Expect he would have taken it with him if he could have found a way."

Later that day, at the dinner hour, Gwyneth said, "The valley is growing with settlers, and Bessie Creek is looking to be established, even to become the county seat. But our original circle gets smaller."

Cob had been holding his news off, hoping to find the correct time to share it, knowing there really was no correct or proper or easy time. But delaying would not make swallowing the pill any easier.

"Gonna get a bit smaller again. Ain't no way to make the telling any easier, nor the hearing of it either. So, I'll just out with it. When I took that letter up to the Creek for you, Gwyneth, there was one sitting there with my name on it, waiting to be picked up. I get so few letters, I knew it was trouble the moment the clerk handed the envelope to me. Wasn't much of a letter, so far as letters go, but it changes everything for me. The message was that Pa is sick and dying. I'm needed at home, on the Hat. My brother, who wrote the thing, said, *please come with all speed*.

"I've ordered rail cars for my herd for one week from now. I started pushing a few of my brand to the side today. Just to get a jump on separating them. No one likes the thought of leaving a home and people you've come to love and respect, but my path is clear. I'll sort out the herd as quickly as possible, get them on the trail to the Creek so's to arrive in time for the cars.

"I know what this will do to all your plans, but way back, when Trent and I proposed this venture, we agreed my part was not to be permanent. That's why it has always been considered to be Trent's ranch. Eventually, I would be leaving. I guess I could say that whatever I thought of as eventually has come."

The silence around the dinner table was like a stone, hard, solid, heavy, unbreakable. Unmovable. No one knew what to say, or even if anything should be said.

Adding to the verbal silence, Gwyneth stood and began clearing the table. She had nothing to say either. Helen joined her, dropping the dishes into the pan of soapy water that had been heating on the stove. Daniel and Night Light eased their two children away from the table and silently left the cabin. No matter what anyone else did, Night Light, being Ute, was not going anywhere. This was her home country, where she could visit with her family from time to time. With Daniel's arm firmly holding her close as they walked, she was sure of his position as well.

THE NEXT COUPLE of days seemed to hold nothing but silence. And most probably a host of memories, specific to each individual. Cob was close to feeling guilty for breaking up the ranch, although everyone understood the history and his current need. For once, Abe had nothing to say, unless it was quietly spoken between himself and Helen, and those words were not shared with the others. Gwyneth's mind was in a complete tizzy. Her emotions and thoughts were rescued by a welcome distraction. Betty rode down from the B/C with one child sitting in front of her on the saddle and the other three riding bareback on a well-broken mare.

"Just came for a visit, Gwyneth. No one is sick and there's no broken bones, so far as I know anyway. And praise the Lord for that. As wild as this bunch is, I'm half expecting trouble with every new day. How y'all doing anyway?"

Late that afternoon, Betty left for her own home feeling sad at the news about Cob but somewhat mollified by the fact that Gwyneth had said nothing about leaving. She had come to lean on her neighbor for medical help and advice as well as a friend. She hoped nothing would break that bond.

To everyone's surprise, at the breakfast table a couple of days after receiving Cob's news, Gwyneth said, "On my visit to the Creek yesterday, I made some arrangements. Cob. Daniel. Abe, I'd like it if you would round up all the Mirrored W stock. Ready it for a drive to the rails. I've got the loan of a couple of B/C riders. We'll drive the two herds about a day apart. That should keep them from mixing and yet hold them close enough so we can help each other if that should become necessary.

There's graze enough up there to hold them while we wait for cars."

Her announcement was almost as startling as Cob's had been a few days earlier. Knowing there were questions that would need answers, she continued, "A woman alone can't hold down a ranch. Although I have come to enjoy ranch life, the cattle business was Trent's dream, not mine. My dream was to become a doctor. I settled for nursing because I fell in love with a cattleman. But no more needs saying on that topic. It's time for me to be free of the cattle."

The men went silently to their work while Helen and Gwyneth dallied over their cold coffee cups. Helen, after a couple of false starts, finally dared to ask, "What are your plans from here on out? There's little enough purpose in staying here if it's just a place to live. Pretty lonely and perhaps not altogether safe for two women alone except for one aging man. Oh, don't ever tell Abe I said that. He still sees himself as being capable of doing anything he sets his mind to, and often enough, he can. But it still puts a lot of pressure on him. And then, other ranchers will come along wanting the grass. You may find a better life for yourself in Bessie Creek or even in a larger town. I'm willing to guess you've thought of all those things. But for my and Abe's sake, it might be best if you were to lay it out."

"I have thought of those things, Helen. Perhaps without giving much thought to the pressure Abe could be feeling. That will, of course, change with Cob gone and with Daniel having no reason to hang around the Mirrored W. Abe always seems like a rock. A man sure of himself. Willing and able to do whatever the situation calls for. I apologize. I have to give more thought in that direction."

～

THE NEWS REACHED THE B/C ranch when Gwyneth rode up to make the deal for the loan of two riders. The very next day, Ty rode down, accompanied by his mother and the four little ones. The past few months, since the loss of his father, Gwyneth had been pleased at how Ty had grown and matured, taking a firm hold on the family ranch. While Ty lifted the children to the ground, Betty practically threw her arms around Gwyneth.

"Oh, Gwyneth, whatever are you going to do, all alone down here with no cattle to hold you and no company? Please don't tell me you're pulling out too."

Gwyneth laughed and held her friend and neighbor at arm's length. "Whoa down there, Betty. I'm still here. And Abe and Helen are staying with me. I haven't talked with Daniel and Night Light yet, so I don't know what they'll be doing. There's still much for me to think about. You lost your man too, so you have some idea of what I'm facing. Of course you have your children, and Ty, who has matured into a fine man. Still young but showing himself for what he could become. If I still had Trent, none of this would be happening. But it is what it is. I have disciplined myself to where I'm making slow, careful decisions. That's about all I can promise you."

Although Ty indeed was maturing nicely, he still carried the bluntness of his father. After putting the horses in the corral, he strolled over to where his mother and Gwyneth were talking.

"I'd buy your bulls if you're making them available. Perhaps twenty or so young heifers too. We'll be sending some mature stuff up the line in the next few weeks, so I'll have the needed funds."

Daniel and Cob were just riding into the yard after a morning of sorting out the brands. Gwyneth called them over. "I'd like it if you men would help Ty sort out some animals this afternoon. He wants the W bulls and a few heifers. He'll ride with you and point out what he wants. Maybe you could even help him move them up to the B/C."

Without a word, the men watered their mounts and turned them into the corral. They hung their saddles on the top rail and saddled fresh animals for the afternoon. With that done, they went to the house. Helen would have lunch on the table. Ty, assuming an invite, went with them, leaving the children to play and his mother to visit with Gwyneth.

Chapter Thirty

BACK WHEN THE MIRRORED W FIRST LAID CLAIM TO their section of the valley, and the cabin was built in the small runoff canyon cutting into the hills, Trent, at Gwyneth's suggestion, created a notice post of sorts to advise all involved that the deep pool in the creek that had been set aside for bathing was in use. It was a simple system, nothing more, really, than a bright blue towel that was rolled up and placed in the wooden box Trent had built and nailed to the trunk of a tree.

When someone intended to wash the day's dust and grime off, the towel was spread out and hung from the branch adjacent to the storage box, as a notice and a warning. Failure to take notice and adhere to the agreed-upon warning would carry severe consequences. Those consequences had never really been outlined nor applied since no one had ever ignored the message the blue towel carried.

The now ragged towel, faded and showing the passage of time, was hanging on the limb when Abe was approaching with a bar of soap in one hand and his own towel in the other. Seeing the warning, he turned back. It was Cob who was bathing, but Abe had no way of knowing and wouldn't have cared if he did know. As the bather scrubbed and rinsed, by ducking fully below the surface of the creek, rising to blow water out of his mouth and nostrils, his skin tingled from the abrasion of the rough homemade soap. He washed almost mindlessly as he went over his plan.

The weaknesses in the plan were obvious even to him, but, formulated during his many hours of riding during the past few days, it was the best he could put together. *Pretty clumsy, Cob, old boy. If the words are going to impress anyone, you're going to need the Lord's help. You're aiming higher than you really know. But you got it to do, and delaying ain't going to make it any easier.*

Shivering so as to think he'd never be warm again, Cob climbed to the grass bank and vigorously applied his rough towel, starting with his hair, he admitted needed a trim, and moving downward to his ankles. He would dry his feet after he was dressed in clean clothes and ready to step into his boots.

Shaved, bathed, brushed my teeth with salt on the end of my finger, fresh clothing. Not much else I can do. And if I don't get 'er done pretty soon, I'm going to lose my nerve. Silly, I know, but there's the truth, nonetheless.

It had been common from the start for the evening meal to turn into a coffee and visiting time, with some going quickly to other free-time activities while two or three leaned back and relaxed in the pleasant warmness of the woodstove-heated room. Daniel and Night Light, with the two children to care for, exited quickly. Abe and Helen were freed to go when Cob said, "Helen, you and Abe go and take your ease. I'll stay and dry dishes. Must be my turn. I haven't been called on for past a week."

He rose from the table and began scraping the dishes into the scrap pail before placing them in the hot water. Gwyneth usually did the washing with a rotation of the others taking on the drying. As they worked, an uneasy silence and tension grew between Cob and Gwyneth, almost as if Gwyneth knew what was coming. Cob was unsuccessful in the couple of times he tried to pick up a conversation.

Finally, knowing the time was upon them, he folded the drying cloth over the edge of the wooden cabinet he and Trent had built to hold dishes. He leaned one elbow on the cabinet, looked fully at Gwyneth, and said, "Gwyneth, I'm pulling out in a couple of days. You have no real reason to stay here, and I'm pretty sure you understand how I feel about you. I've been having trouble hiding it. My home country is a lovely part of Texas, and the Hat is a well-established ranch. You'd like my family, and they'd welcome you with open arms. And I'm never going to find another woman... Oh, fiddle. What I'm trying to say, Gwyneth, is, come with me. I've always—"

Mercifully, Gwyneth, with a single finger pressed lightly on his lips, stopped him from saying more, although he had other words on the tip of his tongue.

As Cob was speaking, she had lifted her hands from the wash water and dried them on her apron. She somehow couldn't bring herself to turn and look directly at him. Remembrances flashed through her mind. Remembrances of two young, strong men. Friends. Who had a dream of ranching in the west. Even then, she knew of Cob's thoughts toward her and respected him greatly for not competing with Trent for her affection. No man could have lived a more proper life, watching his friend marry and live with the woman he himself loved. But Gwyneth couldn't return that love, even though she had been a widow for over two years.

"I know what you're trying to say, Cob. And I greatly respect you for not saying it before, when it would have caused unfixable problems between you and Trent. I have a strong fondness for you, Cob. You're a good man. A man I trust and value as a friend. And if my feelings were to be named as love, Cob, it would be the love of a brother. I know that's not what you're wanting to hear, but I also know you would want me to be honest."

Into the uneasy silence, Cob finally managed to lighten the conversation by saying, "Anyway, we do dishes pretty well together. I wish you every good thing in life, Gwyneth. Now, knowing your feelings, if you were to ever ask my opinion, I would tell you that if you're settled on not coming with me to Texas, take the money from cattle sales and go to college. Get your doctor's degree. Don't let anything stand in your way. You'd make a great doctor. And I'll always remember you as a bright light in my life."

As he walked outside, Gwyneth turned and watched. With a deep sigh, she thought, *There's a good man. Perhaps someday I'll find my own good man again. Or perhaps once is enough. I just don't know.*

Chapter Thirty-One

Daniel agreed to accompany the cattle as they were shipped to Pueblo. There, the buyers would make their bids and, with Gwyneth trusting him, Daniel would make the deal. He would be gone for over a week. During that week, Gwyneth invited Night Light and the children to join her in the cabin. The spot Daniel and Night Light had chosen for their small dwelling was about as isolated as it could be, given the terrain. Although the isolation didn't seem to bother the Indian girl, it troubled Gwyneth. Anyway, the ladies had so little time to visit that Gwyneth was looking forward to the company.

Gwyneth had picked up a good bit of the Ute language and Night Light could well be considered as fluent in English. The little boy, their eldest child, prattled away constantly, it seemed, slipping easily from one language to the other without even realizing what he was doing. Enjoying the company in the cabin, the first since Trent's death, the days slipped smoothly away. When Daniel returned, Gwyneth remained silent, but inwardly she was sorry to see the family return to their own cabin. Even with no further work for Daniel on the Mirrored W, they had decided to remain where they were. Perhaps later, the need for an income of some sort would push them into exploring options.

The summer slipped away in Gwyneth's quiet corner of her world, with no real work for anyone except keeping the firewood supply at a comfortable level. Abe seemed to enjoy the first few days, but it soon became apparent that he was restless and ill at ease. He said nothing until the morning the first bite of frost gave warning of what couldn't be avoided.

Sharing breakfast in the cabin, Abe, sounding almost philosophical, offered, "Sure miss ol'Cob."

After a short pause while he stared out the window, he completed his thoughts, "Winter country. Ain't no way of holding 'er off."

Gwyneth recognized the introduction to a wanted conversation. "What are you thinking, Abe?"

Helen seldom entered into Abe's talk, but she did this once. "It's much more about what you're planning, Gwyneth. For my part, I'm still enjoying this lovely little corner of the world, but at the same time, I'm having trouble making sense of it all."

All Gwyneth said was, "We'll have to make a decision soon."

The decision was eased when an oversized, heavily loaded wagon, its once-white canvas cover sun-faded and storm-lashed, pulled by a team of horses with feet as big as dinner plates, arrived from the south. A tall, big-shouldered and heavily bearded man, loud and jovial in his talk, hollered, "Billy Wilmore here, sir. We're told there's a nurse and midwife somewhere around these here parts. If those folks ranching down to the south can be believed in their directions, I'm figur'n this must be the place."

He had been aiming his talk at Abe, who was the only person within sight, but the little bit of distance between the wagon and the cabin couldn't hold back the volume of his natural voice. Gwyneth stepped onto the porch, shading her eyes from the late morning sun. The wagon driver noticed her arrival and turned his attention toward her, with a finger to the brim of his hat.

"Be you the doctor, ma'am? Fella down south asked me to pass on that he was walking pretty good again, with just a bit of a limp, which I can confirm, if that matters at all. Said even with the limp, it's still a sight better than being dead from the gangrene. Said to bring his thanks along with us. Also allowed as how his boot was beyond repair. All that mean anything at all to you?"

"Yes. That means something to me, and I'm happy to hear that he's walking. Some think of me as a doctor, but they're only partly correct. I'm a nurse. Do one of you have a medical problem?"

"Me wee wifey, a-sett'n here beside me, she figures it's com'n to her time. We left the boys and the eldest girl with the herd, but they'll be com'n along. We came directly on to find you. Glad that worked out. Might it be you could attend while herself delivers another son into our small world. Bein' alone on our ranch, it was m'self that had to come to her aid the last time. She's bound and determined that she'll tend to herself this time rather than submit to me own tender and merciful care agi'n. Kin ye imagine sech a thing?" The boisterous laugh spoke to the admitted truth of his own ineptness when it came to delivering his new namesake.

Gwyneth replied, ignoring the comment about the last delivery, "Yes, I'll be glad to help. But what makes you so determined that it will be a son?"

"Simple to figure that out. The Lord knows it's sons thet are needed to keep a ranch under control. Boys thet 'er gro'in into men. Men that can do a day's work. Girls ain't of much use other than cook'n and clean'n an' such, and we already got enough girls fer that."

A little girl, perhaps six years old, who had been sitting between her parents, dropped off the seat to stand on the floor of the wagon. With her hands turned into little fists placed on her hips, she did a half turn to look at her father and said, "Daddy, that's not right. Girls can do lots of things."

Billy Wilmore broke into a delighted laugh, ruffled the little girl's hair, and said, "Well, on second thought, perhaps you're right. You just might be right on that, Sissy."

"I am right. And don't be calling me Sissy. My name is Summer."

"And right ye are again, Sissy."

The mother, who had yet to be introduced, said, "Billy!" in a way that could not be misinterpreted.

"Yes, yes, of course, me dear."

He swung his foot onto a spoke on the big wagon wheel and dropped to the ground. He rounded the wagon and assisted his wife out of the rig, lifting her into his arms and carrying her as if she weighed nothing at all, although she was not a small woman. The lady herself appeared to be perfectly at ease with the situation, trusting his abilities. Gwyneth had walked to the door of the small medical clinic. Billy took the hint and followed.

"Miss nurse, this here be me wife. Gladys, we be call'n her, all except the wee ones who call her mother."

"Hello, Gladys. My name is Gwyneth. We have this nice clinic set aside from the ranch business. I think you're going to have to set her down, Mr. Wilmore. It's doubtful if you can get through the door carrying Gladys. And it's a sure bet that she can't deliver you another son, or a daughter either, lying in your arms."

Billy turned sideways, putting Gladys's feet and legs through first, and then turned carefully the other way so he could get through the doorway himself and then, with another quarter turn, the patient's head was clear of the door jamb, and they were fully into the room. He then gently laid her on the already prepared table. He stepped back, and with the first serious look on his face said, "Me and the little ones, we'll be pray'n fer ya, Mother."

Abe squeezed through the door with an armload of split firewood. Without saying anything to the patient, he bent before the small iron stove and kindled a fire. The process took only a minute, or perhaps a bit more. With the flames licking the dry wood, he rose and stepped away, leaving the tending of the fire to Gwyneth. Before he could get far, Gwyneth said, "I'd appreciate it if you would call Night Light for me."

Gladys Wilmore was a bit taken aback when Night Light entered and closed the door behind herself. Gwyneth noticed, and to set the patient's mind at ease, said, "Gladys, this is Night Light. She married one of our cowboys. She's from the Ute Nation. She and Daniel have a cabin a bit up the draw from us. They have two little ones of their own. Night Light has been helping me and teaching me at the same time. I teach her our ways, and she teaches me her ways. She's a genius on the subject of herbs and natural remedies. I've come to appreciate her knowledge and rely on her help. You'll come to love her as I do once you get to know her."

The child wasn't quite ready to enter the world, but by mid-afternoon, there was new action. Night Light was walking carefully beside Gladys as the patient exercised her muscles. Day after day on the wagon seat had left her cramped up. But the slow steps with the Ute girl ready to help if the need should arise were stretching out her muscles and loosening her joints. After a particularly strong contraction that caused her to stop and grasp Night Light's hand for support, she very quietly said, "It's time."

An hour later, she was resting with a baby daughter nestled to her breast. Night Light, not yet having been able to understand all the ways of her non-native friends, said, "Your husband, maybe he won't be happy with not son."

Gladys smiled at the remark. "Don't let Billy's talk fool you. It's all just teasing. He loves his daughters every bit as much as the boys."

As if to prove the truth of Gladys's statement, Billy let a

hoot out of him as he was invited into the clinic. His first words were, "Are ye all right then, m'love? You and the child?"

"We're fine, Billy. I'll not be wanting to ride the wagon for a day or two though." That brought out another burst of laughter from Billy.

～

THAT EVENING, Billy insisted on taking a seat in the clinic, balancing a plate of dinner on his knee while he ate. Helen had insisted he take it, along with a smaller plate for the new mother. She had taken the two children who were traveling in the wagon into the house for the simple dinner.

Gwyneth invited Billy to join the others on the porch for coffee after the meal. Gladys was left to rest by herself. A more serious Billy waited until there was a lull in the talk before he spoke, looking directly at Gwyneth, "Abe has told me of the short history of your ranching in this valley. In truth, I'm guessing no one has really been here long. Excepting for the Utes, and they didn't ranch. Still don't. I was sore struck by the tell'n of the tale of los'n yer man. Now you've said farewell to yer animals and yer left with this nice cabin and the clinic alone. De ye have plans fer the land then? And the buildings?"

"Why do you ask, Billy?"

"My purposes should be clear enough. We've come look'n fer grass and a home. We've more than a thousand head of beef critters just a few days away. We've a need, and the funds to make a deal. You've given up yer herd, so you've no more use for the grass. And the thought has come to me that ye jest may be more help to the folks around with yer doctor'n, if ye were to be in some town, perhaps this Bessie Creek Abe tells me about. Would ye be interested in mak'n a deal then?"

Gwyneth knew this question would be asked. Abe came close to bringing up the subject just the day before. And that was after Helen mused, earlier, about it being a secluded place for women alone, with just one aging man. In her silence, she had gone over every option she could come up with. The comfort was that she had adequate funds at her disposal to pretty well do anything she wanted. She had lost track, if she had ever been counting, of the times she had called out to Trent for a word of advice, knowing the foolishness of the exercise. From the time she had left home against everyone's opinion, including her family's, to volunteer in the medical service during the war, she had been making her own decisions. Only after their marriage had she deferred to Trent, and she did that knowing he would listen anytime she had a contrary thought.

To sell and move placed her face-to-face with the unspoken question that always seemed to arise in her private musing, would giving up the last remnants of the Mirrored W be a rejection of Trent's dream? Or had Trent's dream, in fact, died with him? She was alone. She had no child to grow and carry on the dream. Abe and Helen weren't really old, but nor were they young. As the past winter had settled in upon them, Abe had been seen rubbing his hands together even as he sat by the wood stove. He commented just the once when he said, *"Gets chilly, time to time down in Texas, but not like this. Don't last like this here country neither."*

It got to where he left the cabin only reluctantly. Gwyneth rose from her rocker and, before stepping off the porch to check on the new mom and her baby, said, "We'll talk in the morning, Billy."

THE FOLLOWING MORNING, Gladys insisted on getting up. This was her fifth birth, and according to her memory, all had been easy. Gwyneth wondered if her memory was dulled a bit by the love for her children. But in any case, even as she mentioned getting up, she was swinging her feet off the bed. She had nursed the child and trusted her to Night Light, who offered to clean her up and get her ready to meet her father and Summer, or Sissy, as her father teased her, the girl who rode the wagon.

As Gwyneth steadied her first few seconds of standing, Gladys asked, "Did Billy deal you out of the place yet?"

Gwyneth searched for words for a few seconds before answering, "You talked about it did you? And did you approve of his plans?"

"We didn't talk about it. No need for that. I know most of Billy's thoughts before he does. Don't you do anything you have doubts about, Gwyneth, but if you wanted to sell, I could see us settling in here quite happily. We would have to build onto the cabin, but Billy's good with tools. Yes, we'd be fine here."

AN HOUR LATER, after breakfast was over and the dishes washed and put away, Gwyneth joined Billy and Summer on the porch. Billy stood and again touched his fingers to the brim of his hat. He said nothing, but the question was written all over his face.

Gwyneth went directly to the question. "I wouldn't know what to ask for the buildings, Billy, and the grass is free. We took out a homestead on the half section around the building site, one quarter each for Trent and me. We proved up and have the title. Make me a reasonable offer and we'll shake on it."

When the time came, just a few minutes later, to complete the deal, Gwyneth felt a tear rolling down her cheek as they shook, silently saying goodbye to everything Trent ever wanted in life. Billy was gentleman enough to not notice.

ABE WAS amazed when Billy offered to purchase the wagon, pup, and all the horses on the Mirrored W. As if that wasn't enough, Billy said, "What'cha all be haul'n in the wagons then, Abe."

Abe explained about the trading post they had held as a home and business place down to Conville. "Got these here as leftovers from that adventure. Might find a buyer for it at the general store at the Creek. I'll have to hold the wagon and team till that's settled and we've had a chance to load our own goods from here."

At Billy's urging, Abe unloaded enough of the wagon so Billy and Gladys together could look over the remaining stock. Coffee, beans, flour, sturdy boxes of crackers and hardtack, some packaged candy, cases of canned beans, peaches, pears, and tomatoes. There were also hard goods, ammunition in several calibers, two shotguns, and three Winchester carbines. In the pup was a wide variety of tools, from hand saws to buck saws, shovels, picks, an adze, two post hole diggers, and a variety of hammers from the carpenter's style to post mauls, and three axes. There were also several closed wooden boxes. Abe couldn't remember what was in them.

"Name me a price," was Billy's booming response to what lay before him. "We'uns always lay up for winter. This will be a good start, wouldn't you say, Mother?" He was looking at Gladys when he asked the question.

"We'll be needing more flour."

"There ya go, Abe. Mother wants the lot. Name me a price."

Abe scratched his head, whapped his hat on his pant leg, looked over at Helen, and squinted his eyes as he was trying to silently put numbers together. He finally resorted to a piece of paper he tore off a brown paper-wrapped package in the wagon, licked the end of his pencil, studied on Billy for a short bit, and silently laid out the numbers, curling the paper in his hand so Billy couldn't see. He reduced the matter to just four lines—

wagons, horses, food and clothing, and hard goods. He added it up, printed out the number, and circled it before holding it over to Billy.

Billy took the paper and held it to where Gladys could see. When she said nothing, Billy said, "Wagons, all right, horses a bit steep, food and what have you, all right. You take fifty off, and we'll start unloading."

After an internal struggle, Abe finally fessed up, "I'll take a hundred off. I was expecting to have to waste a lot of time going back and forth."

"Done," Billy practically shouted. Another crushing hand-shake sealed the deal.

THE NEXT MORNING, the big wagon still lay heavy with goods. The pup had been unloaded. Abe, Helen, and Gwyneth were loading their personal gear into it, while Daniel prepared the team. By late morning, they were seated, ready to go. At last, when Helen was carrying the final armload of bedding from the back room, Gladys came in holding the baby. Gladys and Helen were just in time to see Gwyneth rubbing her hand along the leading edge of the still-warm stove. This was one thing she would like to have saved, but there was no practical way to do it, nor any real purpose. She couldn't travel the country, wherever she settled down, dragging a cast-iron stove along with her. But to give up the single special thing Trent had bought for her was the final test in her leaving.

Abe would drive the team to Bessie Creek. Daniel rode along on his own gelding to drive the wagon back. He had been hired by Billy to work cattle on the Mirrored W, now to be known as the Billy-4, or, as shortened, the B-4. He and Night Light would retain their own cabin.

Chapter Thirty-Two

THE NEWLY BUILT TOWN OF BESSIE CREEK OFFERED little to nothing in the way of accommodations for arriving settlers. Abe and Helen camped in their wagon, as they had all along the wide trail from Texas to Kansas and onward to Colorado. Addy Quinlan, the lady whom Gwyneth had helped through a difficult birth, heard the nurse was in town and quickly tracked her down to offer her the tiny back room in their cabin.

"We ain't got but that small cot. Room's no bigger than a closet, but the roof don't leak and the walls hold out the wind, and yer welcome to lay up there until ye find something more to yer position, bein a near enough doctor, and all."

"Thank you, Mrs. Quinlan. That's very kind of you. I'll try to hold my stay to just a day or two. My father-in-law, Abe is his name, he's on the hunt for a cabin to rent or purchase. The search won't take long in this small town."

∼

THE SEARCH, indeed, didn't take long. Abe walked through the settlement, asking everyone he saw, getting the same answer each time. "Got just enough space for me and mine. Don't know anyone that's any different."

At noon, Eustice Ward, who had settled down in Bessie Creek, at least temporarily, while he sorted out the possibilities of beginning a regular church there, trotted his horse into town looking for Abe. When the two of them finally got together, Eustice said, "Heard you were in town looking for somewhere to hang your hat. Might want to take yourself a look out of town just a bit, by perhaps a short quarter mile, there to the east. Just an easy walk, really, up on that crest of the hill you can see right over there." He pointed his thumb over his shoulder to aid Abe in his visual search. "Couple up there is moving on. Going further west on the rails. Seems the Creek's promise doesn't match up with the vision they hold in their hearts. If you're willing to part with fifty dollars, you've got yourself a cabin."

Eustice stepped down and passed the reins to Abe, who swung into the saddle. On Eustice's borrowed horse, Abe rode out and made the deal. A sheet metal stove and two cots, one large enough for two, were included in the transaction. A small table and four crude chairs also.

By noon the next day, they were moved in, the pup wagon was unloaded, and Daniel was on his way back south. Their parting had been difficult, with everyone knowing there was little chance of ever meeting up again.

Abe and Helen had little to do in Bessie Creek. Helen fussed around the small cabin, cleaning and fixing, while Abe wandered into town, meeting folks and asking questions along the way. Through a conversation that led from one topic to another, Abe discovered that the man sitting beside him on one of the sawn-off tree sections someone had laid out close by, keeping an eye on an energetic, but poorly taught fella who was stumbling through the construction of a livery stable, was a trained carpenter.

"Offered to stand in on the raising of this here stable, but

the fella figures he can do it himself. And who's to say? Perhaps
he can. First winter's snow or heavy wind will tell the tale."

Abe felt a moment's excitement. "Are you a builder then?"

"Aye. That I be, as the fella who trained me back in our little
seaside town would have said."

"Would you be interested in adding a couple of rooms onto
a shack we purchased just two days ago?"

"If you've the coin to lay out for the time spent, I'm your
man."

THE RESULT WASN'T FANCY, but in ten days, there was an
addition of two rooms in the cabin. One room would be
Gwyneth's private living space, and a smaller space would be
held aside for a clinic, with an outside door, if ever such was
required.

There was, as yet, no structure to the settlement. No mayor
or town councilors. No formal law. Their single attempt at law
had ended when the marshal climbed the three steps onto the
passenger car and bid Bessie Creek farewell. There was no town
plan. Folks in town knew the situation could not long exist, but
everyone was busy doing what they came west to do, offering a
trade or a store of some kind, or looking for ranch or farmland.
There was little spare time or energy left for town planning. The
toughs that had plagued Bessie Creek for a few weeks, the ones
that Big Beef Cameron had trouble with, and who eventually
put three bullets into the man, had moved on. But everyone
knew there would be others. Talk and wishing would have to
become action soon.

Word got around that Abe had nothing but free time and
that he had been talking up the need for a town government.
During a long evening at the saloon, visiting and meeting folks,
Abe held his liquid refreshment down to a single glass while
some others didn't have any such intention or moral reserve. As

the glasses clanked together and the talk got louder, someone suggested that Abe should take upon himself the role of organizing the town. A raucous round of shouted applause followed, with laughter and cheers, as if their vote settled the matter.

Somehow, the revelers failed to consider those who were not in their immediate company. But the next morning, the liquor-generated motion to turn it all over to Abe morphed into a more sober assessment of what was needed in the town to encourage growth and hold off the rougher types that roamed the country.

When a couple of the more responsible store owners approached Abe with the proposal, he agreed, with no promise to stay for the long run. "I'm just passing through for now. Don't know the future. Ain't look'n for no new line of work. Just staying till my daughter-in-law gets herself settled." He stepped into the position on his own terms and went right to work writing out a plan.

Along with the gossip about Abe's planning, the news that Gwyneth had taken up residence at the Creek spread like wildfire. The tale of her delivering Addy Quinlan's baby had not been forgotten. Soon there was a steady demand for medical assistance, mostly childhood diseases, scrapes and cuts, common in rambunctious young ones, and a broken bone or two. A small few offered her a sweaty handful of coins in payment. Some offered nothing, clearly embarrassed to be asking for help with no means of repayment. To prevent further embarrassment to the struggling settlers, Gwyneth graciously smiled and replied, "Glad to help."

Privately, back in the cabin, she confessed to Abe and Helen, "I'm having trouble understanding why most of these people are even here. They have little to nothing, and I see no way they're going to improve on that."

Abe quietly offered his thoughtful opinion. "There's been hard times, Gwyneth. Hard times in more places than just

Bessie Creek. The big boys back east have fancy words to hide the truth that the country is in serious trouble. A person would think that being so long after the war, the nation would have pulled itself together so everyone would have a chance. But even the scripture says, *the poor you will always have with you.* It just seems that there are an awful lot of poor. And many of them are coming west, following the paths sprinkled with gold nuggets they've heard about. The hard times may change when the country sees itself as one again, but it might take a while too. And to be honest about it, I'd rather be poor here, in the Creek, than in some big heartless city. Here, at least a man might do something about it. In the cities he's just run over and cast aside."

The melancholy mood lasted throughout the evening, but by morning, Gwyneth was feeling better again. She took a solitary walk through the town, talking to a couple of merchants and having lunch in the small café. The last stop was at the general store, a half-walled structure with a waxed and oiled canvas roof. Looking around the small space, she smiled to herself, thinking, *Abe and Helen had more trade goods in their wagons than there are here.* Still, she admired the young couple for trying. She bought a small bag of hard candies, introduced herself, wishing the owners well, and continued her walk.

Outside the saloon, another half-walled shack with a canvas roof, there was a homemade bench, sheltered by the only walkway roof in town, where people could sit out of the sun and visit. For her first time since their arrival, Gwyneth was truly uncomfortable. The eyes and grinning smirks of the three men sitting there followed her from the moment she came into sight until she crossed the street and walked back to her own cabin.

ABE DREW up a list of the matters that would have to be addressed if the town were to develop in anything but a haphazard manner. The two most troublesome issues were the hiring of a law officer and the taxing of citizens to cover that cost, and other simple matters such as road grading and extensions, the building of wooden walkways, etc. He called for a meeting to be held in the saloon. The saloon would offer no services during the meeting. Probably no one had bothered to count the folks who were calling Bessie Creek their home, but Abe was surprised when the small saloon filled to overflowing, with more folks outside wishing to get in.

Among the crowd were a good number of women, who were interested in the small politics of the village, a situation that was unheard of in the east but was becoming more common on the frontier. When the advertised time for the meeting arrived, Abe stood to his feet and began, "I'm going to talk as loud as my old vocal cords will allow. I'm hoping you folks outside can hear."

The meeting lasted a bit more than one hour, and nothing was settled, but at least no fights broke out, so Abe called it a success, promising to have another meeting when he had thought more about the issues brought up by the citizens.

GWYNETH'S NAME and medical skills continued to grow. She, along with Abe and Helen, were seen as among the more responsible and trustworthy citizens of the little town.

On one typical nursing call, Gwyneth was advising a young mother on how to deal with the childhood plague of impetigo, instructing her on the use of hot compresses and the application of diluted vinegar for short periods of time. "I'll also leave you a bit of this salve. It will help keep the skin soft and should prevent scars from forming."

To the mother, she said, "This is a common childhood

disease, but it's very contagious. You need to wash your hands thoroughly after you've treated the boy, and keep him away from other children, your own or others. And if the boy can refrain from touching the infection, it will heal much better and might not spread to other parts of his body. You'll more likely avoid further outbreaks if you keep the kids clean and the home as well. Until he's healed of this, don't share anything with your son, towels, bedding, clothing. Call me if you have further problems."

Chapter Thirty-Three

As fall was closing in with the promise of winter not far behind, Gwyneth and Helen were sitting with their afternoon tea, discussing their situation.

"Exactly why are we here in Bessie Creek?"

"I'm not sure I have an answer for that, Helen. I'm even finding it difficult to picture the town existing in five years. But I could be totally wrong on that too. I've known of your doubts from the start, Helen, but what about Abe? He doesn't say much."

"Truthfully, Gwyneth, Abe and I would both rather be back in Texas. We have three young ones wandering the country somewhere. If they are still alive, that is. We could have grandchildren we don't know about. We've sent letters to the last two towns we lived in, but there have been no replies. But still, Texas is home and always will be, at least in some part of our thinking."

Gwyneth was quiet for a while, thinking about what brought Trent and her west. Some days, she found it difficult to realize that Trent's dream died so suddenly. A poorly broken, fidgety horse was all it took. That and a coyote. Not much when she thought about it. But effective. Since that day, she and Trent's parents had simply been hanging on, with no clear idea what their next steps should be.

"I have to go check on that boy with the broken arm. We'll talk again about this, Helen. Soon."

ABE WAS at his usual table in the saloon, making a single glass of beer last all afternoon while he and a group of citizens discussed the future of the town. Against all the well-understood rules governing access to saloons, a boy of about ten years, all out of breath from running, threw back the saloon door until it crashed against the wall, skidded to a stop at Abe's table, and nearly collapsed, gasping for breath. The startled men said nothing, giving the boy a chance to speak.

"Mr. Mr.... You've got to come. A drunk fellas at the cabin a whopp'n on the nurse with his fists. The nurse and that other lady. He's a shout'n and the women are scream'n and crying for help. I heard and went to see. The older lady, she's ly'n on the floor. The nurse, she's bleeding and fight'n the fella. She's got herself a stick of firewood. The fella, he's bleeding some too."

The telling only took a few seconds, but even so, Abe didn't hear the last part. He was up and out of his chair and through the door while the boy was still talking. Two others were running close behind him. People on the street had to scurry out of the way or be bowled over. A woman rushed out of the store hollering, "What's going on?"

Abe didn't stop to answer, but one of the other runners, who was having trouble keeping up, said, "Come along. We'll need a woman's touch. Someone's been beating up the nurse. Another woman too."

I<small>T WAS</small> a sizable crowd that was gathering in front of the cabin. Abe had charged in alone at first. Then the woman from the store eased her way in. There was no sign of the intruder. The cabin was a mess, with a few broken dishes, and the table lamp smashed on the floor from when the table was flung aside. Helen was sitting upright on the cot, still dazed, but conscious. Gwyneth was crumpled on the floor with her legs folded awkwardly beneath her. Blood flowed from a nasty cut on her forehead and another on her cheek. She appeared to be unconscious. Whether more serious internal injuries had been inflicted on her was unknown.

Abe went to Helen first, but she brushed him aside. "Go to Gwyneth. I'm fine, or I will be soon. I'm thinking Gwyneth's badly hurt."

Abe made as if to kneel beside Gwyneth, but the woman who had been running beside the men said, "Leave her to me for now."

Another two ladies entered the cabin and fell to their knees beside Gwyneth. They eased her flat onto her back with a rolled-up blanket under her head. She was breathing unevenly, clearly in pain, but she was alive. There was some doubt when Abe first looked at her.

As the ladies gained more assurance, they carefully pulled Gwyneth's one leg straight, and then the other. They modestly arranged her dress. Abe passed another blanket down to the comforting ladies. They wrapped it tightly, leaving only Gwyneth's head exposed, and eased away from her. The woman who had assumed authority over the situation asked, "Where can we lay her? Is there another cot?"

Abe opened the door to Gwyneth's room and said, "In here."

Together, the three ladies picked Gwyneth up and carried her to the cot. The leader came back into the front room with instructions. "Someone get that stove a-perk'n and heat some water. The rest of you, outside, be gone with ya."

Abe watched the cleaning and gentle treatment long enough to assure himself that Gwyneth was in no danger and then turned again to Helen, who was also being ministered to by a pair of town women.

"Helen, can you tell me who did this?"

"Not by name, I can't. But he's a big fella. Wearing a cowhide vest and a gray hat. He was hoping to sweet-talk Gwyneth, I'm thinking. He got angry when he seen me here, and that Gwyneth wasn't home alone. He made as if to reach out and touch Gwyneth, but she pushed him away, telling him to get out. He was pretty drunk, judging by smell and actions. When he was pushed away, he got even more angry. He reached for Gwyneth again and she slapped his face. It was like that set him off, and that's when he started to beat us, Gwyneth first and then me and then back to Gwyneth. We're too far from folks in this cabin for anyone to hear. But I think it was a boy who finally heard the screaming and the angry shouts of the drunk."

"You have any idea where he went?"

"No. I was just glad to know he was gone. I was going to try to help Gwyneth, but that's when y'all got here."

Abe gently touched Helen's cheek. "If you're all right, I'll go take me a look."

"I'm all right. But Abe, don't do anything foolish." She had that burst of anger in mind that occasionally escaped from under the restraint of Abe's willpower. It was too late. Abe was already stepping out the door. To one of the attending ladies, she said, "Abe can be quite stern when provoked."

ABE HAD NO MORE run in him. He couldn't have remembered the last time he had run more than a step or two if he had allowed his mind to move in that direction. But his steps toward the business section of Bessie Creek were steady and solid. The look on his face was grim to the point of menace. He was well on his way when the thought of a weapon entered his mind. He had his Colt hanging at his side and a camp knife in a scabbard strung on his belt. But although he hadn't yet had time to think it through, somehow, *don't kill him* entered into his thinking.

The first and most logical place to look was the saloon. He burst through the door into sudden silence and staring eyes from every man in the place. Abe asked no questions, simply looking at each man, one by one, looking for a cowhide vest or wounds of some sort that Gwyneth might have inflicted with the length of firewood. He saw nothing suspicious, and when the bartender, a man he knew and trusted, offered a slight shake of his head, he turned and left.

His eyes fell on the saddled horses tethered at the rail in front of the drinking establishment. With a new thought in his mind, Abe stepped around the rail to a gray standing patiently in the sun. He knew it was theft, but at the moment, he didn't care. He lifted the loop holding the coil of rope in place and continued his determined walk with the rope firmly held in his left fist, with a ready loop in his right hand.

From door to door, he stomped with the same result as he'd had in the saloon. Then he thought of the station house, which was separated from the town by a few hundred feet of grass and native shrubbery. He had no more than put the last building behind him when his eye caught motion in the long grass. He turned that way. Almost without thought, he said aloud, "You may outrun me. I'm an old man. But ain't no way you're going to outrun a round from my .45. Stand up and be a man."

There was no further movement for a few seconds, but suddenly the cowhide vest came into view as a man of perhaps six feet and something short of two hundred pounds came erect before him. The terrified fugitive stood frozen for no more than a second before turning and attempting to run. His forward movement was halted when a loop of hard rope dropped over his head and was pulled tight as it reached his elbows.

A frightened and angry squawk burst from his lips. Abe, an old cowhand familiar with angles and the leverage required to bring a full-size steer to his knees, and with all his sympathy for wrong-doers erased during the war, gave just the right tug on the rope to bring the man down. Abe rushed to take advantage of the fall, and with a few rapid moves, there was a double wrap of rope around the man's chest and another, plus a half hitch, around his ankles.

With the downed man rolling and trying to shake the rope loose, Abe tugged, the rope tightening with every pull. It was a heavy load, but Abe dragged him out of the grass and onto the walking space in front of the buildings. An onlooker stepped forward and laid a hand on the rope, and then a second man stepped in to help. Abe said nothing until they were in front of the saloon and under the overhanging roof. Only then did he find breath enough to say, "Stand him against that post."

With another quick wrap of the rope, the woman beater was helplessly secured, with his face against the post. Abe pulled his belt knife and slit the man's shirt down the back and then did the same with his underwear. He spat on his hands and wiped them on his canvas pants before taking a grip on the tail end of the rope, leaving about six feet hanging free of his hands. With the realization of what he planned, a murmur went through the crowd. Two or three women mildly voiced objections. A man standing at the front of the gathering turned to them and said, "And what if it was you who was beaten with this man's fists?"

That stopped the complaints, although one quiet voice was heard to say, "Might be best to just shoot him."

The first swing of the rope brought a further gasp from the crowd, as they began to realize what a whipping really looked like. The gasp was nearly drowned out by the scream of pain from the tied-up man. Abe gritted his teeth and swung again. And again. And again, rhythmical and steady. At first, red welts appeared and then, with lashes on top of lashes, the welts broke, and blood dribbled into sight, beginning with a trickle, then more generously. And still, Abe swung the rope.

If he had a point of satisfaction in mind, he showed no sign of it. The beating victim had passed out after screaming and begging for the punishment to stop. He hollered that it was the drink that made his mind go crazy. That he wasn't a woman-beater. That he wasn't a drinker. But he foolishly drank of the rattlesnake firewater someone put before him in the saloon. He was sorry. He apologized. Just before he passed out, he whimpered, "Enough. Please. Enough."

WHEN ABE FAILED to return to the cabin, Helen worried. With supreme effort, he had held his temper in since they had left Texas. But she was sure the anger he brought home from the war had not disappeared, but was somehow stuffed down somewhere, under his normal consciousness. When she could wait no longer, she struggled free of the fussing women and ran, as best she could, toward the town center.

The screams of pain and the encouraging yells of a few of the onlookers fell on her ears. Frightened at what might be happening, she ran all the harder. Abe was set for another swing of the rope when Helen's arms wrapped themselves around the fist holding the torture weapon. "No, Abe. Enough. You'll kill him."

Abe took a few seconds, but he finally appeared to come to his senses. He dropped the rope and stepped back with Helen still holding him. She cried, "Oh, Abe, what have you gone and done?"

One of the onlookers answered, "He done no more than what should have been done. Me? I'd have tied this brute behind my horse and dragged him all the way to Pueblo, where he could be jailed."

Before turning for home, Abe said to no one in particular, "Untie him and leave him where he falls."

Helen hollered over the multitude of voices, "No. Carry him to our cabin."

Several men started untying the rope. That reminded Abe that he had stolen the rope. He looked at the man standing beside the gray he had lifted the rope from. "That your horse? I owe you a rope."

"Better use for that rope than I ever found. You owe me nothing."

~

ABE AND HELEN slowly walked back to the cabin with four men, each holding one of the beaten man's limbs, following behind.

At the cabin, Helen instructed the men to lay their burden face down on the cot she and Abe had been using. There were a few gasps from the gathered women, but one strong voice, the one Abe remembered as being from the woman who had taken charge of the injured Helen and Gwyneth, agreeing with the one heard by the saloon earlier, said, "Should have shot him and been done with it."

All heads turned toward the sound of the back bedroom door opening. Gwyneth, unsteady on her feet but walking, even if slowly, having heard the directions poured out by Helen, emerged. Her face was a startling sight with a puffy nose and the remnants of dried blood on her cheek and forehead. Her normally tied-back hair had fallen loose. Both arms were wrapped across her mid-section as if she was hoping to stave off the pain of being struck there. She took only a quick look at the whipped man before saying, "Someone get my black leather bag."

Abe and the attending women stepped aside as Gwyneth moved, slowly and awkwardly, to the man on the cot. She said nothing as she pulled a chair over so she could sit beside what was, an hour before her adversary, but who was now her patient. Her medical bag was set on the floor beside her. Abe dragged another chair over and lifted the bag, laying it on the seat where it could be more easily reached. She ignored everyone in the room, concentrating solely on the man's heavily lacerated back. She didn't ask who had administered the punishment, but she had a pretty firm opinion. She whispered, as if speaking to herself, "At least it's clean."

One of the women set a pan of hot water on the chair beside the medical bag.

With the first application of a warm, wet cloth, the whipped man screamed and tried to twist onto his side and rise from the cot. Gwyneth, as sternly as anyone had ever heard her speak, responded, "Lay still if you want to one day heal from this. I don't care how much it hurts. Lay still."

The words were lisped a bit, passing through Gwyneth's swollen lips.

The remainder of the treatment was applied with the man burying his face in the pillow while shudders ran through his body. When the dried blood was soaked off and most of the new, seeping blood was stanched, Gwyneth asked Abe to twist the lid off the can of salve. She administered the salve and leaned back in her chair, wiping her hands on a cloth. To her patient, she said, "I can't do more than that. Your wounds are clean, and if you keep them that way, they will heal. It won't be fast, but they will heal. Now sit up and hold your arms above your head. The man's struggle was immense, but he managed to do as he was told. Rather than look face-to-face with the woman he had used his fists on, he tilted his head toward the floor and held his eye closed."

Gwyneth looked at the neighbor lady who had helped all the way through the process. "In the back room, there's a large roll of cotton bandage material."

With no questions asked, the woman found the roll and returned it to Gwyneth. She said, "Thanks. But I don't need that. From here on, it's up to you and Helen. Wrap the cloth around his chest to keep the wound clean."

She turned her attention to the man. "Don't remove the cloth for two or three days. And don't leave it on longer than that, or the healing wounds will grow into it, and you'll never get it off without tearing it all open again. Now remember, keep it all clean."

When he stood up, the remnants of his cowhide vest, shirt, and underwear were lifted away by one of the other women. The shirt and underwear were put in the stove. The cowhide vest, now in two pieces, was thrown outside to be dealt with later.

Abe had left the cabin earlier to walk to the store. He purchased a new shirt, the largest they had, and when the bandaging was complete, he passed it to the women. "Mister, you put that shirt on and get gone. I've brought your horse down. At least it's the horse the liveryman said you rode in on. You get into the saddle the best way you know how and get gone. Get gone fast and far. You need to be very careful that I never see you again."

Abe had more warnings fighting to be released, but Helen gave him a hug and a silent message. He said no more.

The man rose from the cot and realized every eye in the small cabin was staring hatred at him. He could not have found a way to express his embarrassment at his actions and his regret and humiliation. He simply spoke to Gwyneth, who was at the basin washing ointment off her hands. "You won't have any reason to believe me, ma'am, but I'm just as sorry as I could ever be. I apologize. It was that cursed rattlesnake whiskey. Thank you for fixing me up, ma'am. That was more than I ever could have expected."

Another glance at Abe reminded him that he best take advantage of the opportunity to mount and ride. The mounting was nearly as painful as the whipping had been, but soon he was riding.

Chapter Thirty-Four

THE NEWS THAT NURSE GWYNETH HAD CARED FOR
the very man who had struck both her and Helen repeatedly
endeared her more than ever to the community. But Gwyneth,
herself, was having serious doubts about Bessie Creek. She had
been badly treated but was healing, if slowly. The ranch was
gone. The cattle were sold. Even the dog, who had attached
himself to them way back in Kansas, had been left with the kids
at the B/C ranch. There was nothing left of the Mirrored W.
That dream, Trent's dream, was dead. She had only to look after
herself now. Abe and Helen had hung in with her out of caring
and family loyalty. And perhaps a bit of well-hidden pity. But
she knew they would prefer to be free to move back south.

Gwyneth hadn't seen her mother in years. And no matter
how many childhood diseases she treated or how many broken
arms she set, she was never going to make a living in Bessie
Creek. That had become clear to her. After setting her personal
dream aside to join her husband in his dream, she was again
alone, free to think only of herself. Perhaps it was time to do
that very thing. She had done more than she ever thought a
nurse could do, but to advance, to serve some community well,
she had to have *doctor* written out, along with her name. Dr.

Gwyneth Wycome. There was a nice ring to that. In her mind's eye, she could picture it written on the door to her clinic. Written too, on the sign swinging in the breeze on the roofed-in walkway. Perhaps even printed on the billing pad she would keep handy on her office desk. *Doctor*. What she wouldn't give...

Gwyneth and Helen both avoided being in public for the first week after the beatings. Gwyneth's stomach was sore from the blows, and her face was a combination of slowly healing, bluish-purple bruises, along with a seriously blackened eye and a puffy nose that was only slowly healing. Helen was feeling better, but she had not suffered the blows Gwyneth had lived through.

They were having coffee one afternoon when Gwyneth broke the silence that had so often shadowed the cabin in the past week. "Abe, I'd like it if you would borrow or rent a wagon for tomorrow. I'm leaving on the afternoon train. I'm figuring you'll want to see the last of Bessie Creek too. Let's go together. We'll travel light. Take only what we want and can use. Throw that old bedding on the fire. Give anything usable to some young couple. Leave the rest where it is."

Helen was the first with a question, "Where do you figure to go, dear?"

"Pueblo first. I need to straighten out my banking. Then I figure I would lie up in a hotel until I can be out in public again. These blue bruises should be gone in another week. Perhaps two. Then I'm taking the train back east to visit Mother. It's been too long. I have a plan for after that also, but it's not fixed yet, so I'll have to let it lie for a bit." She hoped those few words would be taken as a release of obligation by her in-laws. She was afraid to suggest they weren't really needed anymore for fear of sounding ungrateful. It was up to them to sort it out.

Abe loaded the small collection of personal possessions, all carefully arranged in canvas panniers, onto the wagon. The kid from the livery drove it to the station while Abe, Helen, and Gwyneth walked. The comments from the folks they passed on the way were encouraging, but not enough to entice them to stay at Bessie Creek. They had no one to say goodbye to. No one who would be wishing them well. Soon they were seated in the passenger car and on their way to Pueblo. It was a short run. They would be in the hotel that evening.

Chapter Thirty-Five

THE TELLER AT THE BANK WAS ADAMANT THAT
Gwyneth would need more proof of the death of her husband.
It was his account that most of the cattle sale money had been
deposited in. Gwyneth, still showing a poorly healed eye and
some puffiness on her nose, was getting frustrated with the
argument. How does one prove a loss from hundreds of miles
away in an unsettled territory, where there is, as yet, no government, no authority, no records kept? She was saved further
complication when Abe and Helen walked into the bank. They,
too, had opened an account on the way west, leaving the bulk of
their funds there.

The now angry teller had called for the manager. That
gentleman assured Gwyneth that there would be no releasing of
funds from Trent's account without some proof beyond her
word. His overbearing and condescending manner was more
than Gwyneth knew how to cope with.

Abe heard, rather than saw, that there was a problem. He
stepped up on one side of Gwyneth while Helen stepped up to
the counter on the other side. "Is there a problem here,
Gwyneth?"

"There shouldn't be, but there is. They don't want to believe what I've told them about Trent, and further, they've made it clear that in their minds, women have no real authority in these matters. They refuse to give me the ranch funds."

Abe put his hand on Gwyneth's shoulder and squeezed just a bit, as if to say, *leave this to me*. He then pierced the teller with his stern eye before turning to the manager. "Gentlemen, hear me. And hear me well. This young lady is our daughter-in-law. She has the unfortunate experience of now being a widow. Her husband, Trent Wycome, was killed in a fall from a horse. Not only did she lose a husband, but we lost a son. A much-loved son.

"That was a couple of years ago. Since that time, she has run their ranch alone, along with a couple of trusted riders. The cattle sale funds, I believe, have been added to the account in this establishment. I see on the counter before you the receipts from the cattle sales. Do they match the deposits in Trent's account?"

Being assured on that fact, Abe continued, "So, you see that the ranch money is in the account, and now you have heard it from Helen and I that Trent is, in fact, no longer with us. You'll find no more reliable evidence than that. Trent's parents and his widow. Now lay out the funds and no more fooling around." The last was spoken as Abe would have spoken to a reluctant corporal during the war.

GWYNETH SOON HAD a large sum of money in her reticule, and both her and Trent's accounts were closed. They walked closely together to another large bank where Gwyneth opened a new account. She would transfer the money east after she was settled somewhere.

Another week in a Pueblo hotel, resting and pondering choices, firmed Gwyneth's resolve. At dinner that evening, she told Abe and Helen her plans. "I'm going to make every effort to pursue medical training. There are a few training colleges that are accepting women. I'm told that one college is only for women. But most of the big schools are down east. I have no desire to travel that far when there is a school in Chicago that might accept me. I want to visit my mother first. She's in Illinois, not too far from Chicago. Then I'll go on to the college to make an application in person, rather than by mail. I'll be applying for a two-year course that will give me my doctor's certificate if I can pass all the tests.

"I know you have been expecting something like this, and I love you both even more for having stuck with me over the years. I'm pretty sure that if I asked, you would come east. But I'm also sure you would rather take the train south and join up with the eastbound that will take you home. Home to Texas. I urge you to go, with my deepest love and gratitude. I wouldn't have made it on the ranch without you. Thank you both. Go home. Put all your effort into locating your other family. As you said a while ago, you probably have grandchildren by now. I'm sorry Trent and I were not able to deliver one for you to love. But any others you have will need you. And you need them. I'll be fine. Don't worry about me. Who knows? Perhaps I'll open a clinic in some Texas town one day. I'll leave you my mother's address. If you write and advise me of your new address, we can keep in touch."

There was more talk and more planning, but most of it had been gone over several times already. There was nothing more to do than purchase a ticket south in Pueblo, while Gwyneth purchased hers to Denver and home.

Gwyneth stood at the top of the steps leading to the passenger car and waved one final time at Abe and Helen. Their responding waves were more melancholy than sad. When the northbound finally rolled out of sight, with much black smoke and chuffing of steam, they turned to the other part of the station where the southbound was building up steam for the long trip ahead. Their luggage was already stowed. They had but to step into the car, say goodbye to Colorado, and look to the soon coming day when they could say hello to Texas. Again. For the last time. They had vowed no more traveling, and Texas was home.

Chapter Thirty-Six

GWYNETH HAD BOUGHT HERSELF A WHOLE NEW wardrobe, more fitting for the big city. She had visited for a week with her mother and one brother who still lived in the vicinity. Thinking better of her plan to simply arrive at the door of the college to plead her cause, she had exchanged correspondence with the college admissions officer. She had outlined her experience from the time she first walked into a civil war medical tent, ending with a brief outline of the treatment of the various illnesses and accidents at Bessie Creek.

She ended her correspondence with a plea for serious consideration of her application as a medical student. The returned letter had been not only positive but laudatory about her experiences, ending with encouragement to apply at the college. She had mailed off her formal application as a student in the study of medicine, along with the required admission fees. The new semester would begin in the fall, just weeks away.

Now, having traveled to Chicago, she was standing alone, across the street from the college entrance, with her single suitcase and her medical bag lying on the sidewalk on either side of her, and with people walking unnoticed all around her, with her eyes and ears blotting out the cacophony of sound and movement on the busy road, and with her heart fluttering with a sense of unbelief, over and over she read the last two words etched into the sandstone lintel over the big double entry doors.

MEDICAL COLLEGE

The reality of attending college, after so many years, and so many diversions in life, was beyond a dream come true, it was in every way a gift from her loving God. She would treat it as such.

As it was the day for student registration, other people were arriving, in small groups and in pairs. They were all men. They entered the big doors laughing and joking with each other, as if they had the matter of becoming a doctor all sewn up. She was alone. She had often been alone. She had offered her services during the war, alone. She was alone when she met and fell in love with Trent. She had been essentially alone since his death. Against all odds, she had persevered and succeeded, alone, for the most part. She would succeed again. Alone.

She picked up her suitcase and medical bag and took a step. A male voice asked, "Carry those for you, miss."

"Thank you, but no. I'm fine."

Fine, but alone. She crossed the street and put a hand to the brass door handle. She pulled the heavy oak door open and stepped inside. Alone. The only female student in the college. She paused again, looking at the wide granite stairway leading to the lecture rooms. *Just one step at a time, Gwyneth. And one day you'll walk down these same stairs. You'll walk down alone, your Trent will still be gone but for the memory, but you'll have a paper in your hand, assuring you that it was all worth it,* Dr. Gwyneth Wycome, physician and surgeon.

Teaser: Gwyneth Arriving (Frontier Dreaming 2)

The big oak doors of the medical college burst open. A gaggle of boisterous men surged out into the late spring Chicago sunlight. It had been a long, sometimes tedious, sometimes enlightening two years. Each graduate was relishing the dream they had fostered before entering the school. To be a doctor. Physician and surgeon. The right to open a medical practice anywhere of their choosing.

But first, an evening celebration. There had been many evenings spent at the Turf and Suds. And many a morning of regret. This would be the last. Tomorrow, it was off to show the world their learning.

Gwyneth purposely hung back. There would be no pub time for her. There never had been. The men had even quit inviting her. For the last time, she straightened out the compact space the college had set aside for their one and only lady student. Her presence represented a new era for the school and a challenge to the men, most of whom had never considered the idea of a female doctor. Gwyneth had mostly kept to herself, studying and going for long walks when opportunity allowed.

When the raucousness that had reverberated through the school's hallways faded, to be replaced by a welcome silence,

Gwyneth took one last look around her room, picked up her suitcase and her medical bag that she had carried over so many wagon and horseback miles, moved into the hallway, made her way to the oak doors, and hesitated. As she had done so often, she again thought of Trent, her long-deceased husband. *You would have been so proud to see this. You made it all possible, my husband, with your planning and your hard work. Thank you, Trent.*

Among her possessions was a certificate saying that Dr. Gwyneth May Wycome was qualified to serve as a medical doctor, physician, and surgeon.

With just a small, satisfied smile on her face, Dr. Gwyneth May Wycome pushed the door open and stepped into her new life.

A Look At: Gwyneth Arriving (Frontier Dreaming Book 2)

She has the skills to save lives—but who will save her from the quiet ache of loneliness?

After years in Chicago's bustling Women's and Children's Hospital, Gwyneth has become a standout physician—respected, capable, and quietly rebellious in a world that demands conformity. But prestige isn't enough.

Longing for the open skies and rugged soul of the American West, she leaves it all behind for Pueblo, Colorado. There, she opens a modest one-woman frontier clinic, bridging two worlds—urban medicine and wild-country healing. From factory burns to typhoid outbreaks in Ute encampments, Gwyneth finally finds the challenges she craved...but not the fulfillment she expected. Nights stretch long. The house is too quiet. And though she tells herself one great love was enough, the loneliness is harder to ignore with each passing season.

Until Cob returns.

Trent's old friend—and the man who once stayed behind to help her grieve—arrives from Texas with a bold proposition: partnership, purpose, and a second chance at love.

Can Gwyneth trust herself to say yes to something that feels too easy? Or is this the life she was always meant to live—on her terms, with the man who never stopped believing in her?

For fans of women's historical fiction, clean Western romance, and independent heroines, *Gwyneth Arriving* delivers heart, history, and a hopeful path toward home.

AVAILABLE JANUARY 2026

About the Author

Reg Quist's pioneer heritage includes sod shacks, prairie fires, home births, and children's graves under the prairie sod, all working together in the lives of people creating their own space in a new land.

Out of that early generation came farmers, ranchers, business men and women, builders, military graves in faraway lands, Sunday Schools that grew to become churches, plus story tellers, musicians, and much more.

Hard work and self-reliance were the hallmark of those previous great generations, attributes that were absorbed by the following generation.

Quist's career choice took him into the construction world. From heavy industrial work, to construction camps in the remote northern bush, the author emulated his grandfathers, who were both builders, as well as pioneer farmers and ranchers.

It is with deep thankfulness that Quist says, "I am a part of the first generation to truly enjoy the benefits of the labors of the pioneers. My parents and their parents worked incredibly hard, and it is well for us to remember".

www.ingramcontent.com/pod-product-compliance
Lightning Source LLC
Chambersburg PA
CBHW021003260626
47169CB00006B/1916